FREECYCLING
for beginners

Misha Herwin is a Staffordshire-based writer. When not writing she works with youth groups at the New Vic Theatre, and runs events such as the 6x6 Story Café for Stoke Libraries. She also runs workshops for museums, theatres and schools. She spends what little spare time she has with family and friends, reading, working in her garden, and baking. Scones are a speciality!

By Misha M. Herwin
> *House of Shadows*
> *Picking Up the Pieces*
> *Shadows on the Grass*
> *Belvedere Crescent*
> *Freecycling for Beginners*

By Misha Herwin (children's fiction)
> *The Awesome Adventures of Poppy and Amelia*
> (with Maddy Harrisis)

The Letty Parker series:
> *City of Secrets*
> *Bridge of Lies*
> *Island of Fear*

Misha also has published short fiction in anthologies across the UK and the US, including *Mslexia*, and has scripted plays for both schools and professional theatre companies.

She tweets as @MishaHerwin
Blog: https://mishaherwin.wordpress.com
Facebook: http://www.facebook.com/misha.herwin

FREECYCLING
for beginners

Misha M. Herwin

The Penkhull Press

First edition

ISBN 978-1-9162865-0-4

Published by The Penkhull Press
Staffordshire, UK

ACKNOWLEDGEMENTS

Thank you to everyone who was involved in bringing *Freecycling for Beginners* to publication. I am eternally grateful to my wonderful editor Jan Edwards, brilliant beta-reader Barry Lillie and meticulous proof-reader Jeanne Wood.

Many thanks too, to Peter Coleborn for all his work on designing and formatting the book, and to my sister Anuk Naumann for the picture of the red chair, which is the perfect image for the story.

I would also like to thank Renegade Writers for their feedback on the early drafts and their support throughout.

And my family for being there for me.

For Mum

ONE

"I can't put it off any longer." Jane walked into the room she still thought of as Hugh's study and looked at the chair standing in the bay window. The sun streaming in from a clear blue sky picked out the faded patches on the wine-coloured plush, the tiny holes where ash had dropped from Hugh's pipe, and the dent in the seat where the cushion sagged. She'd had it cleaned but even so, it showed its age.

Taking out her phone, she found the Freecycle site. She had never posted anything before but it was her best hope of finding a home for the chair. After a moment or two's thought she wrote, Offered: One wing chair. Upholstery a little faded and worn.

Who was she kidding? The chair was not only scruffy, it was so heavy and out of date no one could possibly want it. She deleted the post and was about to put the phone back in her pocket when it rang.

"Hi Mum. I'm just checking in to see how things are going, seeing as moving day is coming up soon. How are you getting on with the packing?"

Jane looked around the room. Everything that had made it hers was gone. The furniture had been sold, or recycled, the books and pictures given away or packed ready for the removal men. All that remained was Hugh's chair.

"It's almost done." It was impossible to lie; her daughter would hear it in her voice.

"You still haven't sorted out Dad's chair, have you?"

"Not yet. I can't take it to the tip. It feels wrong to dump it. It was the only place he—"

"I know what you're going to say," Anna interrupted. "That's where Dad spent most of those last weeks, when he couldn't make himself comfortable anywhere else. We know that. I do see why it means so much to you and I don't mean to sound harsh, but he's gone, Mum. It's been two years."

Her daughter was right. It had been two years since Hugh died but Jane still found herself making a note of something she must remember to tell him, or turning to make a comment about what she was watching on television. She'd talk to him too, telling him what she was doing, or even asking his opinion. It was crazy but she was beginning to accept that was how it had to be. At the same time she was growing used to coming home to a silent house and was more-or-less accustomed to sleeping in an empty bed with no warm back to curl into and no irritating snore to keep her awake. There were even times when she almost felt content. Days when she thought she'd finally got used to the idea of being on her own.

"Look, if you can't face doing the final bits I'll come and help you. We'll do it together. I'm free on—" there was a pause and Jane could imagine Anna scrolling down her appointments "—Saturday at two-thirty. Suit you?"

Don't treat me like a client, Jane thought irritably. "There's no need," she said. "I'll deal with it."

"Are you sure?"

"Positive," Jane said more firmly than she intended and ended the call. Walking over to the chair she ran her hands over the threadbare upholstery and was swept by a sudden almost overwhelming wave of grief.

"I miss you so much," she whispered. "So much," she repeated. "Why the hell did you have to go and die on me?" She thumped the arm. "You were only sixty. That's no age. No age at all. Don't you know how much I need you, you stupid, stupid man?"

She shut her eyes to keep in the tears as the memories came flooding back.

*

Buffeted by the autumn wind, Hugh and Jane had laughed and called out to each other as they ran, hand in hand, along the pavement. Because Hugh was taller, his stride longer, there were times when he was so far in front of her that their arms were stretched to their full length. When that happened he would stop, pull her close and kiss her, then off they would go again racing down the hill.

Turning the corner, a sudden sharp pain in her side brought Jane to a halt. They had reached the main road and a row of small shabby second-hand shops. Their doors were low and narrow, their windows dusty and dark. Most were shut with a yellowing "Closed" sign hanging askew on the inside of the door. One shop, however, was still open, the shopkeeper a vague figure scarcely visible through the dirty glass. Leaning against the shop front, Jane caught her breath as she steeled herself against the ache in her gut.

"Are you all right?" Hugh's face creased with concern

as she winced and clutched her side.

"I'm okay. It's only a stitch." A gust of wind brought a flurry of raindrops and another spasm.

"Let's get out of the rain." Hugh's hand was on her elbow, guiding her into the shelter of the shop doorway. "Give it a minute or two and it'll ease off."

"Shouldn't I bend over and touch my toes or something?"

"Only if you want to butt me in the stomach. If you really have to, I'll get out of your way."

"Don't be silly," Jane giggled. "The stitch is almost gone." She lifted her face to be kissed. He leaned forward and she must have stepped back because in the depths of the shop the doorbell tinkled. Lips touching, they looked at each other. It was too late to run.

The door had swung open and a voice said sharply, "Well come in, why don't you." It was hard to see anything in the dim light or to make out more than a burly shape as a small square woman bore down on them. "I was shutting up for the night, but you may as well have a look around, now that you're already in." Glaring at them, she stood aside daring them to enter.

Jane glanced at the open door. "Let's go," she whispered, tugging Hugh's hand.

"In a minute. First, we'd better pay the dragon her dues," he replied, his beard tickling the back of her neck.

"Okay," she said reluctantly. "But we won't stay long."

"Not a second longer than necessary," he murmured, gently pushing her forward.

The shop had a dusty damp smell and was stuffed with furniture and knick-knacks. Every available space was taken, leaving narrow pathways for any potential buyers who wanted to browse the stock. Rickety tables creaked under the weight of teetering piles of books, stacks of cracked china, baskets of tarnished cutlery, and boxes of broken toys. There were coal scuttles filled with fir cones and spiderwebs. Walking sticks and torn parasols were crammed into umbrella stands. A tailor's dummy sported a trilby hat, a rusty sword hung from its waist. There were washstands with marble tops, moss-covered garden ornaments and spindly bedroom chairs with split-cane seats. There was a chaise longue piled high with old jackets and one or two overstuffed armchairs.

Along the back wall, in front of a line of bookshelves stuffed with crumbling volumes, stood a dressing table. It had three mirrors, the centre one hinged so that it could be moved up and down. In front of it was a jewellery box. A tangle of necklaces spilled out onto the surface, mostly dull and uninteresting, but among them was a row of amber beads that drew Jane like a ray of sunlight through the November afternoon. Unable to stop herself, she picked up the necklace and was stroking the smooth warmth of the beads when Hugh called to her.

"Jane, you've got to see this." He was standing by a chair, his face alight. She started towards him, the beads still in her hand.

"Buy it or put it down," the woman growled. Jane's fingers closed around the necklace. She didn't want to let it go. It was one of the most beautiful things she'd ever seen.

"How much?" she asked, her insides fluttering in

anticipation.

"Ten pounds."

"That's more than a week's rent!"

"Humph!" the woman snorted. "It's a very unusual string of Baltic amber with sterling silver fittings. I bought several pieces from a Russian princess and yes, they do have provenance, not that it would bother someone like you. The better ones sold straight away, but it's still a quality item. I think you'll find that ten pounds is a fair price."

"I'm sorry, I can't afford it," Jane stammered, flushing with embarrassment. She and Hugh had married only a few months before and were eking out their student grants by camping out in an almost empty flat. She reminded herself that there was nothing wrong with not having much money and her anger at the woman's condescending sneer swept away any feeling of awkwardness. Lifting her chin and looking the shopkeeper in the eye, she said, "Even if I could, I wouldn't buy it." She dropped the necklace back in its box and sailed over to Hugh.

Oblivious to the whole encounter, he was patting the back of the chair like an old friend. "My granddad had one of these," he said delightedly. "And —" he looked at her "— we could do with something to sit on. Those orange boxes are damned hard."

The chair reminded Jane of the old people's home where she'd found a few hours work to stretch out their funds. St Martin's was a bleak place where the residents sat in rows, their eyes vacant, limbs trembling, but she was still smarting from the shop woman's manner and the way she'd blurted out their poverty.

"How much?" she asked. Hugh fumbled about and pulled out an ancient price tag.

"It says seven and six," he said hesitantly.

"We'll take it." Jane peered through the murky window and saw that the rain had stopped. "We'll carry it home, or since it's got wheels we'll push it." She stifled a giggle as she imagined them taking turns pushing each other like oversized babies up St Michael's Hill.

"It'll be a struggle getting it up the stairs." Hugh grinned, ignoring the woman as she handed him a written receipt. "Come on, my lady, who's having first turn on the chair-mobile?"

It was a tricky task getting the chair out of the shop. They had to tip and tilt it past the over-laden displays, taking great care to avoid knocking any of the precariously balanced piles of china and glass. When they'd finally succeeded in manoeuvring it out onto the pavement and the daylight revealed its desperate shabbiness, Jane was struck by the stupidity of what they had done.

It's musty and it smells, she thought miserably, but Hugh had looked so pleased with their purchase that she couldn't bring herself to spoil his moment. *We'll get rid of it. As soon as we can afford it, it'll be the first thing to go,* she promised herself.

The chair was every bit as awkward to get up the hill and into their first floor flat as they had envisaged. After heaving and tugging it up the stairs with Jane pulling and Hugh pushing it step by step, he managed to balance it against the bannister while she searched in her pocket for the key. As soon as she had the door open Hugh tipped the chair from its perch and leaned his shoulder against its back. There was a moment of resistance, then he gave it a hard shove and it burst through the frame like a cork from a bottle and skittered across the bare floorboards until it came to rest beside the hideous gas fire, as if this was where it had always belonged.

"Result!" Hugh thrust his arms into the air as if he had scored a winning goal. He strode over to the chair and plonking himself down, waved a lordly hand in Jane's direction. "Tea, woman," he commanded.

"Oh no you don't," Jane said. "Just because you've got the chair you don't need to think I'm going to wait on you hand and foot."

"And why not?"

"Because…" She sat down on his lap and put her arms around his neck. "Because—" she whispered "—we don't do it like that here."

His lips met hers. His hands slid beneath her T-shirt.

Later they made tea together in the narrow kitchen and carried their mugs back into the living room. She drew the curtains shutting out the cold night while he lit the fire, and they sat together by the flickering gas flames, Hugh in the chair and she on the hearth rug toasting her toes and leaning back against his knees.

"You know something," Hugh said after a while. "The chair makes it…"

"Look like home," Jane finished.

*

"I love you," she whispered to the boy he had been and the man he had become. From the moment she first saw

14

him she knew he was the one person she wanted to be with for the rest of her life. Or his life, as it turned out.

The house was now sold, her belongings packed; but Hugh's old chair would not fit into her sleek modern apartment overlooking the river.

"Move on," Anna had told her and now Jane was ready. She would never forget Hugh and the years they had together, but it was time to be practical and start the next phase of her life. There was only one thing left to do. She pulled out her phone, found the Freecycle site, took a picture of it and posted, Offered: One old-fashioned armchair. Upholstery a little worn. Then she pressed send.

TWO

Taking a deep breath, Frankie strolled out of the main gate of Clifton Park Academy. It was half-past two and she had finished for the day – the year – this whole part of her life. GCSEs were over and she was free of the place forever. Without looking back she walked over to where Emma and Amy were waiting. The sun was hot and Amy had pulled off her tie and unbuttoned her blouse to knot it under her breasts.

Emma loosened her shirt and as Frankie approached reached into her bag for a hip flask. "Vodka?" she offered.

Amy took a swig. Frankie shook her head. "Go on have some." Swinging her long blonde hair, Amy looked back at the school buildings. "They can't do anything to us now. We've left. We've done our exams and got our references for college." She took a long drink. "I needed that. That last English paper was so hard."

"What I want is something long and cold," Frankie said.

"Sorry I didn't manage the ice and tonic." Emma smirked.

Frankie shrugged. Mostly she went along with the other two, but on this hot afternoon undiluted vodka was the last thing she wanted. *They're only doing it to look hard.* The thought crossed her mind and was quickly dismissed. Amy and Emma didn't need to prove anything to anyone. They were the two girls in the class that everyone looked up to and envied. They were clever and got top marks and, unlike Frankie, they worked how and when they chose. No one could tell them what to do. Even some of the teachers were scared of them.

The boys wanted to go out with them and the girls wanted to be part of their group; but they had no time for anyone else but Frankie. Quite how that had happened, Frankie wasn't sure. The three of them had been in the same class since primary school and had been friends, on and off. Mostly it was Amy and Emma, with Frankie sometimes included and sometimes not. It didn't really bother her. The trouble was that if everyone thought you were with Amy and Emma, they stayed clear of you, and the times the three of them had fallen out there had been nowhere for Frankie to go. If she didn't want to be a Billy-no-mates it paid to keep in with the other two.

"A few more weeks and then, after the prom, we're off to Florida. For the whole summer." Amy pouted and sighed dramatically. "I told my step-dad I wanted to go to the Caribbean but he said it will have to wait until Christmas. Apparently, the weather's better then."

"We're going to Spain – again." Emma sighed and raised her eyes. Her family owned an apartment in one of the resorts and she and her mum and her little brother went there every holiday. Her dad, who was a builder, joined them whenever he could.

There was a pause which Frankie hurried to fill. "Great." She hoped she sounded suitably impressed, but she wasn't going anywhere. Her mother couldn't afford a trip to Weston let alone a holiday abroad.

"Have you got your prom dress yet? You can't leave it too late or all the best ones sell out." Bored with the topic of holidays, Amy changed the subject.

"I ordered mine weeks ago and I'm having a fitting at Elvi's tonight. I've lost that much weight I expect I'll have to have it taken in," Emma boasted.

The other girls looked at her approvingly.

"My dress was three hundred pounds." Amy hated not being the centre of attention. "And the shoes! You should see the shoes."

"Not?" Emma gasped.

"Yes," Amy smirked. "Jimmy Choos. My mum got them on eBay."

"My dress is off eBay too. Designer," Frankie added, trying to sound nonchalant.

"I'm having the 'California' spray tan before they do my hair and makeup. And now I'm sixteen I get complimentary champagne," Amy said.

"At Beautique?" Emma asked.

"Yeah," Amy drawled casually as though Beautique wasn't the coolest and most expensive salon in town. "Mum says nothing's too good for me, so the step-dad has to agree."

Linking arms, the two girls walked on ahead, chatting about what pampering they were going to have done on the day of the prom. Frankie lagged a few paces behind, feeling more excluded from the conversation with every step. How could she admit that her mum was going to do her hair and nails, and that her coffee-coloured skin had no need of a fake tan?

At last Amy turned round to Frankie. "You are coming

in the limo, aren't you? I told them you were coming with us."

"Sure." Frankie did her best to keep the relief from her voice. It had somehow been taken for granted that she would go to the End of Year Eleven Prom with the others, but until now it had never actually been stated.

"I'm getting a shower, some sun, then I'm going to get ready for tonight," Amy said.

"Are we celebrating?" Emma asked.

"Too right. I'm getting off my head."

"Totally out of it," Frankie added. "Totally," she repeated under her breath as she watched the others saunter across the road. When they reached the other side, Emma threw back her head and laughed loudly at something Amy had said. Then they were round the corner and out of sight. Frankie shrugged and tried to ignore the rapid beating of her heart as she hurried home.

The closer she got to the small terrace house she shared with her mum, the tighter the knot in her stomach. It must have come; it must be there today. Bargains like her dress didn't turn up very often and Mum said her bid had been accepted, but that was days ago, and the promised dress still hadn't arrived.

A frantic barking greeted the sound of her key in the lock. Frankie pushed open the door and bent down to give Tigger a quick pat. The terrier panted and slurped and jumped up and down on his three legs until she gently pushed him out of the way and went into the kitchen.

Debbie, her mum was sitting at the table with Onions, the cat, on her lap, while Smokey-Joe, his brother, crouched over the parcel in front of her. Fluff, the little grey female, purred from her sunny spot on the windowsill, one eye on the rabbits in their run on the scruffy piece of lawn in the back garden.

"It's here." Debbie jumped to her feet, dislodging Onions, who stalked off into the scullery. Frankie's hand flew to her lips. "Go on," her mum urged. "Open it. I've been sat here staring at it for what feels like forever."

"Okay." Frankie studied the package carefully, then picked it up, turned it over and delicately plucked at the tape with a fingernail.

"Oh, for God's sake, get on with it. I can't stand the suspense any longer." Debbie grabbed the kitchen scissors.

"Careful Mum." Frankie could hardly bear to look. "Don't cut it."

"I know what I'm doing," Debbie responded, but her hand shook as she sliced into the padded envelope. Very carefully, she unwrapped a layer of tissue paper and pulled out a fall of pink silk.

"It's gorgeous," Frankie gasped. "Even better than I thought it would be." She took the dress and held it up against her body. The rose pink glowed in the hot sunlight. She flattened the bustier against her chest and smoothed out the skirt. "What do you think?"

"I think I want to see you in it. Go and try it on then you can show it off properly."

"Okay. You stay in the kitchen so I can do the grand entrance bit on the stairs."

"Don't trip when you're coming down."

"Mum!" Frankie groaned, already halfway up.

In her bedroom, she laid the dress carefully on the bed and stripped down to her skin. Leaving her school uniform and underwear in a heap on the floor, she rifled through her drawers for a thong. She reached for her dress, then stopped, sniffed under her arms, sprayed herself first with deodorant then perfume. Finally, reverently, she picked up the pink silk and stepping into the billowing skirt she twisted her arms around her back and began to pull up the zip.

*

"Mum!" The voice that wafted down to the kitchen was full of anguish. "Mum!" Debbie's skin prickled. She went hot then cold. *What now? Why does everything go wrong for me?* she thought as she raced up the stairs, Tigger yapping at her heels.

"What is it?" She burst through the door.

"It's too big!" her daughter wailed. Tigger in sympathy began a frantic barking.

"Is that all?" Weak with relief Debbie collapsed on the bed.

"Mum, it's a disaster," Frankie howled. She held up the sides of the bustier. "I look stupid. I can't wear it. It's useless. What did you order? You know I'm a size eight."

"That's what they said it was." Debbie grabbed the dog and put him outside the door. She was seized by a terrible doubt. She must have made a mistake. It wouldn't be the first time; her life was full of unlucky choices and disastrous decisions. Had she done it again? Had she sent off for the wrong size? She couldn't have. The dress was too important for that. She had checked and checked again. She was sure she had.

21

"How could you?" Frankie moaned, mascara trailing down her cheeks. "What am I going to do? I can't wear this crap." She kicked petulantly at the skirt. "I can't."

"I know." Debbie was close to tears, but if there was one thing life had taught her, it was that when everything went wrong it paid to keep calm. Ignoring Frankie's hysterics, Debbie studied the dress. "It's only a little bit big on the top. The skirt fits okay," she said at last.

"Great. Fantastic. I'll go in the skirt, shall I?" Frankie tugged viciously at the zip.

"Don't do that, you'll break it."

"So? What does it matter? It's all pants anyway."

"No it isn't. It's fine. It needs to be taken in a bit, that's all. Stop shouting and screaming and let me see."

"You can do something?" Frankie's tears dried almost immediately.

"I don't know." Debbie walked slowly round her daughter, noting where the dress gaped at the back and sides. "If it wasn't for the bones, I suppose I could try."

"But it has got to have bones in it." Frankie's lip trembled.

"Yes it has, but it's not a total disaster. There are places where you can get stuff altered."

"Yeah. Like where?" Frankie glowered miserably.

Debbie frowned, trying to recall where she had seen a notice for alterations. There was that house in Raleigh Road where Mrs Schmidt, the dressmaker lived. She couldn't remember the number but there was a sign on creamy card with lovely curly writing that hung in the front room window.

You're losing it. Debbie shook her head. Mrs Schmidt

was back in the days when people made their own clothes, or had them mended and made over to pass down to other members of the family. First communions, confirmations, posh dances and weddings were big business for Mrs Schmidt. If you couldn't afford to go to an up-market bridal shop she would make your dress for less than half the price. Debbie had been taken there when she was a flower girl for her Auntie Maureen; she couldn't have been more than three years old. The business and its owner was long gone. Debbie sighed and stared out of the window at the perfect summer sky.

"Mum?"

She turned round to see Frankie gazing hopefully at her – and the solution came to her. It was so obvious she almost burst out laughing. The dry cleaners in the High Street, the old fashioned one, they did alterations.

"It's all right. I know what we're going to do. Get your clothes on. I've got it sorted."

*

The teenage girl behind the counter wore earbuds and was staring absently out of the window. Debbie cleared her throat but Frankie kicked at the counter and the girl slowly unplugged an ear. "Yeah?" she said.

"You do alterations." Debbie nodded towards the notice sellotaped to the door.

"Yeah," the girl said again.

"We've got a dress that needs taking in."

"Right." The girl reached for a pad. "Name, address?"

"Oh give it here." Debbie snatched the pad and pen and filled in as much of the order form as she could, stopping only when she came to the section on measurements. The girl, thinking she had finished, stretched out her hand. "Nah," Debbie said. "It's this bit here. What do I put?" She slid the form over to the girl who examined it carefully.

"Yeah. Measurements," she said at last, lifting the pen to her lips and nibbling at it. "It's the size you want," she said slowly, almost as if she were explaining it to herself. Frankie scuffed her sandals against the floor. She was, Debbie thought, ready to explode. "Yeah," the girl said more firmly. "Well?" she held the pen above the form.

"Size eight. It's got to be a size eight. Frankie's a size eight. Aren't you love?"

"Yes Mum."

"Right." The pen hovered above the page. "What's that then?" the girl asked at last.

"Oh my God." Debbie snatched back the form. The blood pounded in her head and the words jumbled on the page. "I can't make any sense of this."

"Mum," Frankie pushed her to one side, "Let me see. Oh yeah, it wants my waist and my bust measurements."

"Right." The girl sighed as if the mysteries of the universe had suddenly become clear. "Okay. How big are you round the waist?"

"I'm not sure," Frankie said.

Debbie turned to the girl. "Haven't you got a measuring tape?"

"Dunno. I don't think there is one." The girl rummaged beneath the counter, before emerging shaking her head. "Sorry."

"Bust thirty-two," Debbie said. "Waist twenty-two."

"Mum!" Frankie blushed furiously.

"Right." The girl wrote down the figures. "That'll be twenty pounds. Ready in three weeks."

"But the prom's at the end of term. What if it doesn't come in time? What if they don't get it right?" Frankie wailed.

Debbie's hand holding the money froze in mid-air. The girl half-shrugged, filling Debbie with an almost overwhelming urge to smash her fist into the bland acne-spotted face. Frankie gave a sharp sob of disappointment. The girl put down her pen.

"There's the express service. Ready in three days," she said helpfully. "Forty pounds."

"Guaranteed?" Debbie demanded.

"Guaranteed," the girl confirmed. Debbie searched through her purse, found the extra money and thrust it at the girl, who with infuriating slowness rang the amount up on the till and handed them their receipt.

"Oh Mum. Thanks!" Frankie threw her arms around her mother and twirled her around the shop. The girl stuck her earbuds back in her ears and continued staring out of the window as mother and daughter, arms linked, went out into the street.

*

Frankie sat up in bed and tried to rub the grit from her eyes. The music from last night was still thudding in the back of her brain, and her mouth tasted as if she had been eating cat litter. Dust trembled in the ray of sunlight that slanted in under the blind. Closing one eye, she squinted at the clock and fell back on the pillow in disbelief. It was three in the afternoon. How could she have slept for so long? Why hadn't Mum woken her? Okay, she had crawled in about two in the morning, but today was the day she was due to collect her dress.

She imagined herself wearing it, the bodice tight as a second skin showing off her tiny waist, the skirt billowing out over her hips and skimming the tops of her ballet pumps. She'd wanted the silver stilettos she'd seen in a charity shop, but Mum said that pumps were more classy.

Frankie half-turned to the cupboard where the shoes nestled in their box. The room tilted and began to spin. Forcing herself to focus on a spot on the wall, she took a sip of dusty water from the glass that stood beside her bed and gradually the room settled. Why oh why had she drunk so much last night? It had been her way of making the party more bearable. She hadn't wanted to go but Emma and Amy had insisted and Frankie, as usual, had given in.

The bedroom door opened a crack and Fluff came in. The cat jumped on the bed and began to lick Frankie's arm. Very gently Frankie put her to one side and taking great care to move her head as little as possible slid out of bed. Stumbling into the bathroom, she scrubbed her teeth and had a shower. Once she was dressed, she put on a pair of sunglasses and hurried down the street to the dry cleaners.

*

"Frankie? Have you got it? Frankie!" Debbie's voice faltered.

The house was strangely silent. No thumping thundering music from her daughter's room, no giggles and screams, not even the drone of daytime television from the front room. Nothing but the happy panting of

Tigger, glad to see his mistress back from a long day at work.

Something was wrong. Very wrong. Slowly, heavily, she climbed the stairs. Frankie's door was shut so she tapped on it, softly at first, then louder. When there was no reply she slid it open and stared into the gloom.

Frankie was lying on the bed, her face to the wall.

"Frankie, love, what's wrong?" Debbie touched her daughter's shoulder. There was no reaction. Swallowing her fear, she said, "You can tell me. Whatever it is."

"It doesn't fit. It's useless." Frankie's voice was cold and hard.

"No!" Debbie snatched the dress from the back of the chair where Frankie had thrown it. With a snap she raised the blind.

"It's too tight." Frankie rolled onto her back and stared at the ceiling. "We got the measurements wrong," she had the grace to say.

Thank God she's not blaming me, Debbie thought. "If it's not right they can do it again," she said.

"No they can't. There's no material left. And the zip's broken. I pulled too hard when I was trying to do it up. It's okay," she added flatly, "I won't go to the prom and that's it." She shut her eyes and lay rigid.

Debbie tugged and pulled at the dress. She examined it from every angle hoping against hope that there was something that could be done. At last, however, she had to admit that Frankie was right. The dress was ruined.

"We'll get another one."

"Not like that," Frankie said and Debbie knew she was right. That dress had been a one-off bargain. They would never find another one. Unless she won the lottery, or found a fairy godmother, there was no money for something brand new. Their only hope was to buy second hand or get something from a charity shop.

Cradling the prom dress in her arms she went down to the dining room. Chasing a cat off the table, she laid the pink silk down carefully and rested her head on her hands. This shouldn't be happening. Not to Frankie. Her daughter was a star. She'd done well in school and was going on to college, not like her mum who'd left at sixteen and got pregnant at seventeen. From then on life had been a struggle, but Debbie had done her best to make sure that Frankie didn't miss out. The prom was supposed to be the best day of her daughter's life. The day she deserved. The day that all her friends took for granted. If only they'd gone for something hired, or from the catalogue range of prom dresses but no, she'd had this great idea of getting an exclusive designer gown from the internet. She'd let Frankie down and there was nothing she could do to put it right.

Fluff came and rubbed herself round her ankles. Smokey Jo purred and jumped onto her lap. Debbie stroked him absently; at least the cats still loved her. She sat there for a long time, then, scarcely daring to hope, she got out her phone and logged onto Freecycle. Wanted: one prom dress, she posted. Without pausing, she poured out the whole sad story, ending with, Thank you for reading this. I don't know if there is anyone out there that can help, but if you can I would be really, really grateful. Thanks again, Debs.

Then she pressed send.

THREE

After two days in Bangkok, sorting out a problem with one of his suppliers, Dan was glad to be back. On this summer evening, the air was warm and clean, not humid and thick with traffic fumes. Instead of the choking Bangkok atmosphere there was the smell of the river, a not unpleasant mixture of mud and water. The sky was still blue, and round white fluffy clouds hung over the horizon. Looking one way he could see the Dundry Hills; opposite them, like tiers of a wedding cake, were the terraces of Regency houses that rose above the Cumberland Basin. In contrast, the square red brick converted warehouse with its row upon row of windows, where he had his apartment, was a reminder of Bristol's trading past.

Dan locked the Aston Martin and rested his hand for a moment on its silver flank before he went inside. He picked up his post from the entrance hall and summoned the lift. Usually he took the stairs but today he was tired from the long flight.

It was good to be back and in a place that reflected his own style. The walls were un-plastered brick. The thick ceiling beams were supported by iron pillars. There were no curtains or blinds, no rugs on the wooden floors and the furniture consisted of two leather sofas. The only pictures were a series of black and white photographs from all over the world. These were vivid depictions of global conflict that showed the unflinching effect of war on people and places. The subjects were grim but, as art, had their own unique beauty. Rather like the woman who had taken them, Dan's friend and one time lover, Paola Veronese.

The air in the apartment was stale and dusty with summer heat and Dan flipped the switch that opened the windows before pouring himself a gin and tonic. The evening sun was beginning to sink behind the hills, turning the sky to molten gold. Soon it would be dark and although he was tired he knew that he shouldn't sleep. He was still functioning on Thai time and if he gave in the jet lag would be worse the next day. He had to keep awake until at least midnight.

Finishing his drink he stripped off and went to have a shower. After he'd washed off the plane journey, he turned the dial to maximum cold and let it run until he couldn't stand it any longer. The muzzy feeling in his head had gone and wrapping a towel round his waist he turned his attention to his messages.

The first came as a shock. "Dan. Darling. Sorry to be a pain, but there's a huge box of your stuff you still haven't collected, and I seriously need to clear out the spare room before the weekend. So if you could come over as soon as? I'd be so, so grateful." Antonia's voice was as soft and seductive as always.

Damn. How did she know I was going to be home today, and who the hell gave her my new number? Dan pushed a strand of hair from his forehead. If he never saw his ex-wife again it would be too soon. He poured himself another drink and scrolled down the rest of the messages. If the first had been a shock, the second also took him aback. It was a woman's voice, hesitant and a little nervous.

"Um, it's Lindsay from Friends Wining and Dining. You left your name and number and um, asked if I could ring you back. Well I'm ringing and yes I would like to meet up some time."

Dan hadn't the slightest recollection of who this Lindsay was and what she was talking about. Deciding the message must be a mistake, some sort of promotion, or even someone's idea of a rather poor joke, he was about to delete it, when he remembered. Wining and Dining was a site he'd joined before he'd gone to Thailand. It had described itself as a social group – your chance to meet new people – but it felt like a dating site. Scrolling down to find Lindsay's profile, he wondered why the hell he'd bothered. He didn't need anyone new in his life. He had his brother and his family and plenty of friends, some of them going back to school and rugby club days, though he didn't see as much of them as he used to. Most were married with children. Those few who had stayed with the same woman were in the throes of problems with their teenage offspring. Others, who'd started again with a younger partner, were whipping out photographs of their new babies before they'd even got to the second drink.

He and Antonia had agreed that children would never fit in with their lifestyle. In the early days he had spent a lot of time abroad, sourcing stock for his shop, while Antonia globetrotted with her modelling career, and neither had been home more than one week in three. It was then they, or rather she, began renovating Combe

Farm, and her natural talent had blossomed into a thriving interior design consultancy. Or so she had told him. But how much did he know about the woman who had been his wife? He had never seen any hint that she had someone new in her life, or that she was throwing him out like an old shoe. She said they'd grown apart, that they didn't talk to each other anymore, which must have been true, otherwise he would have realised that the marriage was over.

When she'd told him, he hadn't protested or argued. He'd simply packed his belongings and walked away. Too stunned to react and too proud to let her see how much he hurt. That was months ago and after much negotiation between their solicitors he knew that none of his things could have remained at the farm. So what was her agenda? Whatever it was, he had no intention of playing along.

He looked at his phone wondering whether to ring this unknown Lindsay. Did he want another relationship? Even before his split with Antonia he had grown used to a pared-down lifestyle. It had suited him then, and now that he had the apartment, his import business, the gym and his extended family, what more did he need?

His stomach rumbled, reminding him it was a long time since he'd last eaten. There was nothing in the fridge. He rarely cooked as it was easier to get a takeaway and the neighbourhood was full of good places to eat. The thought of eating out reminded him of Lindsay. Was she waiting at home hoping for a call? He considered getting in touch then decided it was too late in the evening.

The sun had gone down. Through the skylights he

could see a bright sprinkling of stars, and lights shone in the windows of the houses on the hill. Perhaps the best way to deal with the Lindsay question would be to send a text. He reached for his phone and his towel slipped. He moved to save it and made up his mind. No entanglements, no dates.

He was about to order a Chinese when his phone rang. "Darling, at last. I suppose you've been away again and too busy to talk?" Antonia breathed. "Anyway, all I want to know is if tomorrow will be okay." There was a pause while Dan remained silent. "For the things. You know. I left you a message. Don't say you didn't get it because I know that's not true. You're too efficient not to check your messages. So how about tomorrow?"

"Bin it. Take whatever it is to the charity shop."

"I can't. It might be important," she replied. Dan said nothing. "Look, I'll tell you what. If you can't make the time to come round I'll drop it off at the shop. I'm coming into town. It'll be no problem."

"No." He didn't want her invading his Antonia-free space. "I'll come and get it. Since you think it's so important."

"Wonderful, darling," she said lightly. "See you soon." She broke off the connection leaving him feeling wrong footed, as if he, not she, was being unreasonable.

*

The feeling of being in the wrong continued the next morning when Dan realised that they hadn't arranged a time for him to visit Coombe Farm. He either had to get in touch with Antonia or wait for her to call. On the other hand, he could simply turn up, but if she was out, or in the middle of one of her consultations it would be a waste of his time. Cursing, he gave in and rang his ex-wife. Apparently, it was no longer convenient.

It was not until the following day that he drove to the Cotswolds. The sun swept shadows over the curve of the hills. The road dipped and rose until he pulled up in front of a honey-coloured farmhouse, its walls draped in sweet-smelling wisteria. As soon as the Aston Martin crunched to a halt on the gravel drive the door opened. When Coombe Farm had been his home he would have gone straight to the kitchen door; today his ex-wife was treating him like a visitor.

In contrast to their previous conversation Antonia was brisk and efficient. She ushered Dan into the front room and handed him a slim cardboard box, very different from the bulky package he had been expecting.

"It's all there."

"Thank you."

"Aren't you going to check?"

"There's no point. I don't know and I don't care what's inside."

She flushed, a rose-petal tint on her porcelain skin. "Oh, it's something of yours I found when I was clearing out a cupboard."

"Fine," he said briefly, eager to get away.

"Good," she replied.

Is this it? he wondered. *Is this all? Why had she been so insistent that I came to fetch it in person?* The box was small, it could easily have been posted.

"I'll see you out." Antonia was already moving towards the door when she stopped and stood sideways

34

to him so that he could see the faint swell of her stomach, the same stomach that had been as flat as a board throughout their married life.

"I'm sorry there's no time for coffee, I've an appointment in half an hour. Besides, I don't do coffee – it doesn't agree with me." She rested her hand on her stomach and glanced at him from under long dark lashes. "Darling, aren't you going to ask me why?"

"Why?" The word came out like a bark.

"Because I'm pregnant. It's a bit unexpected, to put it mildly. But utterly delightful." She put her hand on his arm and he did his best not to flinch under her touch. "We're having the spare room done out as the nursery." She looked up at him with little-girl eyes. "That's why I needed it cleared. You are pleased for me, aren't you?"

He must have nodded, said something, but whatever it was he had no memory of it. All he could remember was accelerating out of the drive and roaring down the country lanes to get away from her as fast as he could. This was what the charade was all about, calling him back for a final twist of the knife; telling him was not enough, he had to be there to see her blossoming, happy, fulfilled, contented. All the things that were missing when they were together; showing him, yet again, how he had failed her.

If there had been a rubbish bin between the farmhouse and the apartment he would have stopped and chucked the box and whatever was in it away, but as there was not he carried it up the stairs and dropped it on the kitchen counter where he eyed it suspiciously.

He stabbed at the lid with the kitchen scissors, then

ripped the box open from end to end. Inside, wrapped carefully in tissue paper, was a shirt. An expensive white evening shirt with thick cuffs. It was some designer label that Antonia had said was absolutely the thing. She was always going on about how he had no style and couldn't be trusted to buy anything decent, by which she meant expensive, so she'd bought it for him for a charity ball they'd attended. Dan had a sudden vision of them side by side, Antonia glowing in a slinky blue gown, he in his evening gear. Afterwards the suit had been sent for cleaning, the shirt washed, folded and put away. It had been a devil to iron, he remembered. It looked brand new, far too good to be thrown away, but he knew he could never wear it again, not when it reminded him so vividly of Antonia.

Dan opened his laptop. Logging on to Freecycle he posted, Offered: Calvanetti dress shirt. White, silk/cotton, collar 42cm. Worn once.

FOUR

Tracey Brown hurried round the corner into Benbow Close. A few more metres and she was home. Holding one carrier bag under an arm, propping up the other bag with her foot, she managed to unlock the front door, wiggle herself inside and slam it shut again before a frenzy of brown dog flung himself at her.

"Down Jake. Get down. Now!" Ignoring her commands the dog frantically wagged his tail and did his best to jump up and lick her face as she struggled past him and dumped her bags on the kitchen table. "Don't do that you stupid dog. It's disgusting." Her hands free, Tracey grabbed Jake's collar and pushed him into a sitting position. "The one time your master hasn't taken you with him in the lorry, you're all over me." Jake looked at her with soulful spaniel eyes. "You hadn't better have done anything you shouldn't while I was out." Tracey cast a quick glance around the kitchen. Everything seemed to be all right until she noticed that the door to the lounge-diner was open.

"You haven't? You can't have. You've not messed anywhere, have you?" If he had, she'd kill him. Eddie first, then his beloved water spaniel. No, the dog first then her husband. After all, it would be the animal that had done the damage. Hardly daring to look she walked into the lounge. To her relief there were no rips in the shiny leather sofa, the big plant, whose name she didn't know, still stood in its pot, and the ornaments on the mantelpiece were unbroken.

But was the smell still there? She had to check every time she went in. Tracey wrinkled her nose and sniffed. Not a hint of dog pee, just her lovely Blue Grass air freshener. She looked at the corner where Jake had messed as a puppy. It was the only time he'd ever dirtied in the house. He couldn't help it, he was so young, and he'd looked so scared when she'd yelled that she had felt awful for shouting; but he had stained her beautiful cream carpet. With a great deal of scrubbing and bottles of upholstery shampoo she had finally managed to get the marks out. Everyone told her it was as good as new but as far as she was concerned she could never forget what had happened.

Back in the kitchen she put the kettle on. Her feet ached terribly after a day filling shelves and although there was so much to do, she wasn't going to go round the house with the hoover until she had a rest. She'd seen the effect of always being on the go had had on her mum and she wasn't going to let it happen to her or her family.

There was time for a cuppa before her mum brought Milly home from school. Tracey moved the bulging supermarket bags onto the counter and decided that unpacking the shopping would have to wait. It wasn't because she was being lazy. All the magazines said how important it was to have time for yourself. *Me time* they called it. She was going to sit in her lovely sleek kitchen and flick through the latest *Interiors* magazine to pick up some ideas. They couldn't really afford it, but the lounge could do with a make-over; those pale-blue walls were looking a bit tired and if she changed the colour she would definitely need to do something about the carpet. In any case, there was nothing to stop her from dreaming.

Sitting at the small round table, Tracey kicked off her shoes, stretched out her legs and massaged one calf with her foot. Taking a sip of tea she opened the magazine. *Interiors* was so stylish it gave her a thrill just handling the glossy pages. The summer issue was already preparing readers for the winter season. The newest colours were browns, burnt orange and amber, so at least she wouldn't have to change the suite. There was a lovely set of curtains in a rich gold-and-chocolate pattern with a touch of acid green and a slash of purple. Tracey looked up and stared at the lounge door, trying to visualise those curtains at the windows. They were very striking, perhaps too striking for the room. She might do better to stick to something plain. Mulling over shots of drawing rooms in large country houses and penthouse apartments overlooking the river, she was distracted by a sharp knock. Jake bounded over to the back door barking with excitement as five-year-old Milly came running in waving an ice lolly. She was followed by her gran.

"I see you've made us a pot of tea. Pour us a cup and keep that dog away from me. These—" Sheila smoothed her hands down her immaculately pressed jeans "—are clean and they're going to stay that way."

Tracey shooed Jake into the utility room, wiped Milly's hands and sent her into the lounge to watch television.

"It's not stewed, is it? You know I can't stand stewed tea." Sheila held out her cup.

"I can make fresh," Tracey offered.

39

"No, this'll have to do. I can't stay long." Sheila flicked a manicured nail at the magazine on the table. "You're not thinking of decorating again, are you? It's not that long since you did your bedroom."

"Three years," Tracey said quickly. "And things wear out."

"Hmm." Sheila snorted. "We had to make do at your age. None of this changing the curtains every five minutes. Things had to last. There wasn't the money when your dad and I got married. You couldn't put everything on the credit card, not like you do now."

"It's different now." Tracey suppressed a shrug. Things had changed since she and her brothers were growing up. Her mum and dad might have had to scrimp and save but she and Eddie had credit cards. So what if the mortgage was bigger than they could really afford and they were a bit behind? They'd pay off what they owed soon enough. When she compared the house she'd been brought up in to the one she had now, she could hardly believe how far she had come. The strangest part of it was that Benbow Close was not more than a five-minute walk away from where she'd lived with her parents until she got married.

There had been seven of them: five children and her mum and dad crammed into a place with only two bedrooms and a bit, as her mum always called it. Being the only girl, Tracey got the sliver of space – the bit – between the two big upstairs rooms. There was only enough room for a single bed and a chest of drawers, and they were jammed in so tight that you couldn't tuck the sheet into the bottom of the bed because it was right up against the wall. But at least she got a bit of privacy. Her four brothers had the biggest bedroom, Mum and Dad the remaining one. The boys had to make do with two double beds and there were always fights about taking each other's stuff and who snored the loudest, or talked in his sleep. The only bathroom was tacked onto the end of the kitchen and when they were all together in the front room there wasn't the space to swing a cat.

Not like now with her long lounge-diner leading on to the breakfast-kitchen, with utility off. One day, they'd have a conservatory with wicker furniture and a plant or two, which would give them even more room. Even without it, Tracey loved her house, every centimetre of it. Best of all was the master bedroom with its en-suite. In Drake Road, there had always been someone banging on the bathroom door. If it wasn't her dad needing a shave it was one of the boys wanting the toilet. Her mum was constantly moaning at her to hurry up, telling Tracey that she wasn't the only member of the family who needed to get out of the house before half-past eight.

In Benbow Close there was none of that. There was a family bathroom, which the children used, and she and Eddie had the en-suite where she could stay all day if she wanted. Eddie didn't get in her way because he worked shifts. When he was on earlies he'd get up and make them both a cup of tea. If he had time he'd sit on the side of the bed and drink it with her, but mostly he'd have to hurry to get Jake walked before they both set off, so he'd have a shower and a shave while Tracey sat in bed and drank her tea. He'd leave the shower in a mess, damp towel on the floor, soap smears on the glass, but after she'd tidied it up she could stand under a stream of constant hot water enjoying the feel of it on her face and skin for as long as she liked.

Behind the utility room door, Jake began to whimper. Tracey looked at the clock on the cooker and drained her cup. "I'd better get on. The shopping wants putting away and Jodie and Josh will be home soon."

"I'll be off then." Sheila got to her feet. "Bye, my lover," she called to Milly through the lounge door.

"If you go now you'll miss the other two." Tracey felt a pang at the thought that her mum wasn't going to wait to see her older grandchildren. But that was Sheila. She liked them when they were little; it was when they grew older she wasn't so keen. Twelve-year-old girls like Jodie, Tracey had to admit, weren't that easy, but Josh at eight was a sweetie with an air of his granddad about him. It was a shame his gran didn't feel the same way, but having brought up a large family, and with the youngest of them still at home, Sheila made it obvious that she'd had enough of children.

It was no surprise. When Tracey and her brothers were young, Sheila had spent as little time with them as possible. When she wasn't at work she was washing and cleaning and cooking and making a big deal of it. Tracey remembered how the oven had to be cleaned every week after the Sunday roast. The rest of the family might be allowed to sit down and relax but not Sheila, who spent the rest of the afternoon putting the kitchen to rights. When she got older, Tracey was expected to help around the house but she could never do anything right. Whatever she did, her mum would find fault with it, while the boys could get away with anything. Luckily, her dad would stand up for her when Sheila went into one of her tirades.

"Your Mum's stressed," he would say and there was plenty to get stressed about. For a start there was never enough money to go round even though Sheila was expert at making every penny count. Sadly, things were beginning to get easier for her parents when her dad died. It was totally unexpected. He was sitting in his chair in the front room, a glass of beer in front of him and a cigarette smouldering in the ashtray, when he had a massive heart attack. It had happened not long after Tracey and Eddie's wedding, and she was forever thankful that her dad had been there to walk her down the aisle; he'd been so proud of his only daughter. He'd looked as fit and healthy as ever; no one had any clue of the state of his arteries.

"You look lovely. Bright as a summer morning," he had told her as they waited for the car to take them to the church. There had been tears in his eyes when he said it. Tracey had to wipe hers as she remembered that wedding day. Her dad had been such a lovely man and it was one of the saddest things in her life that he'd not lived long enough to know his grandchildren. He'd have loved them to bits – unlike her mum whose only concern was for herself.

The kitchen door swung open. Tracey sniffed back her tears and yelled, "Josh, take your shoes off."

"Mum." He rushed in, threw himself at her for a hug then, before she could gather him close, shrugged her off. "Can I have a lolly?"

"Get one from the freezer, but take those trainers off first."

"Okay." Halfway to the freezer Josh shucked off his shoes. The soles were badly worn, the uppers wearing thin. She really should replace them this month, but Jodie's birthday was coming up, and Tracey hated her children not having stuff. When it came to being generous, Eddie was even worse; he said it was because, having been brought up in foster care, he knew what it was like to go without and he was never going to let that happen to his kids. They were his priority – and hers too.

There was that other credit card she could use and, if she was careful with the food shop, she could get what the children needed and still have enough for a down payment on a new carpet from that bargain place by the river. It was only a bit of a risk and it was a long time since she'd done something for herself. That article she'd seen last week said that every woman should sometimes put her own needs before those of her family. It had given Tracey the shivers when she'd read it. It sounded so wrong, but it went on to explain that a happy mum made a happy family, and knowing that there was no trace of a whiff of dog pee in her lounge would make her very happy.

She flipped open *Interiors* and holding the magazine in front of her walked into the lounge. Should she go for the Berber with a greyish fleck, or the pale brown with slightly raised squares? Or the far more daring burnt orange? It was so hard to choose. Then she saw it, the perfect carpet in a lovely warm coral colour. With the walls off-white and coral piping on the new curtains, the room would look as good as anything in one of *Interiors* special features. A few scatter cushions in matching shades from the discount shop and she'd be done.

Tamping down the last of her doubts, Tracey took out her phone, logged into Freecycle and posted, **Offered: Cream carpet. Almost new.**

FIVE

A strand of hair twisted around her neck as Robyn struggled to free herself from her dream. Night after night it was the same. She was back in the manor house at Coombe Magna, running down the terrace steps, across the lawn, into the woods. Ancient trees loomed over her, their branches filtering out the light and making the path hard to follow, but she knew her way too well to get lost.

As she neared the lake the trees thinned. The bank was slick with moss; the steps leading down to the water slippery with damp. Her feet were bare and her toes gripped the stone giving an illusion of safety, until her foot slipped on a patch of weed. Throwing out her arms to regain her balance she fought to save herself, but there was nothing to grasp and no one to help. Her mouth moved into a scream. No sound came out. Slowly, inexorably, she slid down the remaining step and into the water. The ground sloped steeply and she was instantly out of her depth.

The lake was clogged with weed making the water thick and murky. Cold and green, it closed over her head. Struggling for breath, she kicked and fought but tendrils of water lily roots dragged her down to the mud-filled depths. However hard she tried, however desperately she battled to regain the surface, she could not save herself.

"Stop it, Finn!" A scream broke through her panic. Her

eyes opened. Sunlight rippled above her head. Was it too late? Had the water claimed her? Was she in some sort of afterlife?

Phoebe's voice rising from the kitchen brought her back to reality. "That's my job. I make tea in the morning for Mum."

Grief, I've overslept. Robyn flung back the covers. Her nightdress was soaked in sweat. Her heart was beating too fast and she could not get enough air into her lungs. Her head spun as she stood up and she had to grip the metal rail of the bedhead to steady herself before she could hurry down the stairs to deal with whatever catastrophe awaited her.

In the kitchen every single cup she owned had been set out on the table. Each one had been filled with cold water to exactly the same level and in most of them there was a limp soggy tea bag. Four-year-old Finn was sitting on a chair holding a teaspoon and staring intently at the cups. Glaring at him was a tubby ginger-haired eight-year-old girl.

"I told him," Phoebe growled, "but he wouldn't stop. He never does." She scowled at her brother and stamped out of the room.

"Finn." Robyn knelt beside him but there was no reaction. It was as if she simply did not exist. She stretched out her hand then thought better of it. Her son did not respond well to being touched. "Finn," she repeated. "It's Mum."

Finn leaned forward. He pressed his spoon into a tea bag and began grinding it down into the bottom of the cup. A thin spiral of brown rose to the surface and in a sudden spurt of rage he swept the cup from the table. As it smashed on the tiles he moved onto the next one, then the next, dashing them to the floor, one after the other, his arms flailing like a machine.

Robyn grabbed her son and pulled him away from the table. Finn kicked and screamed. She wrestled with the distraught child until she managed to drag him onto the rug in front of the Aga and pull him onto her lap. Red faced with fury he thrashed about until suddenly his limbs went limp, and sticking his finger in his mouth he fell asleep. Relaxing her hold Robyn cradled him in her arms. It was only at times like this that he would let her cuddle him.

Holding him close she drifted back to that faraway period when her children were happy and contented and she was still married to a man that loved her. When Kit was little and Phoebe had just been born, she would sit by the Aga and feed the baby while the rest of the family was asleep and the marmalade cat lay purring at her feet. With Finn's arrival all that had changed. No more quiet nights in the kitchen – instead, endless pacing of bedroom floors with a screaming angry baby.

"What's for breakfast?" Kit's voice broke through the memory, brought back to the present. Robyn looked up at her ten-year-old son and thought how cruel genes could be. In her family, Phoebe had inherited her grandfather's thick set frame. Kit had both good looks and a keen brain, while Finn's was scrambled. No, she corrected herself, Finn was not scrambled. He was not joined up in the same way as everyone else. He saw the world differently and while for some people that was the source of their talent, in Finn's case it seemed to cause him nothing but anger and frustration. Or was it fear of what he could not control?

"If only I knew," Robyn murmured, stroking Finn's cheek with a long paint-stained finger.

"Is there any cereal?" Kit opened the larder door, looked inside, turned and screwed up his face. "There's nothing to eat in here."

"There's Weetabix. There's got to be Weetabix," Robyn said desperately.

"There isn't. There's only Coco Pops." Kit pulled out the box and shook it. "There aren't many left and those are for Finn." Kit looked reproachfully at his mother and as if on cue his brother woke up.

"Coco Pops," he said, struggling out of Robyn's embrace.

"All right, Finn. I'll get the milk out of the fridge, then Kit and I can have some toast." Robyn stood up.

"You've got bare feet," Kit said. "There's broken cups all over the floor. You'll cut yourself."

"I'll sweep it up."

"Coco Pops," Finn said, seating himself at the table.

Robyn stepped carefully around the shattered china. "I'll clean up after he's eaten." She measured out the precise amount of cereal for Finn and poured in exactly enough milk to cover it. As she tipped the carton she held her breath, a millimetre too much and Finn would throw a tantrum. Today she had it right and he picked up his spoon and began drowning each piece until the whole bowl was full of a slushy chocolate mixture.

As soon as Finn had begun to eat Robyn turned her

attention to her other son. Taking the remains of yesterday's loaf out of the bread crock, she said, "I'm afraid we've only got brown but it will make good toast."

Kit shrugged. "I'll watch it," he said, turning his back on her and lifting the lid on the Aga.

Robyn's eyes filled with tears. "Sorry Kit, I said I'd go shopping yesterday but I had to do some work. I know Finn gets whatever he wants but that's how he is and if he doesn't, we all suffer." She waited, hoping for a reply and when it didn't come gave up and spooned coffee into the cafetiere.

"It's ready." Kit held up a slightly charred piece of bread. "I'll get the butter and marmalade," he added, walking away in case his mother suggested something more healthy.

Just for once it won't hurt and I've no idea what else we've got, Robyn thought. She would shop when she had time, but first she'd have a coffee and, if she were lucky, she might manage to get dressed before Finn's babysitter came. Sue would give her a couple of hours to finish off her latest commission and, when she'd earned enough to pay the electricity bill, she'd finally be able to get back to the work she had in mind for the exhibition at the Royal West of England Academy. She glanced across the table where Finn, sitting bolt upright, was raising his spoon to his mouth. Up and down it went like the arm of a crane. The mechanical movement was in such complete contrast to the delicious roundness of his body that she had to draw it. Robyn reached for her sketchpad and was searching for a pencil when a ringing sound broke her concentration. Still thinking about her drawing, Robyn looked round to see where it was coming from.

"Mum. It's your phone." Kit put down his toast.

"Yes," Robyn said vaguely. The phone was ringing but where was it? She gazed hopefully at the pile of papers on the wooden draining board; decided that it couldn't be there and turned her attention to the plates on the dresser.

"Here." Kit handed her something smooth and plastic.

"Thank you, darling." Robyn reached out to stroke his hair but he'd gone back to his breakfast. "Hullo. Who is it?"

"Robyn are you okay? You don't sound quite yourself." Sue's voice, with its warm trace of a Bristol accent, sounded concerned.

"I'm fine. I didn't sleep well. I need a coffee to get my brain in gear."

"That's all right then." Sue's sigh of relief was so heavy that Robyn could almost feel the breath in her ear. "I'm sorry but I can't come and look after Finn this morning. Mum's not well. I'm waiting on the doctor as we speak."

Robyn felt as if she had been punched. Her plans for the day were ruined. Without her sitter she could do nothing. When Finn was younger, and the other two were at school and nursery, she would put him in his playpen where he would sit for hours stacking and un-stacking his wooden blocks. The game, if that is what it was, kept him safe and gave her the freedom to work. What she should have done was to find him a nursery place but her instinct had been to keep him close. Now he was older he should be learning to socialise, but his behaviour was so unpredictable that no nursery or playgroup would take him and she had to rely on Sue for a few hours respite.

What made it worse was that today Sue had promised to keep an eye on all three children as schools were closed for a teacher training day.

"I'll let you know when things are back to normal," Sue finished.

Robyn shook her head. The phone in her hand was too heavy to hold and she had to close her fingers tight around it to stop it from slipping from her grasp. Things for her would never be normal. Finn would never be normal. She would never have enough time to finish all the paintings she had in her head. The thought of days without Sue's calm and competent help, and the interminable summer holiday stretching out in front of her, Robyn was filled with despair.

Finn finished his Coco Pops and ledged his spoon at precisely the right angle along the top of his bowl. "Sue," he said.

"Wash first. Then get dressed," Robyn said, hoping that Finn would not be upset at the change in his routine. Finn got up from the table and trotted to the door.

"Wash teeth," he said. "Wash teeth. Teeth wash."

Kit raised his eyes to the ceiling.

Please God, don't let him stay stuck on those two words all day, Robyn prayed.

She waited until Finn was halfway up the stairs. If she followed directly behind him he would stop and scream until she went back to the bottom. Maybe he felt crowded or somehow threatened by her action. Who knew what went on in his head? Whatever it was she had learned to give him space.

Finn went straight to the bathroom and stood at the

basin. Robyn joined him as quickly as she could, checking any impatience as she measured out the toothpaste. If she wanted any time to herself there was no hurrying the morning ritual.

Robyn left her youngest sitting on his bedroom floor with his building blocks set out in front of him.

"Kids, can you give me ten minutes, keep an eye on Finn," she called. *Please look after him for ten whole minutes. I won't ask for anything else, not for the rest of the day.* Robyn ran along the landing and was already at her studio door when Phoebe, her face creased and earnest, trundled out of her bedroom.

"I'll do it Mum. I'm sorry I was cross."

"Thanks!" Robyn breathed. "Thank you, darling. Make sure Finn doesn't…"

"I know," Phoebe's frown faded. She looked so serious and determined that Robyn, fearing a deluge of guilt, fled.

Her studio had once been the drawing room, but as soon she'd seen its long windows overlooking the river she had claimed it for her own. "It has the best light so it will be my room for drawing in," she'd joked. Philip had laughed and slipping his arm around her waist had hugged her close.

The floorboards were spattered with paint and a half-finished canvas stood on the easel. Robyn went straight to the computer on the pine table in a corner of the room. Unlike the rest of the house this area was neat and tidy with all paperwork filed away in metal filing cabinets. Cards announcing forthcoming events, or bills to be paid, were pinned up on the notice board. She checked for a message from the gallery owner who had said he wanted to exhibit her work, but to her disappointment found nothing.

From Finn's room came the familiar tap-tap of one wooden block on another – her son's metronome beat that so often dictated her every action. For now at least he was safely absorbed and she had a few minutes to herself.

She scrolled through the inbox. Nothing for work or from friends and family, only a stream of postings from Freecycle members. With a faint twinge of guilt she allowed herself to browse the day's offerings, deleting as she went until she arrived at Offered: One old-fashioned armchair. Upholstery a little worn.

A shaft of sunlight slanted across the floor. Robyn gazed at it and was inspired. If she positioned the chair right there in the window, the light would catch it perfectly. A child could be cradled in its old-fashioned arms or an older person supported by its straight back through the lengthy sittings a portrait demanded.

Yes please, Robyn typed, *I would love your chair*. Without thinking how and when she would fetch it, she pressed send.

"Mum," Phoebe's voice shrilled. "Finn says he's blue today."

Blue, Robyn thought as she ran from the studio, *has he got enough blue clothes?*

Finn stood in the middle of his bedroom. He had taken off his pyjamas and was muttering, "Blue. Finn is blue." Over and over again.

"Come on then, darling." Robyn pulled open a drawer and began looking for the only clothes Finn would agree to wear that day.

To her relief her younger son had clean blue underpants, a blue top and a pair of jeans handed down from Kit. Only the socks looked as if they would be a problem. They were blue but with a red stripe around the top. Robyn held them up. Finn looked steadily at them. Her heart fluttered and she wondered how long it would take her to race into town and back for a new pair. Then Finn nodded and the crisis was averted.

Dressed entirely in his chosen colour he went with her to her room where she slid out of her nightdress, and ignoring the musky smell under her arms, pulled on a burnt orange T-shirt and bronze flowing skirt. Her long red hair she bundled up to the top of her head and secured with a couple of grips. She was sticking the last of these in place when Phoebe walked in.

"Mum, Ruby said I could go and play today."

"Mm," Robyn kept her glance on her reflection in the mirror. Antique and spotted with mould, the mirror made interesting patterns on her skin. Perhaps she could replicate that effect in a painting.

"Mum," Phoebe repeated.

"I know," Robyn sighed. Ruby lived a few streets away. The very thought of taking Phoebe to her friend's house with Finn in tow exhausted her. Finn would insist on avoiding every crack in the pavement and the walk would take ages.

"Kit says he's got to go to the library."

"No." Thankfully the word came out as a sigh making it sound less harsh. However much she wanted to, Robyn was too tired to work out how she was going to get her children to where they wanted to be. She knew she wasn't being fair. Ever since Finn was born the older two had had to come second, but what else could she do? Robyn's head ached with the pain of it all. Unable to move, she let her hand drop to her side and stood in front of the mirror watching her daughter, preparing her assault.

"I can walk there on my own and when it's time to go home Ruby's mum will bring me, if I ask her," Phoebe began. "And I can stay to…"

The doorbell rang, breaking her torrent of words.

"Phoebe go see who it is. Please."

"Yes, but what about going to Ruby's?"

"We'll see," Robyn conceded wearily.

Phoebe scowled and went down the stairs as slowly as she could. She hadn't reached the bottom when the bell rang again, the kitchen door banged open and, racing along the corridor, Kit beat her to the front door.

"It's Uncle David!" Phoebe yelled. Coming onto the landing Robyn saw her children charge towards her bother. As he held out his arms and hugged them, the tight feeling in her chest dissolved. The cavalry had arrived. David was here and the day was brighter, more bearable.

"Where's the mum and Finnegan's Wake?" David asked.

"Right here," Robyn called.

David Latimer's hazel eyes crinkled as he grinned at his sister. "It's a great day. I've got the van and there's no gig tonight so I thought we might go for a drive in the country. How about it kids? Shall we give the poor old mum a break?"

"Yes," Kit and Phoebe chorused, all other plans

forgotten. Robyn caught her brother's eye and shook her head.

"Why not?"

She shrugged. He couldn't be asked to take Finn and she couldn't face being left alone with her most demanding child. At that moment Finn himself made an appearance and immediately David understood the problem. "Okay then. We'll all go. We might even make the seaside. At the very least there will be fish and chips and ice cream."

"Finn doesn't eat fish," Phoebe said.

"Quite right too. With a name like that how can he be expected to eat his friends and relations? He can have chips with vinegar if he likes." David spoke to his niece but he was looking at his sister.

"He can," Robyn agreed and it was settled. They would go out in the van, all five of them, and since there was plenty of room she'd ask David if he would pick up the chair on the way.

*

They drove with the windows open, the warm summer air surging past them as they sang the latest song David had written for his band.

"The way you lot do it, Gullswing will have the greatest hit ever," he told them as they swung down country lanes. Finn banged out the rhythm on the side of the van, carrying on long after they had finished singing. "That's drummers for you," David said and Finn's obsessive pounding became funny rather than intensely annoying.

At last they came to an elegant house at the edge of a

village. David parked in the drive and telling the others to stay where they were, Robyn got out. She shook the creases out of her skirt and went to ring the doorbell. *We look like a bunch of hippies,* she thought as she glanced back at the brightly decorated van.

The woman who opened the door was in her late fifties. She was slim and blonde though there were touches of grey in her hair.

"We've come for the chair," Robyn said.

"So you have." Jane smiled. "Do come in."

Robyn looked over her shoulder. "Kit, Phoebe, keep an eye on Finn. Uncle David and I won't be long."

"We want to come too," Phoebe protested.

"I don't think…" Robyn began.

"You're welcome, all of you." Jane forestalled her objections. "It's a big chair and you'll need all the help you can get," she added solemnly.

In the empty study sunlight streamed in through the bay window onto the faded scarlet upholstery of the old wing chair.

"Oh!" Robyn drew in her breath. The chair was even better than she had imagined.

"It's a little faded but still quite sturdy." Jane misunderstood her reaction. "If it's not what you want, I do understand."

"No, no. It's perfect. We'll take it. It's just what I was looking for. Thank you so much."

"Let's get it loaded," David said.

"While they're doing that, I've got drinks and chocolate biscuits in the kitchen. If that's all right with your mum." Jane looked at Robyn but before she could reply Phoebe said, "Yes please."

"Looks like it's biscuits for two, unless you want to go with them, Finn," David said.

"Mum. Chair." Finn moved closer to Robyn.

"Okay. You stay with us," David said and he and Robyn manoeuvred the chair out of the house. Finn followed them and stood by the van as the chair was lifted into the back.

It took a while to make sure it was secure, by which time Phoebe and Kit were back with a couple of foil-wrapped biscuits for Finn. He studied them both carefully before deciding which he would eat first.

"Now to the beach," David declared. "Where the mum will sit on the cliff top in her magnificently ancient chair, monarch of all she surveys, while we paddle in the sea."

"Sea, sea I see the sea, sea," Finn chanted and they all joined in, their voices floating out behind them as they drove towards the wide sweep of the coast.

SIX

Anna set her laptop down on the kitchen counter. She loosened the band that held up her thick blonde hair and it tumbled over her shoulders, as she ticked off her mental list of things that had to be done.

First, there was that report for tomorrow's meeting. When that was complete she might have enough time, before Alistair arrived, to slip upstairs to see how her mum was doing. She had not long moved into the flat above and Anna knew how hard it must have been for Jane to leave the family home. She wished they could talk about it; she wanted to tell her mother how sad she was that such an important part of the past had gone forever, but every time Anna tried to bring up the subject the words had stuck in her throat.

It was probably for the best. If she started talking about her feelings, she would end up doing something stupid, like bursting into tears, which is how she'd reacted when Jane told her that she'd found a home for Dad's chair. When Anna had learned what Jane had done she finished the call and sobbed and sobbed. There was no logic to this grief – it crept up without warning and made you do crazy things. There was certainly no point in weeping over a piece of old furniture, well past its sell by date.

If Mum didn't want it, well, there was no room for it in Anna's apartment with its cool uncluttered interior; the few objects on display drew the eye: a bowl of fruit, carefully arranged, was the only splash of colour in the kitchen. In the living room, an abstract view of Provence by Anuk Naumann, its glowing vibrancy vividly conveying the heat and scent of the South of France, contrasted with the white vase holding a single orchid that stood on a simple black table.

Anna liked things simple, in her men as well as her home. Alistair's ability to focus on what was important was one of the things she appreciated about him, apart from his amazingly good looks and yellow Ferrari.

What am I thinking? When did I become so superficial? There has to be more to him than that, so why can't I see it? Anna raked her hand through her hair. Her mind seemed to have stalled, which was far from surprising after the day she had. Meetings from eight o'clock onwards, then in her role as head of Human Resources she had to tell one of her staff that they had come to the end of the road with him. They had gone through all the legal processes and he was going to be made redundant. He had been upset and angry, refusing to accept that the problem lay with his behaviour. His attitude had left her shaken and upset, and wondering what she could have done better to have achieved a different outcome, yet knowing that with this particular individual there was nothing else she could have done.

Anna kicked off her shoes, took a bottle of Chardonnay from the fridge and poured herself a large glass. That was the trouble with men. However dependable and reliable they seemed, they invariably let you down. The only exception was her dad.

She half-closed her eyes and saw him sitting in his chair, pipe in hand, the smoke rising into the air. A sharp breath and she could almost smell the pungent sweetness of the tobacco. No wonder that chair smelled. *Of your dad*, a small voice insisted, and she shut it off as efficiently as she might delete a spam email. She couldn't bear to think about her dad growing old, then sick. In the last year of his life the red chair was the only one he could use with any comfort. Its firm back supported his increasingly frail body. Resting his head against a wing, he would sit, huddled up in his old corduroy trousers and ancient cardigan, looking out at his beloved garden. If she asked how he was, he would reply that he was thinking, not wanting to admit how exhausted he was by the latest dose of chemo.

Anna shook her head to get rid of the image. What was the matter with her tonight? Where was all this coming from? Selling the old house must have affected her more than she'd imagined. It was only to be expected as that was where she'd spent a very happy childhood until she'd left home to live with Miles. When that relationship hadn't worked out she'd bought her own flat. From then on she'd moved up the property ladder, selling some, keeping others to rent out, until she could afford her riverside apartment.

Now Jane was living in the same apartment block and, Anna had promised herself, she would do her best to keep an eye on her mum. A quick visit once or twice a week so her mother wouldn't feel crowded should do it. With Anna's work schedule it wasn't going to be possible to do more.

Right from the start, Anna was determined to establish boundaries. She had her own life and she didn't need anyone interfering. Whatever happened she was perfectly capable of dealing with it on her own. She'd never been one to come running home for tea and sympathy, and she wasn't going to start now. One of the good things about Alistair was that he understood her need for independence just as she understood his.

Anna wandered over to the glass doors that overlooked the harbour. Beyond the city, the sky stretched like a purple bruise shot through with slashes of scarlet. Lights shone in apartment windows and in the houses across the river. Stepping out onto the balcony she let the evening air caress her skin.

She drank the last of her wine, checked to see if there was time for a refill before supper and was shocked to see that it was almost nine. She had planned to write that report before they'd eaten and if she left it much longer it would be the early hours of the morning before it was finished.

Tuesday was one of their regular date nights and Alistair should have been here hours ago. Had something else come up? She checked her phone. Nothing. Could he have told her about a meeting and she'd forgotten? She had been so busy lately it could easily have slipped her mind.

Where are you? she texted. There was no reply. Anna shrugged. He might be driving, or on another call. He would get in touch when he was ready. In the meantime, she'd get on with the rest of her evening.

Abandoning the planned supper for two, she made

herself a sandwich of pitta bread, hummus, and a salad. She ate in the kitchen, standing in the half-light, watching the shadows spreading across the floor. When she had finished, she poured strong black coffee into a mug and went into the study.

Around midnight she heard the soft thud of the apartment door, followed by footsteps. Anna pushed her reading glasses to the top of her head and leaned back in her chair, waiting for the familiar feather-like kiss on the back of her neck.

Instead of a greeting, keys clunked into a marble ashtray, followed by a blast of water from the shower. Ignoring the unexpected feeling of rejection, Anna finished writing her sentence, stretched and yawned. Moving deliberately slowly she closed down the laptop, packed up her work, put her mug in the dishwasher, and made her way to the bedroom.

Leaning against the door frame of the en-suite, she watched Alistair's outline against the glass as he rubbed shampoo into his black springy hair, then washed it off, shaking his head like a dog, and rubbing the back of his arm over his nose sending the last drops of water flying everywhere. Still dripping, he stepped out onto the wooden duckboard and asked, "Are you going in?"

For the briefest of moments she was tempted to strip off and pull him back into the shower with her. Was that what he wanted too? Even as the question crossed her mind, he wrapped himself in a towel and peered at his reflection in the mirror. Was he going to shave? She hated the stubbly feel of his face at the end of the day, but as he ran a hand over his chin she realised that his skin was smooth, so he must have shaved earlier.

"Where were you?" she said.

"Out." He was still studying his face. "Why?"

"You didn't say you were going to be late."

"Didn't I?"

"No," Anna said, annoyed by his attitude. "I had supper planned."

"That's a first." What might once have been a tease now sounded flat, almost accusatorial.

"Yes." She heard her voice sharpen and was angry with herself for letting her emotions show. "It's Tuesday, or had you forgotten."

"I know what day of the week it is." He kept his back turned to her, although he knew she could see his face reflected in the mirror. "Look Anna." He straightened up and faced her. He was so incredibly handsome her stomach flipped. "We agreed that we lead our own lives. Remember." Walking past her into the bedroom, he finished drying himself.

Anna was too tired for a row. Besides there was nothing to fight about. The deal was that they each had their own flats. He had the key to hers, she to his, and there were so many days in the week when they were together. It had worked well at first. Meals out, clubbing, moonlight walks, weekends abroad. Everything they did was spontaneous, spur of the moment. The only things they ever planned were the extravagant expensive holidays to exotic locations.

"Two adults together, but independent," she said.

"That's right." Alistair pulled on clean clothes. "Anna, I'm sorry." His voice was kind, his eyes concerned. "I can't go on like this... I was going to... Oh hell..." Shaking his head he went into the living room. The curtains had not been drawn and the full moon hung red over the hills of Dundry. "We have to talk. Do you want a drink?"

She shook her head but he ignored her and poured two large malts. She put hers down carefully on the low table, surprised that her hand was completely steady. Their eyes locked and she saw a brief flicker of pain in his before he walked over to the window. "This isn't working."

Anna nodded. She felt completely numb, as if it was all happening to someone else. She picked up her glass and was grateful for the burning sensation as the fiery liquid slid down her throat.

"It wasn't what I wanted." His shoulders slumped and his whole body took on the stance of a guilty little boy.

"It doesn't matter." Wearily she moved towards the bedroom.

"Where are you going?"

"Bed. I've got a busy day tomorrow. I mean today."

"Anna listen. Please. I want to explain. I want to tell you how it is."

Anna sighed theatrically, raising her eyes to the ceiling. "You've found someone else. She's younger, more exciting. You tried to resist but there is something special between you. Something neither of you have ever felt before. You don't want to hurt me, but..."

He looked at her in amazement. "How did you...?" he began.

"Keep it," she said briefly. "I've heard it all before. When I haven't dealt it out myself." There was a pause.

Alistair took a swig of his whisky. "Okay, so it's over. I want you out of here by the time I get home from the office tonight. You still have your flat – you won't be homeless. Or perhaps what's-her-name will take you in." He started to speak, but she cut him off. "No we won't be friends. In fact we won't see each other at all. Oh, and for what's left of the night you can sleep in the guest room."

"Anna!" There was anguish in his tone as he started towards her. "I didn't want things to end like this. When we first got together..." She lifted a hand to stop him, but he went on. "I thought this was it. All I wanted was to be with you. You were everything I'd ever dreamed of." Not wanting to hear any more, she put her finger to her lips, but he took her hand and moved it away. Still holding it he said, "We never had time." Head bowed, his voice cracked. "*You* never had time for us. You were always working. After a while I thought there must be someone else." Dropping her hand, he raised his head. "When I found out there wasn't another man I came to the conclusion that you didn't care about me as a person. I was only here to service you. Escort duties. Bed duties."

"No!" Anna said, pain stabbing through her. "It isn't... It wasn't like that."

Alistair shrugged. "So you say. When Helen came into the office, she..."

"Listened?" Anna turned her head towards the night sky. The pain was getting worse but it was overlaid by a hysterical urge to giggle.

"I couldn't help it," he murmured.

"Of course you couldn't." She reached up and patted his head as she would a contrite dog. Then she went into the bedroom and shut the door.

Anna lay on her back staring at the ceiling as she ran through the list of things she would have to do. Luckily, she and Alistair did not share a mortgage and had separate arrangements for their finances. Perhaps that meant they had known, deep down from the very start, that their relationship wouldn't last.

In the coming days and weeks she would have to let mutual friends and acquaintances know. There would be texts to send and calls to make. Why wasn't there a quick and easy way to do this? An announcement in the paper, on social media, on local radio. *Anna and Alistair are no longer partners.* That sounded like a business agreement, not a relationship. *Anna and Alistair are no longer bonking, seeing each other, are not a couple...* The giggles she had suppressed earlier rose in her throat. She clapped her hand over her mouth to hold back the hysteria and tried to breathe through her nose to relax.

She had to be sensible and stay calm. The betrayal was no surprise. What had shocked her was that it came from him and not from her. If she hadn't had so much to think about she would have been there first. She had known for a long time that the spark was gone. She no longer hurried back to be with him at the end of the day. Instead, she spent hours at the office completing work that could easily have been done at home. If she had been honest with herself and with him, she should have finished the relationship long ago.

Alistair was right. He was someone she called on when she needed him. Someone to spend time with at the weekend. Breakfast in a café on the harbour side. Dinner in a candlelit restaurant, savouring the food and looking at the view. Not saying much because there was not much to say.

Tonight was the first time in months they had spoken to each other about anything that mattered and ironically it was too late. Alistair had already made his decision and she hadn't even bothered to fight it. What did that say about her? Was she one of those women that slid in and out of relationships because none of the men she slept with mattered to her very much? Or was it simply that long term commitments weren't for her? Perhaps she had to face the uncomfortable truth that she was never going to love any man as much as her mum had loved Dad.

What she did know was that she was perfectly fine on her own. Her mum too was moving on and to Anna's surprise, Jane had not fallen to pieces when Hugh had died. After the initial shock she'd gently but firmly declined any offers of help and made her own decisions about what she was going to do, including buying an apartment rather than the traditional little terrace or chic mews house Anna had expected her choose.

I suppose it's all because she's coming to terms with losing Dad. Not that she'll ever get over it. No one could ever get over my lovely dad. A sob rose in her throat and she swallowed it down. She wasn't going to cry. She was and always had been a strong woman – as was Jane. What her mum was doing was getting on with life, because there was nothing else to do. Moving into the city showed she was looking forward, not living in the past. Letting go of the chair was all part of that.

Anna turned onto her side and yawned. She should be

glad the chair had found a home. *That's why freecycling's so good. You put something you don't want on the site and someone who wants it fetches it. Shame it doesn't work for people. If it did, I'd post,* **Offered, one boyfriend slightly used.**

SEVEN

Sitting down to breakfast, Jane realised with a slight pang that she was already beginning to feel at home. Although it was so different from the old house the apartment suited her. The rooms were light and airy with space for her new furniture, and the huge windows had spectacular views over the river and the distant hills. There was a balcony where she could sit out and enjoy the sunshine, although there would be times when she missed the garden. *No, it's not the garden. It's you I miss*, she told Hugh. *But since you're not here…*

Taking a sip of coffee, she decided that today was the day she would explore more of the local area. Anna had recommended the butcher and the health shop in the High Street. There was also a delicatessen, an old-fashioned junk shop where you could browse for a bargain, a brand-new bookshop, as well as a florist and greengrocer. Most tempting of all was the river. With its tree-lined banks and wide pavements it would almost be like being abroad, and there was sure to be a café or a pub where she could treat herself to some lunch.

It was very hot and she walked slowly, relishing the shade as well as the sunlight sparkling on the water. Cars, buses and vans filled the air with a constant hum and a lingering taste of exhaust fumes. On the other side of the road there was a row of elegant but slightly shabby houses. Some of them had been restored to their former glory, others were still bedsits or flats, but she had no doubt that they too were on their way up in the world. Jane wandered slowly past, wondering who lived there and why. When she had lived in the country she knew all her neighbours; here she was anonymous and it gave her an intoxicating feeling of freedom. She could be anyone, she could do anything, and no one would know or care. Engrossed in the idea of being a different person she didn't notice the red-haired woman with two children coming towards her.

"Chair lady." The words came out like a sneeze and Jane was brought to a sudden halt in front of a small boy. There was something familiar about his round face and the eyes that looked straight past her.

"You are her," said a dark-haired boy. "We went to your house," he continued as Jane stared at him in bewilderment.

"Oh I'm so sorry," the woman apologised. "It's Finn." She shrugged as if there was nothing more to say.

"You gave us your chair," the older boy explained.

"Now I remember." Jane smiled. "You're...?" she hesitated, trying but failing to remember his name.

"I'm Kit Latimer-Jones and this is Robyn, the mum—" he paused "—and Finn."

"We live over there." Robyn waved towards the terrace.

"The one with the purple door. That's ours," Kit said. "Are you our new neighbour?" He looked at the "Sold" sign on the house next door. "I didn't see the van."

"No. I live in one of the apartments by the river now.

It's not far from here, and since I've not long moved in I thought I'd come out to explore the area."

"And met us," Robyn said.

"Chair lady," Finn began. "Chair…"

"Yes she is." Robyn turned as if she was going to shepherd her family across the road. The children did not move. Kit stood looking intently at Jane. Finn's hot fingers clutched at her hand and tugged.

"Chair," Finn repeated.

Robyn, her hair rippling down her back, stood at the kerb and looked right then left, then right again as if she were about to cross, and Jane felt a moment of panic. Surely she wasn't going to be left alone with the two boys.

"Oh dear, I'm sorry." Robyn finally noticed her children's preoccupation. "Once Finn has made up his mind there's nothing we can do. He's…" she trailed off.

Kit raised a finger to his temple. "Nuts," he hissed.

"Kit! Don't say that." Robyn glanced at Jane. "Finn is…"

"It's all right. I quite understand." Jane was wondering how she was going to free herself from the child's grasp without making any sudden or startling moves.

"I think he wants you to come and see what we've done with your chair," Robyn said. "Perhaps if you have a few minutes to spare you could stay for coffee? I've got Florentines and macaroons and vanilla slices." She looked down at the basket on her arm. "It's the least I can do to thank you."

"Oh there's no need, no need at all," Jane said, still trying to slide her fingers away from Finn's. Whenever she pulled his grip tightened, and giving up the attempt to free herself she let him lead her across the road and up the path to the house with the purple front door.

Uncollected post lay on the tiled floor. The fanlight was thick with dust and the wooden stairs bare. The walls were painted a deep scarlet and lined with drawings, some framed, others merely tacked to the plaster, and all of them were of children. There were studies of babies, asleep in their cradles, playing on rugs, crawling, smiling, crying, or taking their first unsteady steps. There were quick sketches and full portraits of Phoebe, Kit and Finn.

Jane examined each picture more closely, moving slowly from one to another.

"They're wonderful," she said.

"Thank you." Robyn smiled and swept past her into the kitchen leaving her with Finn.

"Mum, you brought cakes?" Jane heard Phoebe say.

"We'll have them in a minute but first…"

Thinking Robyn was expecting her to join them in the kitchen, Jane started down the corridor but Finn was having none of it. "Chair." He tugged her towards the stairs.

"It's in the drawing room." To Jane's relief Robyn reappeared. "Upstairs." She gestured towards the first floor. "It was a kind of joke at first, you'll see." She slipped past Finn and almost floated up the staircase leaving the little boy and Jane to follow in her wake.

All the doors on the gloomy first-floor landing were closed shuttering in the musty smell of an old house. Robyn flung open the drawing room door and Jane's senses were assailed by a pungent wave of oil paint and turpentine.

Jane stepped into an almost empty room and stood blinking against the sudden brilliance of the light that flooded in through the floor-to-ceiling windows. Finn, however, wouldn't let her pause and pulled her to the window where the chair stood, its worn upholstery glowing in the sunlight. He relinquished his hold and Jane, feeling slightly foolish, had no idea what she was supposed to do. The child placed himself solidly at her side while his mother stood and watched them.

Finally Jane had an inspiration. "Do you want me to sit down?" Finn nodded vigorously. She let out a long breath and lowered herself onto the cushioned seat. It felt strange to be sitting in Hugh's chair, the chair she had thought she had said goodbye to for ever. She wanted to process what she was feeling but Finn's presence made that impossible.

The little boy circled the chair, once, twice, then without a word he turned and walked out of the room. Jane heard him clumping down the stairs and another woman's voice calling his name. A door opened and shut and he was gone.

Weak with relief, she had to make a real effort to stop her eyes from closing. The whole incident, stupid though it was, had brought so many emotions to the surface. She was swept by a wave of sadness and loss, underpinned by a feeling of unease about being in an unfamiliar house with an unpredictable child and people she did not know.

Jane leaned her hands on the arms of the chair and was about to get up when Robyn said, "No, don't move. Please." She was holding a sketchbook and working furiously. One line, then another and another, and her drawing was finished.

"Can I see?" Jane asked. Robyn nodded and handed over a pencil sketch of a woman in her fifties, her face tired yet caught in the moment when weariness gave way to relaxation. There was beauty in the way she held her head, but a sadness in her eyes.

"It's beautiful," Jane said.

"I think I've caught something of you." Robyn stood at her shoulder, frowning as she studied the drawing. "But there is more. I would love to paint you."

"Me? But I'm not sure I could—"

"No," Robyn interrupted. "I didn't mean you should commission me. I want to do it for myself. There is so much in your face, so much experience and suffering, and joy too, I think."

"But you draw children mostly, don't you?" Jane stammered, taken aback by the other woman's honesty and intuition.

"You mean the pictures on the stairs? I've drawn them since they were born, and sometimes I get a commission for someone else's sprogs. Not very often though. People prefer photos and with digital cameras you can't go far wrong. I mainly do adult portraits. People commission them for special events, like important milestone birthdays, a retirement or even graduation. Pictures like those are my bread and butter. Not that you would be," she added hastily. "Painting you would be a joy. I'd love to do a portrait of you sitting in your chair. What could be more fitting? It wouldn't take long. Once I'm inspired I work fast, so please say you will." Her whole face was alight like a child begging for a treat and Jane found it impossible to say anything else but yes.

"I'd be honoured," she added.

"That's that then." Robyn walked over to the table where she did her admin and looked through her diary to book in the first sitting. "Now," she said as she entered Jane's name in flowing purple ink, "let's go and get this coffee I promised you."

They sat at an old pine table in the sun-filled kitchen. The sink was piled high with unwashed dishes, the door to the garden was open, and Phoebe and Kit's voices floated in over the drone of the traffic. Of Finn there was no sign. Robyn explained that Sue, her cleaner, child minder and miracle worker, was looking after him. "I can't leave him with the other two. I think there'd be murder committed. Sue is a total angel. I don't know what we'd do without her. She gives me space to work. Without it we'd be broke and I'd be in a psychiatric unit." She grimaced. "I love Finn to bits, I really do. We all do," she added as if trying to convince herself. "But..."

"He's hard work," Jane finished the sentence.

Robyn bent her head over her mug, letting her hair fall over her face to hide her expression. "Mm," she murmured. "Yes," she added more clearly. "His father couldn't take it. He couldn't stand living with the chaos of it all and went off with an anally retentive, super housewife DT teacher. You can eat off her floors, apparently. When you're not drinking out of the toilet bowl that is."

"How scary." Jane looked round the cosy chaotic kitchen. "Personally, I prefer this."

"Don't tell me. It's got character." Robyn screwed up

her face but her eyes were laughing. "That's what people generally say when they don't want to say it's a total mess."

"That's not what I meant at all. This is real, not like something out of a magazine. It's a room where children can play and adults sit and talk. It's the kind of home that cries out for a large family. You're so lucky." Jane smiled wryly. "Three lovely children, that's all I ever wanted. It's what Hugh, my husband, and I always planned but you know what they say, the best laid plans…"

"You've no children?" Robyn asked gently.

"Only one. My daughter Anna. Hugh and I wanted more but somehow it never happened. We had Anna and then—" She winced even now after all these years the pain lurked waiting to surprise her. "I couldn't carry another baby, as it turned out, so we rattled around in the big old house – until Hugh died." She braced herself against that all too familiar stab of grief.

"And you moved here?"

"Yes." Jane smiled. "I loved my old house and life in the village but now I'm ready for something different."

"Don't you miss the country?"

"I thought I would but I don't. At least not yet. I don't suppose I've lived in town long enough to be sure but something tells me I won't regret the move."

"I like it here too." Robyn flicked back a lock of hair. "With the park so close it's as good as living in the country, and a lot easier with the children. You know something—" she leaned forward, her elbows on the table, and confided "—I wanted dozens of children. I loved being pregnant. The feeling of this new life growing

inside you is so wonderful. There is nothing like it."
Robyn glanced at Jane, who nodded, resting her hands
over her stomach as she remembered sitting in the old
chair, hugely pregnant, Anna safe inside her, kicking and
wriggling, impatient to be born.

"I'm the only woman I know who actually likes giving
birth. I love it all. The way the contractions grow stronger
and stronger until they completely take over, then this
incredible triumphant final push, and there is this baby
all wrinkled and furious. At least Finn was." She
shrugged. "After him that was it. No more. Never again."

The mugs were empty, the cafetiere drained to the
dregs. "I'll make some more." Robyn was pushing back
her chair when the door opened and a middle-aged
woman in a nylon overall came in.

"Finn's busy watching Peter Rabbit so I thought I'd
start lunch," Sue said.

Puzzled Jane shook her head, she was sure the child
hadn't walked past her, so how could he have gone from
the garden to the front room, or wherever they kept the
television? She frowned and looked towards the kitchen
door.

Robyn caught her glance. "Peter is Finn's rabbit. I
thought that getting him a pet might bring him out of
himself. I'm not sure it's worked out in the way I hoped.
All that's happened is that he's got another obsession. He
can sit and stare at that wretched creature for hours.
Literally hours. It keeps him quiet and is better than his
banging but..." She trailed away dejectedly.

"Oh," Jane said. She should have known that anything
to do with Finn was going to be complicated and

different. To bring herself back to normality she looked at her watch.

"Good heavens is that the time? I'm so sorry, I'd no idea it was so late. I've been keeping you from your work."

"No you haven't. I've been watching you. The way the light played on your face. The way you sit and move. Besides, I've enjoyed the conversation so please stay and eat with us. I'm sure there's plenty. Isn't there Sue?"

"There certainly is. I've got some of my soup from yesterday. It's all home grown and organic as I get the vegetables from my neighbour's allotment. We're trying to see if keeping Finn off additives and e-numbers will help. After that there's bread and cheese. The bread's fresh from Lucy's this morning." She looked at their visitor, waiting for Jane to make up her mind.

"No, I couldn't. I really couldn't," Jane flustered. "I must go."

It had been a lovely morning but for a first visit this was enough. She needed a little space to make sense of this unusual family.

"I'll see you the day after tomorrow for your first sitting," Robyn confirmed before Jane was escorted to the front door by a solemn and silent Kit, who stood on the top step and watched her walk away. *That child carries the world on his shoulders,* Jane thought as she waved him goodbye. She liked Robyn and was excited by the prospect of having her portrait painted, but it was the children that filled Jane's thoughts as she walked slowly back to her apartment.

EIGHT

Eddie steered the lorry into the yard and parked. It was late afternoon and he was back earlier than expected. There had not been much traffic on the motorway; he had a good run from Tewksbury where he'd been delivering a load of pallets. As he climbed out of the cab the heat reflected off the tarmac. He held up his hand to shield his eyes from the dazzle of sunlight glinting on the windows of the surrounding buildings. It was so hot he'd kill for a pint. The thought was tempting but he'd still hadn't finished his shift; there might be another small job that could be fitted in.

Eddie had to admit, the way he and Tracey had been spending money the extra cash would be useful. On the other hand, if he went home he could combine taking the dog for a walk with a stroll along the river to the pub. He'd sit outside with a cold beer, and if that nice barmaid was there she would find a bowl of water for Jake. He reached for his bag. He'd made up his mind that for once he would turn down the chance of making some more money when Milton Corbishly, the son of the previous owner, appeared at the door of the office. Still in his early thirties, he was totally bald and as he blinked against the glare resembled a worm emerging from its hole.

Eddie swallowed a sigh. "I was just coming in."

Milton's eyelids twitched. His Adam's apple jerked up

and down. "Good, good," he stammered, nodding rapidly. "I need a word."

"Sure." Eddie shrugged. For a moment he wondered if there was any problem with the delivery, but as far as he knew everything had gone without a hitch. With a regretful glance at the bright blue sky he followed his boss into the gloom of the dusty building where even the calendar seemed to date from old Mr Corbishly's time.

In the cluttered office Milton, his face shiny and white like a boiled egg, sat down behind the desk, cleared his throat and began. "As you know, Corbishly and Brownlow have been going for over forty years. My dad and his mate started the business. They built it up from nothing and we've done well. If I say so myself, we've done very well. But now, Ed, you see how it is. With this economic uncertainty, things are getting tight. Our profits have been falling for months. There's not enough orders to keep the drivers busy so I've had to make the decision and—" His right eyelid winked frantically as if he was trying to convey some slightly risqué joke. "Let me tell you it's not been easy, far from it. I've not slept at night. It's been a nightmare, a real nightmare, but there's no other way around it. We've got to make cutbacks. It's a question of—" The words swirled through the dust, rising and falling in some strange way that made it impossible to make sense of them. Eddie clenched his fists and tried to concentrate. "There will be a few weeks' notice and some redundancy money, but we'll have to let you go at the end of the week," Milton Corbishly finished, his eyes swivelling round the room. "No hard feelings and when times improve … well you've always been a good hard worker." He moved out from behind his desk and gestured towards the door.

Bloody hell, you can't do this. I've got a family to support. Bills to pay. A mortgage. God, the mortgage! They were behind. There had been a couple of months when other bills had been more pressing, so the house had gone unpaid. After all, what did it matter if you were earning good money? You could always pay it off the next month. Or the next. *I'm a good worker, a bloody good worker. You said so yourself, so why the hell are you letting me go?* The words thundered through his brain, choking him with an anger that paralysed his tongue. He thumped the wall as he stumbled out into the brilliance of the afternoon.

The light hurt his eyes. His stomach churned and roiled. What the hell was he going to do? What was he going to tell Trace? How would they manage? A few weeks money was neither here nor there. It wasn't going to get them out of this mess. He was in such a state he couldn't think straight. What he needed was a drink – it would calm him down, help to get his head sorted.

The Green Man was heaving. Eddie fought his way to the bar and ordered a pint. The sun streamed in through the open door and many of the customers had made their way out into the courtyard. The tables outside were all taken. There were people perched on the low wall that ran along one side of the yard, while other drinkers lolled on the steps or stood in knots under the shade of the one rather straggly tree.

Because everyone wanted to be out enjoying the sun, the darker corners inside the pub were empty, which suited Eddie. He needed somewhere out of the light, where he could sit quietly and try to get a grip on events.

He put his glass down on the wooden table and sank into a chair. His legs felt as weak as that time when he'd had the flu. His head was thumping and there was a nasty acid taste in his mouth. This morning he had been working, he had a good job, which he enjoyed, and by this afternoon, through no fault of his own… He banged his fist against his thigh as if to ram home the point: he was unemployed. Out of work, on benefits, on the scrap heap. It couldn't be happening. It wasn't right. He needed another drink, and another and another after that. Eddie downed pint after pint but nothing changed the feeling of utter disbelief. Not even topping them up with a shot of whisky that zipped like fire down his throat made any difference.

The sun moved round and the shadows crept out of the door and into the courtyard. Daytime regulars were replaced by workers stopping off for a quick one before they went home. Eddie did not move except to stagger to and from the Gents. The tally of glasses on his table grew. The girl swept some away and brought yet another beer. It wasn't until the pressure on his bladder made him go again that he could bring himself to leave the pub and start walking home.

The pavement seemed spongy, the line of trees along the river wavered like their reflections in the water. The whole world was out of sorts. Nothing was as it should be. Everything had changed. This morning he was a responsible husband and father, providing for his family, and now what was he?

It was past seven by the time he finally made his way

along Benbow Close. As he neared the house he saw that the windows were all wide open and he could hear the sound of the television coming from the lounge. It was some programme the children liked to watch, so at least they would be out of the way when he broke the news. What would they think of him when he told them? Their dad out of work. Their dad letting them down. Reluctantly, he pushed open the side gate and was greeted by a frantic barking as a large brown hairy dog leapt up at him, almost knocking him over.

"Good dog, good boy." With Jake's front paws on his chest, Eddie put his arms around the water spaniel's neck and buried his face in its hot oily curls. Jake whimpered softly and licked his master's face. He understood. The bloody dog understood. But how was he going to tell Trace? Eddie glanced at the gate. He couldn't go back to the pub. He had to face what was coming. Telling Jake to stay, he went inside.

Tracey was sitting at the kitchen table leafing through a magazine and looked up briefly when he came in. "There's salad and chips for tea."

"I'm not hungry," the words slurred together.

"I didn't know what time you'd be back. You didn't say." Her face set, Tracey turned over a page and put the magazine face down on the table. Eddie waited for the onslaught but to his relief she seemed to be letting him off the hook. "If you're not eating, do you want a cup of tea?" She pushed back the chair and went over to the sink to fill the kettle. "I'm having one even if you aren't."

Eddie grasped hold of a chair back. The floor was rocking and if he didn't steady himself he was going to crash to the ground. Water drummed into the sink. China clattered as Tracey took a couple of mugs from the cupboard. "I put the lounge carpet on hold – nobody's asked for it, anyway – and got Jodie a new tablet and that pair of shoes she wanted for her birthday. I thought Josh could get her a top and Milly that beauty stuff, then her presents are sorted." Pouring boiling water onto tea bags she half-turned towards him. "I can't believe she's thirteen at the end of the month. Our little Jodie." Her voice grew soft and warm. "Remember the day she was born. You took one look at your little princess and it was love at first sight."

"Mm." The sound came out as a cross between a sob and a growl as he thought of that tiny scrap and how her little hand had reached out and clasped hold of his finger. His daughter, the first person he ever knew that really belonged to him. She was his and he'd do anything for her. Anything. And now he'd failed her.

"I thought for her party we could have a barbecue," Tracey continued. "You'll have to clean the dog dirt from the garden, and if you give the grass a cut and I get some of those lantern things to hang on the fence, it'll look really good. Now we've done the house it's time we concentrated on the garden. We can put the drinks in the kitchen to keep them cool. Though sod's law, the weather is bound to change. Still, we may be lucky. Oh, and if you're working that weekend our Ryan's offered to do the cooking. You know me, I'd only burn it all." She giggled. "You could ask Milton Corbishly not to use you. I mean, it is your daughter's birthday so it's not asking too much, is it."

"Nah," Eddie managed to growl.

"So?" Tracey put two mugs of tea on the table.

"So what?" Eddie shook his head. His wife had said something important but for the life of him he couldn't think what it was.

"Are you going to ask for time off?" Tracey spoke very slowly to make the point that she knew he hadn't been listening. Eddie shrugged and at that moment Jake bounded up to the back door. Standing on his back legs he pressed his face against the glass. "Eddie," Tracey snapped, "do something with that dog. He's slobbering all over the place." The kitchen tilted and Eddie tightened his hold on the chair. "Jake," Tracey screamed, banging on the door, "get down." The dog ignored her. "Now!" She whirled round to glare at her husband. "He's your dog. Sort him. If you're not too drunk, that is."

"I'm not drunk," Eddie said carefully.

"Oh no? You're just pretending. Typical. After the day I've had. Mum getting on at me again for not going to see her, though when I do she's never got anything pleasant to say. Then Paula at work mixing up the shifts. And now you come home out of your head. Fit for nothing, with your dog slobbering all over the place, the kids to see to and—" She stopped, lost for words.

He let go of the chair back and lurched towards her. "Bad day?" he mumbled. "I've been sacked. Let go. According to Milton, the firm's broke."

A cold wave of silence washed over them. Tracey clutched at the work surface. Eddie sank down on a chair. "What are we going to do?" she said at last. Eddie forced himself to his feet, walked over to the door and let the dog into the kitchen. Jake flopped onto the floor, tongue hanging out, panting heavily. "There's all the bills." Tracey looked over towards the drawer where she kept them. "They've sent letters about the house and we've maxed out on the cards. Oh my God!" She put her hand over her mouth. "Eddie…" Her voice trembled and her face was white and pinched.

More than anything, he wanted to go over and put his arms around her but the fear of what she might say and do held him back. What if she cried or screamed? He had nothing to say to comfort her. "There'll be something going. I'll ask around."

"There's bound to be. A good reliable worker like you, you'll find something."

Eddie said nothing. Jake pressed against his master's leg and Eddie leaned down and ruffled the dog's ears.

Tracey wanted to scream at him. How were they going to cope? They could hardly manage, as it was, and with Eddie's money gone her miserable part-time job wasn't going to support a family. It wasn't fair. They both worked so hard. A wave of overpowering fury swept over her. It was all Eddie's fault. What was the point of being dependable and loving if you couldn't keep your job?

"Trace," he said miserably, almost as if he knew what she was thinking, and the look he gave her made her forget her anger. What her husband needed was a great big cuddle, like the kids did when they were hurt or upset. She began to move him, but just then Jake whined that he wanted to go out. The dog. It was always the bloody dog.

Clamping her teeth together she rinsed her cup and slammed it in the dishwasher. Whatever happened, no one could say she left her house in a mess. Housework, she thought grimly, was something she was good at. "I'll ask Paula, see if I can get more shifts. Mum will have Milly for me after school." She crossed her fingers as she spoke knowing full well that Sheila, with a new man in her life, would not be pleased to be asked. *Or you can do it.* She almost said the words, biting them back at the last minute, because if Eddie could look after Milly then Eddie wasn't working, and if he wasn't working they wouldn't have the money to pay the mortgage, let alone anything else. Sick with fear, she thrust the thought to the back of her mind.

"If Paula can't do anything for me, I'll get something else. I might be too old and fat to go out on the streets, but there's always cleaning jobs. Lots of girls I know do it. Mum used to, and the pay's much better now than it was. Yeah, that's what I'll do." The idea filled her with hope and energy. "I can work it round the kids being at school, which will be better than doing shifts, but I'll still try for some of those as well." She walked round the kitchen putting things straight, even if they weren't out of place, and wiping over the gleaming surfaces. Anything rather than look at her husband, who having made no response to her plans took the dog out into the garden.

Tracey got the children ready for bed, hoovered the lounge and the hall and washed the kitchen windows. She could see Eddie outside with Jake, but she didn't call him in.

At last, hot sweaty and exhausted, she showered and

went to bed. The room was stuffy; the light from the streetlamp seeped in through the curtains. Eddie came in at some point, reeking of drink and sweat. He pulled off his clothes and left them in a heap on the floor. The mattress sagged and Tracey sat up. "Stick them in the washing basket. And for God's sake have a shower," she snapped. Ignoring her he heaved himself over to his side and began to snore.

Some time before dawn she must have dozed off because the next thing she knew was that Eddie had gone. She could hear Josh and Milly fighting. Her head ached and there was a terrible taste in her mouth. She glanced at her phone – to her horror it was eight o'clock. Screaming at the children to get dressed she pulled on her clothes and hurried downstairs. Rummaging in the drawer of unpaid bills she found a piece of card. On her way back from school she would drop into Lucy's Bakery.

*

The window of the Lucy's bakery was filled with bread sculpture. A branch hung with glass bead necklaces stood in one corner. Posters announcing local arts events were pinned up on a cork board next to the door. Inside, there were round marble topped tables and bentwood chairs; outside, there were metal ones on the pavement in front of the shop where even this early in the morning the first customers of the day sat under the shade of a dark green awning.

Taking a deep breath Tracey stepped into the shop. She'd never been here before. Lucy's was for posh people; people like her bought their bread at the Co-op. White sliced, finger rolls, baps. Nothing fancy, brown, or covered with seeds. The kids wouldn't stand for it, nor would Eddie. Bread was meant to be plain, something you put your cheese or ham between.

The air was sweet with the scent of vanilla and sugar. She could smell freshly roasted coffee and for a moment she almost felt hungry, then her stomach contracted and she had to fight down the sickly feeling that rose in her throat. There was a pretty blonde woman behind the counter. She was slipping some flapjacks into a bag and chatting to her customer. They seemed to know each other and Tracey felt more and more awkward as she waited for the money to be put in the till. "Can you save me a couple of cream slices for tomorrow, Vee?" the woman asked as she put her change into her purse.

"Of course." Vee smiled and turned to Tracey. "Can I help you?" Her smile and her voice were kind but Tracey, who knew that Vee together with Lucy were the owners of the bakery, suddenly found it hard to speak.

"Umm." Her fingers closed round the card she had so carefully written.

"Yes?" Vee prompted encouragingly.

"I, um… I'm looking for a cleaning job," Tracey mumbled.

"I'm sorry—" Vee looked genuinely concerned "—we already have a cleaner."

"Oh I didn't mean here." Tracey flushed. "I heard you put up adverts so I thought…" She trailed off, too embarrassed to say that she had targeted the bakery because their customers were the sort of people who needed someone like her, and it would be cheaper than putting an ad in the local paper.

"No problem. It's all part of the service."

Tracey shoved the card in Vee's direction and pointed at random to a pile of bread rolls. "And two of those," she said hastily. She handed over what seemed to be a huge amount of money and clutching the paper bag hurried out of the shop. Once back on the pavement she sidled towards the shop next door, all the while keeping an eye on the bakery. She waited until she saw her card being pinned onto the cork board and only then did she let out her breath. She'd done it. Now all she had to do was wait for her first client.

Joining Vee in the shop, Lucy glanced at the latest card on the board. "It's not quite straight," she said. Unpinning it, she read, "Wanted cleaning work. Hours to suit. Ring Tracey on… I hope she gets something." Lucy replaced the card positioning it in the centre of the board where it was sure to be noticed.

NINE

Anna rode up in the lift to her mother's apartment. A quick visit then, Friday evening duty discharged, she could get on with her weekend. She was going to relax and give herself some time to adjust to being on her own again. Not that it would be a problem. It never was.

"Mum!" Anna kept her voice light and made sure she was smiling as Jane opened the door.

"Anna. I didn't expect to see you. Is everything all right?"

She knows, Anna thought. *I don't know how, but she always knows.* "Yes. I'm fine."

"Good." There was a questioning note in Jane's voice.

Anna steeled herself. "Alistair and I have split up."

"Darling." Jane turned, half-opened her arms, and for a horrible moment Anna thought she was going to be pulled into a hug.

If she touches me I'll cry, Anna thought. Moving away, she went to the window. "How odd. I thought our views would be the same but yours is even better than mine. Because it's that bit higher up, I suppose."

"I love it." Jane stood beside her. Anna stepped sideways. "Shall I make us a cup of tea or would you rather have a glass of wine?"

"I'll have tea, thanks." Tea took time to brew. It meant that Jane would go into the kitchen and Anna could stand looking out over the city, perfecting her air of calm competence.

"You don't have to tell me if you don't want to but it might help," Jane said as she brought in the tea tray.

"There's nothing much to say. I told you, I'm okay, Mum." Anna sat on the edge of the sofa.

"You've been together for a while now—" Jane prompted, handing her a cup "—I had thought that maybe..."

"Maybe what? That this time it was going to be forever? Don't you know me by now? A long-term relationship is not what I want. It's not how I see my life going. Okay?" Anna took a gulp of tea and stared at the opposite wall. If her mother started on about family and children she'd throw the bloody cup and saucer at her.

"I'm sorry. I know you think it's none of my business, but you're still my daughter and I can't help being concerned."

There she goes again with the mother thing. I know what she's thinking. Alistair was her last hope of having grandchildren and with him gone it's not going to happen. "I told you I'm fine." Anna took a final mouthful and stood up. "Sorry it's only a flying visit, but I've got things to do and I'm sure you have too."

*

Jane waited until the door had shut behind her daughter, then her shoulders hunched and she wrapped her arms around herself. Her poor, poor Anna. It was so obvious she was in pain. She had that brittle look which said don't touch me or I'll break. If only she could let herself go, bury herself in her mother's arms and cry, but that was the last

94

thing Anna would do. She had never confided in her; it was Hugh she had turned to when she was in trouble. If only he was still here…

Don't, she told herself. *There's no point thinking about it. Anna will do what she wants, as she always does. Nothing is going to bring Hugh back. Ever. That life is over. You have to concentrate on the here and now even though sometimes it's so hard.*

Wiping the tears from her eyes she walked out onto the balcony. However bad she felt the view lifted her spirits. The sun was low over the city turning the river into a ribbon of molten gold. *A golden road leading to happiness.* As a mother, you had to face the fact that however old your children were, you never stopped worrying about them. It could be worse. Anna might be suffering but she was coping, as she always did. Her daughter was a strong and resilient woman. *As so many of us have to be.*

Jane's thoughts turned to Robyn. In contrast to Anna, she seemed so fragile, so much on the verge of breaking into pieces, yet she too was coping. Though how on earth she managed with Finn's constant need for attention Jane could not imagine. Perhaps there was something positive in Anna's need to keep her distance. Unlike Robyn's children, she had never leached her mother of energy, being content to get on with her life and let her parents get on with theirs.

I should be grateful, Jane mused. *I may only have the one child but she's turned out all right.* Unlike Finn, who was like some alien being, or Kit who was so strung up and nervy that he looked as if he might come apart at any moment. Then there was Phoebe. A stolid and sadly unattractive child, so different from her delicate-looking mother that Jane's instinct was to reassure the little girl that looks weren't everything, and she too was loved and special. Those children might not be her family but she warmed to them. Her own daughter might not need or want her but they did. Robyn found her interesting enough to paint her portrait and since she refused to take any money the least Jane could do was to help out with the children from time to time.

The only children she had ever imagined looking after were Anna's, but since her daughter showed no sign of providing her with grandchildren in the foreseeable future there was no reason why she shouldn't make herself useful to the Latimer family. It was obvious from what Robyn had said that, apart from Sue and her brother David, she had no support. Jane could see why she was reluctant to ask for help. People were unlikely to understand about Finn. He didn't look different, but his behaviour was beyond strange. It was easy to come to the conclusion that he was spoilt and over indulged, that if his mother handled him better there wouldn't be any problems. No doubt that was why Robyn had been so vague and distant when they had first met. She must be so tired of trying to explain what was wrong to people who thought it was all her fault.

Jane yawned. The encounter with Anna had tired her. What she needed was a glass of wine. Or would a cup of hot chocolate be more comforting? She would sit here on the balcony watching the river, then have a long lazy soak in the bath before slipping into bed with a book.

*

Back in her own apartment Anna opened a bottle of Sancerre. As the crisp white wine slid down her throat the tension slipped from her shoulders. Glass in hand, she wandered onto the balcony and watched as the sun set behind the hills. Car headlights swept past on the Portway; the Suspension Bridge hung wreathed in lights above the dark chasm of the gorge. Sitting at the patio table, Anna rested her chin on her hand and in spite of trying to keep them open, her eyes began to close. Her head fell forward, her fingers loosened. Just before the glass crashed to the floor she woke with a jerk. Tightening her grip on the stem she rose groggily to her feet. It had been a long day and she'd better get herself to bed.

She woke at two, then three, then again at five. The figures on the clock glowed in the dark. The blinds shut out all light from outside and for a while she lay there hoping to be able to drift off again, but the room was too quiet. There was no one breathing beside her and the silence pressed against her ears until she could stand it no longer and flinging back the duvet she got out of bed.

In the kitchen she automatically switched on the radio. First came the farming programme, then the weather forecast, followed by the news, local and national. She didn't want to listen to any of it but it was better than music. Music snagged the emotions. It would remind her. Of Alistair. Of the good times and the bad.

Anna brewed a pot of coffee. Black and strong. She plugged in her laptop and began to work. Three hours later she had finished and the whole day loomed in front of her. What was she going to do? There was the gym but Alistair might be there, and she wasn't ready for that. If they did run into each other, it would be awkward and painful for them both.

She didn't need to go to the supermarket – the fridge was full. There wasn't any cleaning to do, either. The flat was pristine. Floors and surfaces gleamed; the cooker looked as if it had been newly delivered from the showroom.

It was too early in the day to ring friends. Those who went out to work would be busy with household chores; those with kids would be doing family stuff. She could go clothes shopping, but town on a Saturday morning would be heaving with people and she was not in the mood for crowds, yet she craved company.

Without meaning to she glanced at the ceiling. If she didn't want to be alone she could go up and have coffee with her mum, or they could go to Lucy's for brunch, or cake, followed by a walk along the river. Spending some time together would make up for the awkwardness between them the night before.

Anna dressed and ran up the stairs to the top floor. As she rang the bell and waited for the door to open, she rehearsed what she would say. She was sorry if she had upset Jane but she hadn't meant to hurt her. All she had wanted to do was to make it clear that she didn't want any discussion about her life choices.

But what if Jane thought she had come upstairs for tea and sympathy? The whole cycle would start again. Coming up here was a stupid idea. She would be much better off spending the time on her own. When she and Alistair were together she would often have whole weekends alone when he was away on business. *Or with someone else*. The thought intruded before she could wipe it away.

Damn him. Anna glared at the smooth black surface of her mother's front door, turned and went down in the lift. Alistair was the past. She was over him and she wasn't going to let him affect her weekend. When she reached the ground floor she hesitated. A morning spent with her mum didn't have to result in an in-depth analysis of Anna's emotional state. She and Jane could resolve to keep things light. On the verge of changing her mind she reached for her phone, then thrust it back into her bag and plunged out into the sunlight.

The sky, a brilliant blue, arched over the brightly coloured terraces of Hotwells. Sunlight sparkled on the river and people were out enjoying the summer. Anna walked briskly until she came to the High Street where her pace was slowed by Saturday morning shoppers. She wandered past the second-hand shops with their display of bric-a-brac spread out on the pavement, and lingered outside the florists wondering whether to buy some plants for her balcony. There were so many she had no idea where to start. Next weekend she would make the decision but for now she would buy a newspaper and treat herself to a coffee.

Lucy's was full of customers queuing for their croissants and pain-au-chocolat. The air was hot and sweet with the smell of freshly baked bread and the herbs and spices sold in the shop. As Anna walked in, she almost bumped into a tall fair-haired man looking intently at the card advertising cleaning services which had been pinned on the centre of the notice board.

"Sorry. I'll do this and I'll be out of your way." He took a picture of the card then slid his phone into the back pocket of his jeans. "It's your turn. I've been served." He nodded towards the counter.

Anna shook her head. "I'm not buying. I only came in for a coffee."

"There's plenty of room outside," Vee called. "Grab a table and one of us will be out to you as soon as."

"There's no hurry," Anna assured her. Sitting in the shade of the awning and watching the passers-by was as good a way of killing time as any. The coffee, when it came, was excellent. Anna unfolded the newspaper and began the Sudoku. This week's was a challenge and she was staring absently across the road, trying to work out the final sequence, when she almost dropped her pen in surprise.

"Mum," she called, starting from her chair then sinking back in embarrassment as Jane showed no sign of having recognised her. She was busy talking to a thin dark-haired boy. Her head was bent towards him and he was listening intently. Another younger child was walking beside her, his eyes focussed on the pavement as he took great care not to step on any of the cracks. A plump girl trailed behind them, stopping from time to time to look over her shoulder. Following her glance, Anna saw a thin woman in a pale green skirt and creamy long-sleeved blouse hurrying to catch up. Her red hair tumbled over her shoulders and she carried a large basket over her arm. As the woman reached them, Jane turned and smiled and they began talking rapidly, until the newcomer gave a shout of laughter and clapped her hands. The older boy and girl scampered away down the street, the younger one plodding seriously after them as Jane and her companion, still talking, followed.

That could have been me, Anna thought. *If Mum and I didn't rub each other up the wrong way we could have been laughing and chatting like that. Why are we so spikey with each other? I was never like that with Dad. Still, at least Mum's making friends which means she won't be so dependent. Though that ginger-haired woman looks too young to be a friend. She seems more like another one of Mum's good causes.*

Anna blew down her nose. Jane was supposed to be starting a new life, not finding a needy family to help. That was the sort of thing she'd done in the past. Having moved to the city her mother should be concentrating on herself. But that was Jane all over. There was no telling her. Jane simply didn't listen; she went her own way.

Like I do. Anna dismissed the thought. She and her mother had nothing in common. To start with, Jane liked children and Anna didn't. Her mum had always made it obvious however hard she'd tried not to that she'd love Anna to have a family. Was that what this was all about? Was her mum playing at being a grandma?

Whatever the reason for Jane's behaviour, it showed how little effort she was prepared to put into her relationship with her own daughter. Instead of spending time with Anna she'd hooked up with some random family. Anna settled her sunglasses on her nose and picked up the paper. The puzzle no longer seemed to make any sense but she would solve it. On her own. Without help from anyone.

TEN

Frankie took one of the white plastic chairs from the shed and set it out in the middle of the back yard. She sat down and, resting her legs on a flowerpot full of wilting geraniums, lifted her face to the sun. She could smell the ripe scent of animal bedding from the rabbit cages behind her and the stink of hot fur rising from Tigger, the three-legged terrier, who lay panting at her feet. Onions, the ginger cat, had stretched out on the wall that separated their garden from the next one in the terrace. Fluff and Smokey-Joe slept on the kitchen windowsill.

Closing her eyes, she imagined herself on a tropical beach, the sun shining, the palm trees rustling, the waves breaking gently on the shore. There was a glass of sangria at her side, a book on her lap, and tonight she'd be going dancing with the tall fit lad she met at the pool that morning. He'd admired her legs, her slim body, and told her…

At this point the story stumbled to a halt. What had he told her? Most of the boys she knew couldn't string two words together. The ones that had more than a single brain cell had worked out that it wasn't cool to be clever, so they clowned around with their mates. The one or two seriously academic lads in their year didn't bother with the likes of Frankie, Amy and Emma.

That didn't seem to worry Amy and Emma, who vied

with each other to go out with the sexy hunks that every girl in the class fancied – something that Frankie considered a complete waste of time. She knew that everyone thought she was a stuck-up cow because she didn't flirt and tease like other girls. But why bother when the lads were so boring? Perhaps she was a freak. Or maybe when she got to uni she'd meet someone who liked the same things she did: caring for the environment, animals, books and films, the kind that had subtitles and were on really, really late on some channel no one ever watched.

"I'm off to work," Debbie called from the back door. "Can you make sure that the rabbits have enough water and…" The list continued. Frankie blanked it out. She wasn't speaking to her mum. She wasn't speaking to anyone. There was a chance, a very, very slight chance that she would get something to wear for the prom but most probably, the way her life was sliding into complete disaster, there would be no Fairy Godmother, no last-minute miracle. She would have to tell Emma and Amy that she wasn't going with them, that there'd be space in the limo but not for her. She'd be letting them down and they'd never speak to her again, or worse they'd laugh at her. What was a catastrophe for Frankie would be a joke to them because if something happened to their dress they had the money to buy a new one. They had no idea what it was like for her and now, thanks to that stupid girl at the dry cleaners, the whole of her summer was ruined.

She leaned back and basked in her misery. The concrete slabs reflected the heat from the cloudless sky, the brick walls holding it in like an oven. Sweat trickled down between her breasts. Her shorts stuck to her backside. It was time to go in, have a cool shower, and plaster herself with after-sun lotion. If she could be bothered to move.

The phone in her pocket vibrated and she wriggled round to pull it out. The text was from Emma. Finger poised Frankie wondered whether to delete it. She didn't want to read how wonderful things were right now. She felt like throwing the phone against the wall where it would shatter to pieces, but old habits were impossible to break. Curling her fingers round the screen she read, *No room in limo. Sos xx*, followed by a sad face.

Unable to believe what she was seeing, Frankie stared at the message. It didn't make sense. They couldn't mean it. There had to be some mistake. Only the other day Amy had said she was coming with them. There was lots of room for the three of them. After all, they weren't taking any boys. Then it hit her. Emma and Amy were going with Simon and Toby. They'd met up with them at the club the other night. Emma had left with Simon, then Amy had sloped off, saying she'd see Frankie tomorrow. She hadn't even bothered to see if she'd got someone to go home with. So there she'd been, alone in the city centre at midnight, abandoned by her so-called friends. Luckily, she had her emergency taxi money or she'd have been stuck because Debbie didn't have a car. Her mum said you didn't need one in the city, but the truth was they couldn't afford it.

Rocking on her seat, Frankie wrapped her arms around herself. She'd been so stupid. Amy and Emma didn't want her. They never had. She had been worrying about letting them down and they'd been looking for someone else to take her place. All they had wanted her for was to pay her share. They didn't care if she had no one to go with. No one did. She was what she'd always been scared she would be, that odd girl in the class, the one without any friends.

*

Tracey wiped her forehead with the back of her arm, then stood and looked around the apartment. She was hot and sticky but she had done a good job. The floors and surfaces gleamed, the bed linen was laundered and ironed, the bathrooms smelled of lemon; everything was in its place. Dan Brockman should be pleased when he got in after work.

She picked up the envelope he'd left on the kitchen counter, slipped it into her bag and let herself out of the door. In the hall she looked nervously over her shoulder before pressing the button for the lift. It didn't feel right standing there in this classy building in her dirty old jeans and stained top. What if someone saw her? What would they think? It wasn't that she was ashamed of her job but she didn't want to look like some down-at-heel loser. The colour rose to her already flushed cheeks. The magazines said that if you wanted to succeed you had to project the right image. Next time she'd bring a change of clothes so she could come and go looking smart.

It was five o'clock, rush hour, and the road was crammed with traffic. Cars were bumper to bumper over the bridge and as far as she could see nothing was moving. It was lucky she was walking. That was something to be grateful for, she supposed. Slinging her bag over her shoulders she set off. Petrol fumes slid into her chest, the sun beat down on her head, and her mouth was dry. Trudging past The Green Man she threw a venomous look at the tree-shaded courtyard. Luckily, there was no sign of Eddie. If she'd seen him she'd have killed him. After a double shift at work and a couple of hours cleaning there was nothing she'd like more than to stop and have a drink, but there was no chance of that.

Not like those couples sitting under the shade of the tree with their long cool beers, the girls in their summer dresses, the men in shirtsleeves, obviously stopping off before going home from work. It was all right for some, but Tracey had responsibilities. A husband who was out of work and kids to feed. They were her priorities, never mind if she was tired, hot and thirsty. When she got to her mum's she'd have a cup of tea before the final walk home.

"You took your time," Sheila said as she opened the door. "I'm going out, or had you forgotten?"

"Sorry." Tracey swallowed the lump in her throat. Her mum was all dressed up in a pair of white linen trousers and bright blue top. Her hair and nails were done and she was already putting the front door key in her bag.

"Mum." Milly flung herself at Tracey. Her blonde curls were damp with the heat and her face was sticky with ice cream. "I don't want to go home," she complained as Tracey took a wet wipe out of her bag and began to clean her up. "I want to stay at Nanny's."

"Well you can't." Tracey shot a bitter glance at Sheila who was tapping one long scarlet nail on the hall table.

"Next time, my lover. Then you can stay for the night. Would you like that?" Sheila cooed. Milly clapped her hands and gave her gran one of her light-up-the world smiles. Tracey had to stop herself from saying something mean. It was so easy being a gran: there were no worries or responsibilities and you got all the love a child could give.

"Come on. We haven't got all day." Clutching Milly's wrist so hard that the child winced, Tracey pulled her towards the door. "Can you have her again for me next week?" She turned to her mum and tried to smile, while something deep inside yearned for that look of unconditional love that Sheila had given her little granddaughter.

"I will if I'm not busy. You know what George's like." Sheila's face softened. Tracey winced. Ever since her mum had got together with George she'd been too busy to help out with the children in the evenings. When Eddie was working they used to pay for a babysitter, or do a swap with one of her girlfriends, when they wanted to go out. Now when things were so tight, and she could really do with the support, her mum simply wasn't there for her.

"Get Eddie to do it." Sheila hustled them out of the house and was shutting the front door. "He's got nothing else to do."

Tracey clamped her lips together. Her mum was right. Eddie should be at home looking after the kids while she was working to keep them, but it didn't happen. Suddenly this man, who had always been a loving dad and reliable husband, was never there. Out looking for a job, he called it, when they did manage to bump into each other. Sitting drinking in the pub was what Tracey suspected, though she'd not caught him at it – yet.

Milly, who was hot and over-tired, whined all the way home. By the time they reached Benbow Close Tracey was ready to slap her. Only the thought of what people in the street would do stopped her. Raising a hand to a child was sure to get the Social Services round, which was all she needed. The house was hot and stuffy but at least there was no dog to leap up at them, panting and slobbering. Eddie must have taken Jake out on one of their long walks, but Tracey barely registered the thought as she dumped her bag in the hall.

"Mum, I want an ice cream," Milly moaned.

"You had one at your gran's and you're not having another before your tea."

"Mum." Milly's lip trembled, her eyes filling.

Tracey's heart bubbled with rage. "Stop it," she snarled. "And you two can switch that down." She stormed into the lounge where Jodie and Josh were sprawled in front of the television, packets of crisps on the sofa beside them, glasses of fizzy orange leaving sticky rings on the coffee table. "Now look what you've done," Tracey yelled. "How many times have I told you to put coasters down? I've been working all day and look at the place. Go on, get out." The children scattered. Josh slunk into the garden and started kicking his football against the fence. Jodie stamped up to her room with Milly stumbling after her.

Tracey scooped up greasy crisp bags, thrust glasses into the dishwasher, wiped and vacuumed and aired. She flung chips into the oven, slammed beef burgers under the grill, tore lettuce into shreds and chopped tomatoes and cucumber. She thumped bottles of sauce and relish onto the table and summoned the children. They ate in silence, three pairs of eyes watching her warily, waiting for the next outburst of temper. The strain on their faces was enough to break her heart but there was nothing she could do about it. She was so stressed that everything they did riled her beyond belief. In the daytime she could hardly bear being in the same room as them. It was only when her children were fast asleep that all her love for them came flooding back.

She put Milly in the bath and told the other two to get their things ready for school and not to stay up watching television until late, or their dad would have something to say when he got in. Jodie pulled a face and Josh muttered something under his breath but she managed to ignore it. With a supreme effort she washed and dried her littlest one and got her into bed. Pink and warm, her curls fluffed around her head, Milly held out her arms for a cuddle. Part of Tracey wanted to pick her up and hold her close but all she could do was give her a quick kiss before going into her own room and shutting the door behind her.

Her legs felt as if they were going to give way and she had to sit down on her lovely silky blue bedcover. She was still in her cleaning clothes but she didn't care, not anymore. What was the point? It was all going soon enough. If they didn't find some money for the mortgage company the house would be repossessed – and then what would happen to them all? She wanted to cry. She wanted to lie back on the pillows and let out all the hurt and pain and fear, but there was a cold hard lump inside which stopped her. Her mum hadn't cried for her dad until a long time after he'd died. Maybe Tracey was more like Sheila than she thought.

Tracey's mouth twisted in disgust. She got up, pulled off her dirty clothes and stepped into the shower determined to make use of her lovely en-suite while she still could. She stood under scalding water until she felt boiled, then turned the dial to cold. The water ran down her face and into her mouth, tingling her skin and bringing her out in goosebumps. It was almost as good as crying.

Towelling herself dry, she stepped into the warm evening light. She pulled open the underwear drawer and clicked her tongue at the mess. Wrapped in a towel, she began to sort and tidy. One drawer led to another, then another. Soon there were piles of stuff to bin, to keep, to recycle. Just like the magazines advised. All that was left were the drawers under the bed. Rummaging through them, she wondered why she had kept all those old clothes. She'd never wear any of them again, not even the beautiful turquoise silk dress she'd bought for Lauren's wedding. She wouldn't fit into it, for a start, but it was too good to throw out. Maybe she could sell it. Make a bit of money. Picking it up, she hung the dress carefully over the wardrobe door. Everything else she packed into bin bags.

Finally, the bedroom was tidy. Looking around at the ordered room, Tracey caught a glimpse of herself in the mirror as she started to get dressed. Her hair, which had dried without being combed, stood up around her face and she was wearing nothing but her underwear. Suppose one of the kids walked in, or Eddie. The thought of him seeing her half-dressed made her scrabble for her clothes. The way she felt, the last thing she wanted was his hands anywhere near her body.

She damped down her unruly mop and tied it back behind her neck. Feeling better for having achieved something she gave herself a quick spritz of perfume before taking the bin bags downstairs into the hall. Passing the children's rooms she saw Josh sprawled across his bunk bed fast asleep. Milly was curled up with her thumb in her mouth. Jodie managed a sleepy "Night Mum" before turning on her side and drifting away.

Love you, Tracey thought and smiled.

Bin bags neatly stowed by the front door, a cup of tea at her side, she scrawled through the messages on her phone and came across Debbie's story. *What a shame,* she thought. *That's not right. What if it happened to Jodie? I'd be gutted. Spending all that money and then the dress not fitting. It goes to show that life's a bitch.* She sat back, took a sip of tea, and remembered the turquoise silk dress. What if it fitted Debbie's daughter? She wouldn't make any money on it, but so what? What she could get for it second hand, she thought, wouldn't make much difference to the disaster that was their financial situation. She'd have made someone happy, she hoped. Feeling better about herself, Tracey pressed reply and typed, *Think I got what you want.* And sent the message.

*

"I've got you a dress!" Debbie charged into Frankie's room without knocking. Her daughter was lying on the bed, face down, curtains drawn. The room smelled thickly of hot body and stale air. "It's like Cinderella, love.

You can go to the ball." Debbie was still on a high.

"Whatever. I told you it doesn't matter. I'm not going," Frankie muttered into her pillow.

"Why not? It's all sorted. I rang the woman who's giving us the dress and it sounds perfect. The colour's right for you and she lives round the corner on that new estate so we can go and pick it up tomorrow."

"I'm not going to the prom. I've got no way of getting there." Frankie half-raised her head from the pillow and Debbie saw that she had been crying. "It's a fucking joke. First, I didn't have a dress and now I've got one I've got no way of getting there. Emma and Amy have got someone else to share the limo. No one wants to go with me. Oh Mum!" she sobbed, throwing herself into Debbie's arms.

The mean bitches, Debbie thought as she stroked her daughter's hair. *If they think they're going to the prom and leaving my Frankie behind they've another think coming. She's going to be belle of the ball. That'll show them.* To Frankie she said. "Have you asked anyone else?"

"They're all sorted. Anyway, they wouldn't want to go with me. It's not like I'm the most popular girl in the class."

"That's stupid. You're not to think like that. Remember what I told you, don't let the buggers get you down."

"Yeah." Frankie sniffed. "I know, but I'm still not going. We don't have a car and all the limos are full. Even if anyone wanted me there wouldn't be any room." Her lip trembled. "I might have a dress but I still can't go to the prom."

"You can and you will. We'll think of something.

Come on love, don't cry. I got you a dress, didn't I?"
Frankie nodded. "Well then I'll get you a limo, or
something even better. You see if I don't."

Later, when Frankie had slipped into a miserable sleep,
Debbie took out her phone and bringing up the Freecycle
site, she posted, Wanted: Posh car and driver to take my
daughter to the prom. I know it's a lot to ask but she's been let
down over her lift.

ELEVEN

Anna had had enough: night after night without any sleep and she was finding it impossible to concentrate on the paperwork in front of her. What she needed was a break. She would go home, have a coffee or two and finish off the rest of the day's work on her laptop.

Coming into the apartment block she automatically checked her mailbox and there it was. A thick creamy envelope lying among her pile of bills and circulars. The address was handwritten but looking closely she saw it was addressed to her mother. Anna raised her eyebrows. Couldn't the wretched postman read? Wasn't the difference between Mrs and Miss Poynton obvious?

She debated whether to slip the letter into her mother's box or whether it was urgent and should be taken up to Jane's apartment. If she did that she would have to face her mother, and Anna didn't have the energy for the serious talk they needed to have about that ginger-haired woman and her kids. In the village there would have been no problem. It was all WI and Meals on Wheels. Safe and civilised. Everyone knew everyone else and the neighbours kept an eye on each other, but here in the city anything could happen. Jane wouldn't appreciate being reminded of that fact but Anna had to warn her. After that, it was up to her mother to decide whether she was going to take a risk on a complete stranger and her family.

Anna took the lift to the top floor. Brandishing the letter in front of her like a weapon she stepped out onto the landing. As the lift doors closed behind her a skinny urchin of a boy scrambled to his feet.

"Jane," he began then stopped and stared at Anna. "You're not her."

"No," Anna replied. "I'm her daughter. Who are you and how did you get in here?" She stared at the boy, convinced she'd seen him before but couldn't quite remember where.

"I came to see Jane. She gave me the numbers for the door."

"And?" Anna was determined not to give him any encouragement. The boy raised a shoulder. His foot scuffed at the floor.

"I'm Kit. Kit Latimer-Jones." Remembering his manners he put out his hand in an old-fashioned way. Anna ignored it.

"You're the boy in the street," she said as the memory flooded back. Kit looked puzzled. "I saw you with my mother the other day. There were four of you, a girl, a boy and a woman with red hair."

"That's the mum," he admitted grudgingly.

"And the others?"

"The girl is my sister, Phoebe, and—" there was a significant pause "—the other one is Finn."

"Is he your brother?" Anna said thinking of the angelic looking child with thick fair hair. Kit made a noise which came out as something between a snort and a yes. He stared at the floor, apparently absorbed in working the toe of his trainers into a non-existent crack. The silence

115

between them grew tense. Kit's foot squirmed busily until Anna could stand it no longer.

"What exactly are you doing here?" Kit shrugged and Anna's irritation grew. "Did Mum invite you?" Kit nodded. "Jane is *my* mother," Anna said stupidly. She glanced meaningfully at the closed door to show this scruffy child that if Jane had indeed invited him up to her flat she hadn't really meant it.

As if reading her thoughts Kit muttered, "She said I can come whenever I want." Keeping his eyes on the ground he added, "But she's not here."

"No she's not," Anna said. The boy did not move. "Do you live around here?" she asked pointedly. Taking the hint, the boy's shoulders drooped.

"I'd better go," he mumbled and turned towards the lift. There was something so defeated and miserable about that gesture that Anna was filled with remorse. How could she have treated him like that? He was only a boy and for him to come looking for Jane there must be something wrong. He looked so worn down and unhappy while she, who should know better, was behaving like a spoiled child.

"No wait. You can't go off like this." Kit reached out to press the call button and she put her hand on his arm. "I'm sure Mum will be sorry she missed you, but in the meantime is there anything I can do to help?"

"She said I can come whenever I want," Kit repeated.

"Is there some special reason why you came today? Did you want to talk to her about something?" He shook his head but the way he pressed his lips together, as if to hold back the words, convinced her she was right. "Do

116

you think you could tell me?" He lowered his hand and the lift, summoned to a lower floor, slid downwards. Kit did not move. Anna felt the thinness of his body under her fingers. "Come on, this is silly. Why don't we go inside and you can tell me what you came for?"

"We can't." Kit looked at the door. "Jane's not in and you can't walk into someone's house when they're not there. It's rude."

"I suppose it is." Anna smiled. "Okay then. How about if you came to mine?"

"I can't. I don't know you. You could be anyone. A serial killer, a kidnapper, or —" he cocked his head to one side and studied her carefully " — an alien in disguise."

"Really?" Anna wasn't sure whether she was amused or offended.

"Really," Kit said and suddenly they were both laughing. Anna shaking her head at the silliness of the idea and Kit giggling until he stopped and said, "That proves it. You're not an alien. Aliens can't laugh. At least the robots that look like humans can't. They don't have a sense of humour programmed in. But you're still a stranger and Mum says we're not to speak to strangers."

"Your mum's right." Anna struggled to keep her voice level. "You mustn't speak to strangers but I am Jane's daughter so you kind of know me." She looked at the boy and nodded encouragingly, then when he didn't say anything added quickly, "On the other hand, if you don't feel comfortable with that you'd better go home. I wouldn't want you to do anything that your mum wouldn't like. Okay?"

Kit's eyes swivelled round the hallway. He looked

hopefully at Jane's door. Anna grew impatient; the situation was becoming untenable. She couldn't leave a disturbed child on her mother's doorstep. Anything might happen to him, or to the apartment, and she would be responsible for leaving him without supervision. Jane might be away for hours. Anna had no idea where her mother had gone or when she was coming back. "Go on Kit. You can't stay here forever. Your mum will be worried."

"She won't," he said bleakly.

"Of course she will," Anna replied. Then she realised why the boy was looking so shifty. "She doesn't know you're here, does she?"

Kit chewed his lip. His eyes wandered from her face. "No," he mumbled.

"Why didn't you tell her? If she knows Jane she wouldn't mind, would she?" Talking to Kit was like pulling teeth. What was the matter with the boy? Why was he so closed up, and what sort of home did he come from if his mother didn't know or care where he was?

"Mum's busy. When she's like that she doesn't notice. Anything."

"Okay," Anna said slowly. "What about your brother and sister, where are they?"

"They're at home with Sue."

"And who is she?"

"Sue looks after us. Sometimes. Phoebe's doing her scrapbook. Sticking in her stupid pictures. She thinks they're great but they're stupid."

Anna let out her breath. At least there appeared to be one responsible adult in the household. "And your little brother, what's he doing?"

"Finn's banging."

"Banging?" Anna tried to work out what Kit was really saying. What could a little boy be banging? And why? Was this something she should be concerned about? "What exactly do you mean by banging?"

"He's playing drums," Kit growled. "He's always doing it. It's horrid. I hate it so I went out. No one noticed." He straightened up and looked her fully in the face. He was white, his body quivering. "I hate him."

Shocked by his intensity, Anna stifled a gasp. "Do you want to talk about it?" she asked, sliding Jane's key into the lock. "Sometimes it helps." Kit lifted a shoulder slightly. Pushing open the door she added, "You've been here before, haven't you?" and was relieved when he nodded. "If you're still worried about being with me, I'll keep the door open. See." She wedged it ajar and led the way into the living area. "Are you all right with that?" He said nothing but followed her warily.

Anna sat down on the sofa and patted the cushion beside her. She didn't think the boy would come so close but perhaps he would feel safe enough to relax. Kit remained in the doorway, tensed up as if on the verge of flight. Acutely aware of the child hovering on the threshold, Anna concentrated on making it look as if she didn't care whether he came in or not.

There was a long silence and she was beginning to think that her ploy hadn't worked when Kit said, "You didn't tell me that I don't hate him." The words burst from his lips as if propelled by an unstoppable force.

"No," Anna said as neutrally as she could manage.

"Everybody else does."

"I'm not everyone else and anyway you're allowed to hate your brother if you want." Anna spoke without looking at him. She was convinced no one had ever let him express his real feelings, because most adults faced with such violent emotion in a child couldn't cope and went into self-protective denial. She, however, was determined to give Kit a chance to talk about what was troubling him.

Puzzled by her attitude and still keeping an eye on the door, Kit took a step towards her. "Finn's special," he said defiantly.

"So what if he is? Why should that make any difference to the way you feel about him?" Anna challenged. He looked at her in surprise then quickly looked away. "You might have a good reason for hating him," Anna prompted. "If you like, you can tell me. I won't mind."

"If I do, you won't say it's not true?"

"No I won't. Why should I? Only you know if it's true or not."

"Hmm." Kit was almost at her side and Anna was about to ask if he wanted to sit down beside her when a quick glance at his tense little figure told her that it was too soon. If she said something now he was sure to retreat. The best way of getting Kit to open up was to let him take his time. He needed to be sure he could trust her before he said anything. Pretending that she hadn't noticed how far into the room he had come, Anna concentrated her attention on the dust motes dancing in a beam of sunlight.

Kit shoved his hands into the pocket of his jeans and shuffled his feet, wrinkling up his face and gnawing at his bottom lip as he tried to make up his mind. It took so long that Anna was about to give up when he burst out, "Finn's horrid. He spoils everything. He's always getting upset and when he gets upset, Mum says we have to do what he wants. It's not just me and Phoebe, everyone has to. If we don't, he gets worse and worse. Mum says he's like that because he was born that way and no one can do anything about it. Finn is Finn. You can't change how he is. Ever. But she never tries." His voice rose. "If me or Phoebe do anything wrong we get told off, but she's never cross with Finn. Mum does everything he says and then she gets so tired she has to go to bed. Sometimes he wakes her up in the middle of the night and screams and screams. Mum says it's because he's scared, but what about us? We're not allowed to be scared."

"Are you? Scared I mean."

"No." The boy's face tightened. "I'm not scared. Ever." He clenched his fists, holding them against his thighs as he stared past her.

Anna waited a moment then said, "What about your dad? Does he help?"

"Dad!" Kit said bitterly. "We don't see him. No one comes to our house anymore except Sue, and she's used to us. Other people don't like Finn because there's something wrong with his brain. That's why Dad left. I heard him. He said he couldn't take it anymore."

"That doesn't mean to say he doesn't love you," Anna said carefully. *Bastard,* she thought *leaving his kids when they needed him most.* Kit hunched his shoulders. He looked so much like some scrawny little bird that Anna had to force herself not to lean over and pull him into her arms for a hug. "Sometimes grown-ups find things hard and they decide they can't get on with each other, but that doesn't mean they don't love their children." *What am I saying? I don't know anything about him. But what else can you say to children when their Mum and Dad split up? Their lives are shattered and someone has to help them put the pieces back together.* Looking at the unhappy child in front of her she felt a burst of gratitude to Jane and Hugh for loving each other and giving her a secure and happy childhood.

"No," Kit said. "He doesn't. No one does. Gray, mum's partner, didn't either. He left after the dead baby." Anna searched desperately for words. "It died when it was born. Mum cried and cried and Gray left."

"There must be someone," Anna tried. Kit shook his head. "Someone at school? Your form teacher maybe?" Another shake.

"There's Uncle David." Kit's face brightened for a moment. "He's in a band and has to go on tour a lot so we don't see him much."

"But he cares about you?" Anna cast about for some hope. Kit nodded. "And your mum does."

Kit's face clouded. "She only cares about Finn." He paused. "And her painting. When she's not with him she's always painting. That's all right, because it's what she does. She's an artist."

"Hello?" There was more than a tinge of anxiety in Jane's voice as she came through the open door. "Oh." She stopped as she saw her visitors. "What...?" she began. Anna shook her head and she continued, "Kit. What are you doing here? We thought you were watching television." Her voice warmed and in spite of herself

Anna felt a twinge of jealousy.

"No," Kit said. "I came to see you but you weren't here."

"Oh dear. I was upstairs with your mum. Robyn was painting me." Jane was glowing as she turned to Anna. "She says she wants to put my portrait in this year's summer exhibition. Apparently, I've got an interesting face. She has me sitting in your dad's old chair, which is why I thought I'd wear this." Jane fingered the amber beads she wore around her neck.

Anna looked at Kit and suddenly she understood. All his life he had been second. To his sister, to his handicapped brother, to his mother's work. No wonder he looked so needy and undernourished – he was lacking the one thing she'd always had in abundance: her parent's undivided love and attention.

Oh Kit, Anna thought. Aloud she said, "Now Jane's here shall we have a drink and a biscuit? Knowing my mum, she's bound to have some chocolate ones."

"A whole tin full," Jane responded. "Shall we?" She held out her hand but though Kit nodded he didn't take it and kept close to Anna as the three of them went into the kitchen.

TWELVE

Debbie walked slowly along the riverbank. The trees threw dappled shadows on the pavement. Tigger stopped at each trunk, sniffing for canine messages. "Leave the pee-mails. We have to get a move on," Debbie scolded but did nothing to hurry the terrier. As far as she was concerned, they could stay there all evening, anything to put off the moment when she had to pick up the prom dress. She wanted it. But what if it was wrong? What if Frankie hated it?

"She probably will anyway," she told the dog who balanced on two of his three legs to leave his own message. He was still in mid-flow when a large brown dog, covered in what looked like Rasta curls, bounded up and did its best to upend him.

"Jake, leave." The command broke through her worries. "Sorry." Jake's owner, a thick-set guy with broad shoulders locked the animal's lead. "He's okay. He won't hurt your dog."

"I know that. I'm sure he's just being friendly. Aren't you boy?" Debbie stroked the velvety muzzle and ran her fingers through the dog's long fringe. "He's lovely," she said and Tigger gave a warning yip. "It's all right, I still love you," she reassured the terrier then turned back to the other animal. "What breed is he?" she asked. "I've never seen anything quite like him. He kind of looks like a poodle, but…"

"He's an Irish water spaniel," the dog's master told her. "You don't see a lot of them around. I'm Eddie by the way, Eddie Brown." He held out his hand.

"Debbie Murray." She took his hand and smiled. Eddie's grip was firm, his fingers rough, his skin dry. A good strong handshake. One she could hold onto. What was she thinking of? Debbie hastily loosened her hold. "Nice to meet you but we have to be getting on." She tugged at the lead but Tigger decided that he wanted to play. Tails wagging, the two dogs circled each other. "Come on," Debbie said, "stop showing me up."

"They always do that." Jake's master grinned but when he whistled the water spaniel obeyed instantly. Debbie shrugged ruefully and shook her head at Tigger who trotted meekly towards her and looking up with adoring eyes waited for his mistress to lead him away.

She crossed the road and made her way to the new estate. When she reached Benbow Close she hitched the lead to the gate post and told Tigger to sit. Unusually for him, the terrier did as he was told. Then, with an uncomfortable flutter of nerves, she rang the doorbell. The sound of the television drifted out through an open window followed by children's voices.

A woman shouted, "Get the door for me, will you Jodie."

A skinny girl in cut-off jeans and a crop top appeared. Leaning provocatively against the door jamb she drawled, "Yeah?"

"I've come for the dress…" Debbie began.

Jodie straightened up. "Mum, it's for you," she yelled

over her shoulder and slunk back into the house leaving the door wide open. Debbie stood hesitantly on the doorstep. Was she supposed to follow? She hadn't been asked and if she did go in what was she going to do with Tigger?

"Sorry about that." A slightly over-weight harassed-looking woman came into the hall, a plastic carrier bag in her hand. Her hair was greasy and the colour needed touching up. Her face was strained and pale and there were deep-purple shadows under her eyes. "Here." She thrust the bag into Debbie's hands. "I hope it's okay and your daughter has a lovely time."

"Thanks, that's really kind. I can't tell you how much it means to her. She was so looking forward to her prom, as they all do. It's the highlight of the year."

"Right." Tracey nodded. The two women stood looking at each other not knowing what to say, but somehow unable to make a move until Tigger, who had had enough of being good, gave a sharp bark.

"My dog." Debbie waved a hand in his direction.

"Yeah, well. That's dogs. Worse than kids, I sometimes think."

"Oh, I don't know." Debbie smiled. "But I've only got the one. Frankie." She expected a conversation about children and all the terrible things they did, but Tracey was already stepping back and before Debbie had finished her sentence the door was shut in her face. "Well," she breathed, "talk about rude. The way some people are I'd rather have animals any day." Smarting from the manner in which she had been treated Debbie turned down the path and dragged the protesting Tigger

126

past every lamppost on the way home.

Back in the house the dog sank onto the kitchen floor, tongue hanging out, panting desperately. Full of remorse, Debbie filled his water bowl. "Sorry Tigger, I shouldn't have taken it out on you. You're a good boy, really." She gave him a quick pat and turned her attention to the plastic bag lying on the kitchen table. She dare not look straight away in case she'd made another of her stupid mistakes. But desperate to know, she slid her hand tentatively inside. Her fingers closed around the silky material. It felt gorgeous. Classy, as the e-mail had said. But what would it look like on? Murmuring a swift prayer she pulled the dress carefully out of the bag and held it up against the last of the evening sun. Blue-green silk shimmered like sunlight on the sea. The colour was perfect for Frankie, but what mattered was the fit. Debbie searched for the label. It was an eight. It should be all right. It had to be.

"Frankie," she called. "I've got your dress."

Her daughter strolled into the kitchen doing her best to look as if she did not care, but when she saw what Debbie was holding she let out a gasp. Slim fitting, with spaghetti straps, the dress dipped at the back into a small train.

"Is it okay? Do you want to try it?"

Frankie pouted but already her hand was reaching out.

"I think it will look lovely," Debbie said.

"Dunno." Frankie raised a shoulder. Then she grabbed the dress and pulling off her clothes, lifted her arms for her mother to slip the garment over her head. The silk swirled round her, clinging to her bust and hips. "Does it look OK?" Frankie cried, all pretence at being cool gone.

Debbie stepped back almost knocking over the dog's bowl as she did so. Tigger gave an offended bark but she ignored him as she gazed at her daughter. In the pink dress, Frankie had been a pretty teenager; in this one she was a beautiful young woman.

"Is it all right? Mum?" Frankie's voice was frantic.

"It's more than all right, love. It looks amazing on you. Go on. Go upstairs and look in the mirror." Frankie needed no encouragement. Lifting the skirt she ran. "Be careful. Don't break your neck," Debbie called after her. The dress was only a little too long, but long enough for a careless heel to get caught in the hem.

"It's not a problem," she told Smokey-Joe cheerfully as the black and white cat climbed in through the cat flap. "I'll sort it." Logging on, she posted, Wanted: Someone to shorten my daughter's prom dress. I can't sew and it needs doing as soon as poss. Thanks. And pressed send.

*

Jane flicked open her phone and scrolled down the messages. There was nothing important so she went to the Freecycling site. Reading through the posts she came across Debbie's entry. Hooked by her initial appeal she went on to follow the story of the ill-fated prom dress. This Debbie, whoever she was, might not be able to sew but she cared about her daughter and was doing everything she could to get her Cinderella to the ball.

Jane smiled. She had a lot for which to thank the nuns at her convent school. Not only had they insisted on the highest academic standards, they had been adamant that their girls would all go on to college or university, and also made sure that their pupils had what they considered other basic skills. Leaning her chin on her hand Jane remembered Sister Margaret Mary's needlework class. The tiny nun, she couldn't have been taller than four foot ten, wore a silver thimble on her finger so that she could rap it on a girl's wrist if her stitches weren't small enough. One hard tap and the bruises would last for a week but you never forgot what you had been taught.

Nor had she forgotten those other lessons about being kind and caring for others. The nuns' teaching had been reinforced by her parents and she'd tried to bring up Anna the same way. To a certain extent she had succeeded as Anna had shown in her choice of profession, where she dealt with people and their problems. If she was not as caring in her relationships, hopefully this was something that would one day change. *I'll have to be patient and wait for Anna's good sense and fundamental kindness to kick in, as you always said they would,* Jane told Hugh.

In the meantime there was something practical she could do for Debbie's daughter. *I can alter the dress for you. Tomorrow.* Or was it today? Glancing at her watch she saw that it was not quite midnight, so she pressed send.

*

Tracey was exhausted. In spite of opening the windows, the bedroom had been hot and stuffy. Eddie, when he finally came in, couldn't settle and when he wasn't disturbing the children or the dog by getting up and mooching around the house, he was tossing and turning and muttering in his dreams, until she had to stop herself from pressing a pillow over his face. Lying rigidly beside him she'd longed for somewhere cool and peaceful where she could sit with a long drink and never ever move again. Instead, the time ticked relentlessly on until the alarm went off and she had to get the kids up and dressed ready for school. Then she'd gone to work, done her shift, collected Milly from her mum's, made everyone's tea, and after all that she was on her way to clean for Dan.

"It's all right for some," she grumbled as she toiled along the pavement, her cleaning clothes in her bag. Eddie would have been sitting on his butt all day, the kids would be in front of their screens, and she was off to her second job so that they wouldn't be thrown out onto the street. At least not yet. She was doing all she could to put off the terrible day but the building society had lost patience and the court... A wave of cold sweat broke over her, and her head spun so crazily that she thought she was going to tip over right there on the pavement like some drunken old bag lady. Screwing up her eyes she forced the image of leaving Benbow Close from her mind. She mustn't think about it or she'd sit and howl, and it was up to her to keep her family together.

Shakily, she keyed in the entry code and let herself into Dan's apartment. She was met by a blast of cold from the air conditioning and all at once her evening job didn't seem so terrible. If she took her time the worst of the day's heat would be gone by the time she left, and if she was really, really lucky when she got home Eddie might have got the kids to bed. "Chance'll be a fine thing," she murmured, going to the main bathroom to change into her old T-shirt and shorts, but she was smiling as she tried the door.

To her surprise it was locked. Guiltily, she glanced round the open-plan apartment and saw that the laptop was open on the table. Tracey sighed. Dan must be working from home. This was the last thing she wanted. She hated cleaning round people; she needed space to do it her way. She couldn't stand being watched. It took her back to when she was a little girl and Sheila picked holes in everything she did. What was worse was that being the only girl she was expected to help in the house, but she could never do it right. At least Dan, being male, probably wouldn't notice. On the other hand he was her boss and that was bound to be awkward.

There was the sound of running water and Dan came out of the bathroom. He looked awful, his face grey, black shadows under his eyes.

"Are you all right?" Tracey asked.

"No. But I'll live. I've got some sort of stomach bug. I've been throwing up all night."

"Do you want me to go? I can always come back another day."

"It's okay." Dan shook his head then winced. "I shouldn't have done that. My head feels as if it's about to fall off."

"Can I get you anything?"

"Thanks, but no." He kept his head very still. "I'm fine so long as I don't do too much. I've been asleep most of the day and I was taking a look at my messages to see if there's anything urgent." He glanced across at the screen. "No. Nothing. Just Freecycle stuff."

"You're on that too?" Tracey was surprised that someone who had as much money as Dan would use the

Freecycle site.

"Sure. I think it's a great idea. It's good for the environment. There's less stuff thrown into landfill, fewer resources used to make new things, and people can get what they need for free. It's a win-win situation all round." In spite of herself, Tracey couldn't help looking round the room with its expensive furniture and fittings.

"I know," Dan said wryly. "I don't always practise what I preach, but who does?" He shut his eyes briefly. "God, I feel terrible."

"Go and lie down. I'll bring you a cup of tea or something."

"No tea." Dan went white.

"Piece of toast then?" Tracey suggested. "That's my mum's answer to being sick. Have a piece of toast to mop up the stomach acid, she says. It works too. At least it always has with the children and with Eddie's hangovers. But if you don't fancy it..." She trailed off uncertainly. Why should someone as sophisticated as Dan want to try her mum's old remedy?

Dan's stomach grumbled. He closed his eyes and swayed slightly. Tracey moved forward half-expecting to catch him before he crashed to the floor but he opened his eyes and gave her a wavering grin. "You know something, toast sounds good."

Tracey went into the kitchen and looked helplessly around. Where the hell was the bread bin? The toaster? The granite surfaces were completely clear and she couldn't see any way of opening the stainless-steel cupboards until she remembered the spread in last month's *Ideal Home* magazine. Dan's units were exactly the same as the ones featured in their spread on this year's latest kitchen design. No protruding knobs or handles to catch the dirt. It was easy when you knew how. Feeling totally confident she found what she was looking for and soon the smell of toasting bread spread comfortingly through the living area, where Dan had collapsed onto one of the huge leather sofas.

"What about you? Aren't you going to have any?" he asked as she handed him a plate of toast dripping with butter.

Tracey shook her head but her mouth watered. It was a long time since the tuna sandwich she'd had for her lunch. "I should be getting on with my work," she said half-heartedly.

"There's no hurry. Join me," he mumbled, his mouth full. "This is so good." He licked his fingers appreciatively. "Your mum knows what she's talking about."

"Thanks, I will." Tracey went back into the kitchen and popped more bread in the toaster. The dust and dirt weren't going anywhere and she was in no hurry to get back to screaming kids and a miserable husband, who snapped and sulked and, when he wasn't doing either, was down the pub with the dog. He stank of drink too, most of the time. As soon as he staggered home he fell into bed without bothering to shower. Not like Dan. He might be ill but even in T-shirt and joggers he looked immaculate. His hair catching the last of the evening sun glowed white gold in the shadowy room. Leaning back against the cushions, his long legs stretched out, he was like some film star. The colour had come back into his face and his eyes were blue as the sea. Raising his arms above his head he yawned lazily.

"I'm feeling so much better. I'll grab an early night and be back to normal in the morning. And it's all thanks to your mum's toast." His grin was stronger now.

"I said it worked, didn't I." Tracey brushed the crumbs from her lap and started to get up.

"There's no hurry." Dan yawned again. "I can do without the hoovering today." Tracey drew in her breath thinking of the money but he seemed to have read her thoughts. "Don't worry, I'll pay for the usual hours. You can make a pot of tea and more toast if you like, and can I be very cheeky and ask you to pass me the laptop? I feel too comfortable to want to move."

As she lifted it from the desk, Tracey couldn't help seeing that Dan hadn't closed down. The Freecycling site was open and on it was a message from Debbie. "I know her," she said without thinking. "Oh, I'm sorry. I didn't mean to read your messages. You can trust me with your stuff. Honest. It's just that I saw Debbie today. She came round to pick up a prom dress for her daughter. I'd got one I'd bought for Lauren's wedding and Debbie said she thought it would be perfect. She'd got one for Frankie off e-bay but they'd made a mess of it when they had it altered and…" In her embarrassment she didn't seem to be able to stop. Dan made a gesture of surrender and she finally faltered to a halt.

"Enough!" he groaned. "I get the picture."

"Sorry." Tracey flushed.

"It's OK. Helping each other is what Freecycling's all about. Did her daughter like the dress?"

"Debbie said Frankie loved it. She sent me an e-mail to say thanks. Trouble is, the poor kid's been let down over the limo so it's all been a bit pointless."

"If she's got the dress, surely she can go to the prom."

"You'd think so but that's only part of it. As well as the dress there's the shoes and the bag. After you've got your colour scheme worked out there's the trip to the salon for your hair, nails and makeup – maybe even a spray tan. It all has to be right. Then you've got to arrive in style. So you see the car's really important. Look." She handed Dan the laptop and waited while he read Debbie's plea. "See what I mean?"

"Yes," he said slowly. "Perhaps I can help. If no one else offers I could take her in the Aston Martin." They looked at each other. He shook his head. "I'd be more than happy to do it but what about her mum? How do I convince her I'm not a dirty old man who's after her daughter? Unless…" He looked at Tracey. "You'd be prepared to vouch for me."

"'Course I will. I'll tell her that I work for you and that she can trust you. You offer and I'll tell her you're okay."

Frankie will have a dress and a lift to the prom and all because of Dan and me working together to make it happen. A flicker of joy flared beneath Debbie's ribs as Dan began to type, Offered: Lift to the prom.

THIRTEEN

Finn's scream echoed around the garden. "Gone, gone, gone," he bellowed, banging his head over and over again on the back door.

"What is it? What's wrong?" Hair and skirt flying, Robyn tore through the kitchen.

"Peter's gone," Finn howled.

"No, darling, no. He can't have. I shut him in myself last night. He's there, he must be. Shall we go and see? We'll have a proper look." Robyn tried to sound calm but her heart was thumping at the thought of yet another problem to be solved.

Finn raised his head and whirling round started stamping and pointing wildly round the garden. Robyn could see that something was missing but it took a moment or two for her to realise that there was an empty space on the back wall where Peter Rabbit and his hutch should have been.

Unable to believe her eyes she went over to the wall, her hands held wide open as if she might be able to feel what she could not see. There was no doubt about it, the hutch had gone and so had Finn's beloved rabbit. The unimaginable had happened. They had lost Peter. No. Not lost him, you couldn't lose a rabbit and a hutch. Some cruel hideously uncaring person had stolen Finn's rabbit and now her son was hysterical, rocking backwards and forwards on his heels, his face stained with tears, his nose running.

"We'll find him, we'll get him back," she said pointlessly knowing that nothing she could say would make any difference. "Look Finn." She resisted the impulse to kneel beside him and take him in her arms because that would add to his confusion and grief. Instead, she focussed her eyes somewhere above the little boy's head and tried to make her voice light and exciting, "Perhaps Peter's gone to visit his friends and relations. Or maybe he's slipped into Mr McGregor's garden, like in the story. If we wait a little while he might be back."

"Want him now." Finn balled his fists and lowering his head charged at his mother. Trying to avoid him she stumbled and half-fell against the wall, where she leaned momentarily breathless until she recovered enough to grab him by the arm. Finn's grief and fury was too strong for her and wrenching himself free he ran into the house, up the stairs and into his room where he sat down on the floor. His face turned to the wall, he leaned his head against the plaster and began to howl.

*

The eerie inhuman sound echoed through the house and was the first thing Anna heard as Kit opened the front door.

"Thanks for bringing me home," Kit said.

"It's okay. I—" Anna began but the rest of her sentence was drowned by Finn's keening. She cast a hasty glance at Kit who hunched his shoulders and avoided her eyes.

"Finn," he mumbled.

Hell, Anna thought. Kit had said his brother was

strange but this was beyond everything. Something terrible must have happened to get the child into this state. Had there been an accident? Where was the children's mother? Why wasn't she doing something? How could anyone stand this noise?

The desperate sobs spiralled down to the hall increased in volume, then began to fade to a low concentrated moan. As they did so the door at the end of the hallway opened and the red-haired woman Anna had seen talking to her mother came in. Her hair wisped wildly about her face and she was knotting her hands in her skirt but she made no attempt to go upstairs to comfort her child. Lifting her chin, her eyes clouded with tears, she said flatly, "It's my youngest son. He's autistic."

"I told her," Kit said.

"Oh," Robyn's sigh was so soft Anna hardly heard it.

Not knowing what to say, but feeling an explanation was necessary, she held out her hand. "I'm Anna Poynton. I think you know my mother, Jane."

"Oh yes." Robyn's voice was a little louder and she almost managed a smile. "She has lovely bones," she added, her eyes wandering towards the staircase.

"You're painting her portrait," Anna said. There was something surreal about this situation. All around them was this harrowing noise, as if all the pain and sorrow in the world was trapped in this house, and she was trying to ignore what was going on by making polite conversation.

"I am," Robyn murmured. She looked at Anna for the first time. Her green eyes scarcely focussing as she said, almost to herself, "There's nothing you can do. Nothing any one can do."

Nonsense, Anna thought. *You're giving up.* "There must be something," she said.

"He'll keep going until he's hoarse. Then he'll stop," Robyn said.

"He goes on and on." Phoebe came out of the front room. "For hours and hours and sometimes all night if it's really bad. What's happened Mum?"

"It's Peter Rabbit." Robyn's head drooped.

"Is he dead?"

"No," Robyn sighed, her body slumping as if weighed down by sorrow. "Though that might have been better. At least we could have had a funeral. No Phoebe, someone's stolen him and not only that, they've taken his hutch as well."

"Is that all?" Anna cried in amazement.

"All!" Robyn glanced at her through a curtain of hair. Kit screwed up his face and Phoebe gasped in disbelief.

"It's a vile thing for someone to have done, but if it's upset Finn so badly can't you buy another rabbit? You could get one the same colour and put it in an identical hutch. Surely that wouldn't be too difficult?" The children stared at her as if she was speaking in an alien tongue. "Well," Anna prompted. "Why not?"

"Finn would know," Phoebe said at last. "He always knows when things are different."

"You can't pretend with him," Kit said. "He's not stupid."

Just crazy. Hastily, Anna shut off the thought. "You must be able to do something," she persisted. Honestly, what was the matter with this family? Had they no initiative. Finn was handicapped but there were ways of dealing with kids like this. Weren't there?

Robyn shook her head. Brushing hair from eyes glazed with lack of sleep, she trailed listlessly into the kitchen. Phoebe followed her mother. Anna hesitated. Was she supposed to go with them? Or should she leave? Did it matter? She waited but as no one said anything she decided the best course of action was to go.

"I'll be off now," she said. Kit, who was still standing in the hallway grunted. "Bye," Anna said loudly, in case he hadn't heard her above Finn's moans. Kit said nothing. His whole body seemed to collapse inwardly and she was seized by a sudden urge to put her arms around him. "Come round and see us again," she said trying to sound cheerful. He looked up at her and his eyes were dark with pain. "I mean it. It would be good." She nodded encouragingly. "Come on your own." She looked towards the stairs. "Give yourself some space. Yes?"

"Mm," Kit muttered, biting his lip.

"Okay," she finished a little desperately. She waited for him to respond but all he did was to stare at the floor tiles until Anna could stand his silence no longer, and pushing open the front door stepped out into the sunlight. The door clanged shut behind her but not even the thick wood could shut out the piercing sound of Finn's misery.

Anna hurried down the street eager to get back to the peace and sanity of her apartment. She'd had enough of this family and their bleak despair. If they couldn't get it together there was nothing she could do. Some people were impossible to help, she told herself as she entered the lift, so she may as well forget it. On the other hand, she wasn't the sort of person who gave up at the first difficulty. In her experience there was a solution to every problem if you went about it logically.

There must be places that children like Finn could go, at least part time, to give parents a break, and she was sure she'd read of some innovative new therapy for autistic children. Was it to do with riding wild horses on the Steppes? Or swimming with dolphins? Anna frowned as she tried to remember. She knew she had talked about it with someone. Was it Alistair? Anna blew sharply down her nose. Whoever it was, it wasn't her ex. Disabled kids, kids of any sort, was not something she would discuss with him. Could it have been a member of her department? Possibly. Or was it her mum? Without thinking she pressed the button for the top floor and before she was fully aware of what she had done she was standing outside Jane's door and ringing the bell.

"Anna, come in." Jane tried to hide her surprise at the sight of her daughter on her threshold bubbling with determination.

"Mum, honestly, I don't know where to start." Anna sighed dramatically. "I took Kit home and you wouldn't believe what's going on there."

"Wait." Jane held up her hand. "If you've been to the Latimers you might need one of these." She poured two large glasses of wine. "Tell me everything," she said, carrying their drinks out onto the balcony. She sat down and waited for Anna to join her, but Anna was too wound up to sit. She paced up and down, the wine sloshing about in her glass as the words tumbled out of her mouth. "Though why we should bother I don't know. They're all so defeatist," she finished and staring out across the river took a long drink.

"I know. It is hard seeing what's happening and not be able to help. But…" Jane let the word hang in the air hoping that Anna would take the point.

"Only Robyn and her family can solve their problems but I'm not sure if they even want to," Anna said.

"I don't think it's a question of wanting or not wanting to. It's more like they are totally overwhelmed by the situation."

"So there is nothing we can do."

"Not at the present moment though things could change."

"In the meantime it's none of our business. Is that what you're trying to tell me? Okay Mum, since there's nothing we can do how about I take you out to supper at the Tobacco Factory? In the meantime we can cheer ourselves up with another glass of that white."

"That sounds good to me," Jane replied and the flush of warmth she felt came not from the alcohol but from the sudden leap of joy that she and Anna were going to do mother and daughter things together. Was this going to be a new start for them both?

*

Robyn slumped across the kitchen table, her head on her arms, hair covering her face.

"Mum," Phoebe whined. She tugged at her mother's arm but Robyn did not move. If she kept very still, if all she could see was a cascade of red-gold curls, maybe she could blot out the primitive wailing, the demanding hands, and the blanket of despair that threatened to overwhelm her.

"It's all right, Phoebs." Kit came into the kitchen. He went to the fridge and pulled a carton of ice cream from the freezer compartment.

"Is it chocolate?" Phoebe came over to see what he had found. Kit nodded.

"Get spoons."

"Why do I have to? It's not—" Phoebe began then stopped. It wasn't often Finn left them with any ice cream. Chocolate was her favourite and if she didn't hurry Kit would eat it all. Her brother was already wandering out into the garden with his share. Grabbing two plastic spoons from the draining board Phoebe followed and was just in time to see him crawling into their secret hiding place between the big rhododendron bush and the garden wall. She wriggled her way in and joined Kit who was already sitting cross-legged on the ground. Sunlight filtered in through the glossy leaves making strange patterns on the bare earth. The ice cream was sweet and melty and after a while even the sound of Finn's sobs began to fade.

When at last her youngest child had fallen silent Robyn raised her head. The mellowness of the light told her it was late afternoon. She should get up and find something for her children to eat, though not for Finn who would have collapsed into sleep and was best left until he woke. But the other two would need their tea. She gazed at the fruit bowl and noted the interesting patina on a wrinkled apple, the sinister bruising of a banana skin. Shaking her head, she opened the fridge and stood perplexed in the sudden rush of cold air.

"Mum!" Phoebe's voice seared through her head.

"Darling," Robyn said guiltily.

"I'm hungry."

"There's nothing—" Robyn began helplessly. Phoebe's face puckered. *Oh God please don't let her cry. If she starts I'll scream at her and it isn't her fault. Poor kid. Poor, poor kid.*

"Can we phone for a pizza?" Kit, her clever quick-witted son saved the situation.

"What a brilliant idea!" Robyn said. "Now where did I put the number?"

*

Later, when the children had eaten and she had picked at a slice of something that tasted like cardboard covered in cheese, Robyn went to look in on Finn.

The evening was hot and airless. Kit and Phoebe were bathed and had gone to their bedrooms. Passing her daughter's room she saw through the half-open door, Phoebe sitting bolt upright lining up her dolls against the wall as she scolded them. "Don't do that again. I told you not to bother your little brother," she was saying. Robyn's heart twisted and she pressed her lips together to stop crying out. Next door Kit sprawled on his stomach lost in a book.

She crept along the corridor stepping carefully to avoid the creaking floorboards. Finn's door was shut and she hoped that he had not fallen behind it, but when she pushed it opened easily. The little boy was curled up against the wall, his face filthy with dirt and tears. Cheeks flushed, chest rising and falling, he was deeply and completely asleep. Robyn slipped her arms around him and lifted him onto her lap. "Oh Finn," she murmured, glad of the chance to hold him close. The little boy's eyelids fluttered and instantly she relaxed her hold waiting for the blank stare followed by a terrified scream as he came back to a world that he couldn't control or understand. But Finn didn't wake and instead he slipped deeper into sleep.

Robyn sat with him until it grew dark. Her eyes began to close and it was time to put Finn into bed so he would wake up in a familiar place. Her arms ached and her legs shook as she carried him across the room. He was heavy and she had to be careful not to jolt him, but at last Finn was in bed, lying flat on his back as always, still dressed in the clothes he had been wearing all day. It was the best she could do. She had neither the strength nor the energy to wash him or to put on his pyjamas. "Night-night my baby," she murmured, kissing him gently on the forehead.

The moon hung over the houses throwing silver shadows on the dark river. In her studio Robyn took paper and charcoal and began to draw.

It was almost light by the time she'd finished; a pale grey streak lined the sky. She held up her sketch and examined it critically. The drawing hadn't quite worked. Frowning, she tried to work out what was wrong with it. Then it struck her. She was using the wrong medium. This picture should be a collage and had to be built up layer upon layer to suggest the strangeness of moonlight in the city. What she needed were different textures. She could start with tissue and silver paper. Then she would need something to suggest the solidity of the road that ran alongside the river. Robyn ran her hand through her hair, tossing back her head in excitement. This was going to be a new venture, a technique she had never used before and she could hardly wait to begin.

The sound of a car door opening and shutting brought her back to reality. Her time was not her own. There were the children and the fallout from the theft of the rabbit to consider. Her joy evaporated and the familiar weariness set in. Why did it have to be so hard? Why couldn't Finn be like the other children? Why couldn't he accept that one rabbit might disappear but another one could be just as good? What was it Anna had said? "You could get one the same colour and an identical hutch. Surely that wouldn't be too difficult?" Anna had sounded so sure, so confident. She was the type of person who got things done in life. Not someone like her who was almost drowning in her hopelessness. Perhaps it was worth a try.

On her computer Robyn typed: Wanted: Rabbit and hutch. As soon as possible. Ours was stolen from our garden by a heartless thief, leaving my autistic son totally devastated as he cannot understand where his Peter Rabbit has gone.

Then she pressed send.

FOURTEEN

Anna linked arms with her mother as the two women walked home through the summer night. "The Latimers are such a strange family," Anna said, her thoughts returning to Kit and his siblings.

Jane suppressed a sigh. They'd had such a pleasant meal during which both of them had avoided talking about Robyn and the children. She wished Anna hadn't raised the topic in case it spoiled what was left of their evening. "I suppose it's the artistic streak," she said.

"That doesn't explain Finn. Nor the way they treat him. Honestly, Mum, that child rules the place. They do whatever he wants. It can't be right even if he is disabled. He needs a firm hand."

"I expect you're right." Not wanting to risk an argument Jane was keen to avoid any discussion about what autistic children could and couldn't do.

"Why doesn't Robyn draw the boundaries?" Anna was genuinely perplexed.

Her mother had to hide a smile as she replied. "It's not as easy as that. It never is. When you're bringing up any child it's difficult to get the balance between being firm and letting them express their own individuality."

"You did all right with me."

"Oh darling." Before Jane could tell her daughter how much that simple statement had meant to her, Anna was striding towards the lift.

When Jane joined her, Anna brought the conversation back to Robyn. "She's painting your portrait and I don't know anything about her, or her work. Let's google her when we get in. She's bound to have a website."

"Why didn't I think of that?" Jane said as she let them into her apartment and switched on her computer.

"That's because you're still in the Dark Ages," her daughter teased.

"I'm not!" Jane protested, laughing. "I use my phone and computer every day. In fact, I don't know where I'd be without them." *I certainly wouldn't have met Robyn and her children.* "Here she is."

"Robyn Latimer, Artist," Anna read over her mother's shoulder. "She doesn't use the Jones like the kids do so he must be the ex-husband. Go on, Mum, let's see the kind of thing she does."

Jane clicked on to the paintings. There were one or two portraits, each one distinctive yet capturing something universal about the sitter. Next came some rather fierce sketches of children, then a landscape, where The Downs spread before them in a haze of sunlight before stopping suddenly at the edge of the Gorge. This was followed by another painting of shimmering golden houses, their windows staring vacantly over a slate grey river.

"They're stunning!" Anna said. "But there's also something strange about them, something menacing and otherworldly. And there's another thing: it says here that her last exhibition was four years ago. It looks as if she hasn't done much since then."

"It must be very difficult finding time to work with

148

Finn to look after, and then there are the other two. It's never easy combining work with bringing up a family especially if you're a single mum."

"I'm sure Kit's no trouble," Anna said swiftly and Jane noted how her daughter was standing up for the boy.

"I'm glad you like the pictures. Robyn says she's going to put my portrait into the Royal West of England show," she said as casually as she could and was gratified when Anna let out an appreciative, "Whew."

"You'll be famous. You'll go down in history as the artist's muse." Anna's tone changed and she said more seriously, "Do you think meeting you was the thing that got her working again?"

"Don't be silly," Jane said.

"I'm sure it was. You know what, we'll have to go and see your portrait in the exhibition. Do you think we could get an invite to the opening night or even better, the private view if they have one? Or do they keep the subjects hidden in case everyone sees what a mess the artist has made?"

"Anna!" Jane exclaimed. "I thought you said her pictures were really good."

"I'm only teasing. No really, I am impressed. If I had the money I'd buy one. That one of The Downs has something about it. I don't know what but it kind of stays with you. I wish..." Anna took the mouse from her mother and scrolled back to the picture. "I can't make up my mind whether it makes me feel sad or not."

"It's beautiful."

"Yes, but kind of threatening too, or something. I don't know. Come on Mum, to celebrate you being painted by

149

a top artist let's open a bottle of bubbles."

Haven't you had enough? Jane thought. "I don't think…" she began.

Anna nodded. "On second thoughts, I've had enough wine. If you don't mind, I'll make us some coffee."

"There are some raspberry buns in the tin, if you've any room," Jane called as Anna went into the kitchen.

"I mustn't," Anna's voice floated back but when she brought out the tray, beside the coffee cups was a plate of Jane's tiny cakes. "This is like being at home," Anna said. "I mean back in the old house—" she corrected herself after she'd eaten a couple of melt-in-the-mouth buns and cleaning her plate by scooping up the crumbs and licking them off her fingers.

"The raspberries came from Mary's garden. She brought me a couple of pounds last time we met. You remember the Sawyers, don't you? They were our next-door neighbours."

"Yes I do. Helen and I went to junior school together, and they had a donkey in their field. We used to feed him carrots. Dad would pull them up for me." Anna smiled at the memory.

Jane, feeling a lump rising in her throat, hurried to say, "When you first suggested I move to Bristol I thought I'd miss the country, but I'm loving it here, even if I have to take in sewing," she added mischievously.

"Mum!" Anna gasped in mock horror. "I thought you had plenty of money to buy this place."

"It's all right, I'm not serious," Jane reassured her. "I've offered my services to someone called Debbie on Freecycle."

"That sounds even worse."

"I suppose it does. Actually, it's for her daughter Frankie so she can go to her prom."

"You're playing fairy godmother." Anna laughed.

"I suppose I am." Jane was delighted by the idea and wished she could spread some magic over Robyn and her children.

*

Frankie stood outside the block of apartments. She was sure that this was the right place. She'd checked the address over and over again, but to be absolutely certain she looked again at her phone. Reassured, she pressed the button for the intercom and waited. Nothing happened and she had to try twice more before someone answered.

"Hello." The voice sounded okay but its throat was dry.

"I'm Frankie. I've come about the dress."

"I'm on the top floor. Come on in."

The door swung open and Frankie stepped into the entrance lobby. With its stone floors and brick walls it looked bare and at first she thought she hated it, but as she waited for the lift doors to open she decided that there was something cool about it too.

Jane's apartment was even better. The view from the huge windows stretched for miles over the city. The living area was airy and spacious but it didn't feel empty. *I could live like this*, Frankie thought as she stood on a coffee table while Jane pinned up the hem of the turquoise dress. *It must cost loads. I'd have to earn lots of money.*

"Careful. Keep still or I might stick a pin in you," Jane warned as Frankie jerked her head at the realisation that she could, or rather, she would have a place like this one day. She wasn't going to be like her mum, disorganised and messy. She was going to make something of herself.

"Do you know what you want to do when you leave school?" Jane asked.

"I'm going to college, then uni to study veterinary science so I can be a vet." The idea came from somewhere at the back of Frankie's brain. "I mean, I never really thought about that before but that's what I'm going to do."

"Are you good with animals?"

Frankie laughed. "They're like part of my life. You've no idea. My mum picks up strays like other people get colds. I'm good at science too."

"Then there's no reason why you shouldn't make a great vet. Let me see if I've got this right." Jane stepped back to check the length of the dress. "Yes, I'm happy with that. If you jump down and get changed, I'll sew this up and you'll be good to go. Do you want to wait or will you come back later?"

"I'll stay if you don't mind," Frankie said and sat and scrolled down her phone while Jane sewed.

"All it needs is to be ironed carefully and you'll be the belle of the ball." Jane finished the last stitch and handed Frankie the dress.

"Thanks. Thanks for everything," Frankie said and kissed her quickly on the cheek. It was going to be all right. She had the most gorgeous dress, she was going to the prom, and after the summer break she was off to college where she could finally be herself. Because of the subjects she was going to study she would be leaving

Amy and Emma behind. Freed from their so-called friendship she could settle down and work without worrying about what others thought of her. Whizzing down in the lift, she shimmied out into the bright day. Head held high, she sauntered along the pavement humming under her breath. She was about to cross the road when she saw Robert Mackenzie on the other side. They were in the same science groups and he usually got top marks. Except when she beat him.

Yeah, Frankie thought happily and gave Robert a quick wave. What did it matter if he was the kind of lad Emma and Amy made snide comments about? It was because he was clever and didn't take any notice of them. She was feeling good so what harm did it do to smile? The lights changed. The traffic stopped, she began to cross, so did he, and they met halfway. "See you around," Frankie called as she passed him. Did he say yes? Did it matter? What did she care? She was doing her own thing.

*

It's hanging day, Robyn thought as she looked at Jane's portrait. The words conjured up an image of herself hanging from a tree in the garden at Coombe Magna, her body swinging gently, the soles of her feet green with grass stains, and only the choking feeling around her throat keeping her from soaring into the freedom of the sky.

"Robyn?" David's voice brought her back to the studio. "Is this the one?"

"Yes. Be careful with it," she added as he picked up the painting.

"Like this?" David jerked his arms as if the picture was

153

slipping from his grasp.

"Don't," Robyn cried.

"You know I wouldn't drop it." Her brother tightened his grip on the frame.

"I know. But this is the best piece I've done for years. Or at least I think it is." She frowned and pushing her hair back from her eyes peered anxiously at the brown-paper parcel. "I don't know what's been happening to me recently. While I'm painting, I get carried away and think the picture is wonderful, then when it's finished I can't bear to look at it. There are times when I think I've lost it and I might as well give up. I've even taken to collage," she finished miserably.

"Then you've got nothing to worry about. Your new work is good. So is this or it wouldn't have been accepted." David set the picture carefully against the wall and looked at his sister. "Come on Robyn, this isn't like you. What's wrong?"

"Nothing." She waved vaguely, her hand bone thin. "I'm tired, that's all. So tired I can't think. Some days I can hardly get myself out of bed."

"Is it Finn? Or the kids?"

"No. At least no more than usual. Kit and Phoebe, they sleep, they eat, they more-or-less do what they should. Finn doesn't, but I kind of know how to deal with him now."

"Nanny would say you need a tonic." David spoke lightly to hide a flare of anxiety. His sister looked so pale, so lifeless, so unlike the girl driven by her passion for life and art that she had always been. "She'd prescribe a spoonful of cod liver oil and a visit to the GP."

"Maybe," Robyn admitted with a lack of resistance that worried him even more. "There is something I need to see him about. I just haven't got round to it."

"Idiot. Make sure you do or I'll personally drag you there, by the hair."

"Which won't do me any good." She attempted a smile.

"Mum," Phoebe's voice floated up from the hall. "Jane's here and she wants to know if you're ready."

"Phoebe, I didn't say that," Jane called, protesting, laughing.

"You meant it. Didn't she Mum? Mum!" Robyn put her hand to her forehead. Brother and sister looked at each other for a long moment.

"You promise me you will go to the doctor."

"Of course."

"Scout's honour?"

"And Guides and Brownies and Pixies and the whole of Fairyland, if that stops you worrying."

"Good. Now are you ready?"

Robyn nodded and followed her brother down the stairs where Jane was waiting in the hall with Phoebe.

"It's very good of you to give up your weekend for the kids," he said.

"A Saturday afternoon is hardly a weekend and seeing as it's my portrait it's the least I can do," Jane replied.

"All the same, we're really grateful." David hesitated for a moment then said, "I wonder if you could do us another favour and babysit when Robyn goes to the doctor."

"Of course I will. It's about time she saw someone.

She's been looking so peaky I've been quite concerned. She probably needs some iron pills, but it's better to be safe than sorry." Brother and sister burst out laughing.

"Mum!" Phoebe said. "It's rude to laugh at people."

"We weren't laughing at Jane but at something she said," Robyn told her.

David turned to Jane. "Please don't be offended. We laughed because you sounded so like our old nanny. It's the sort of thing she was always saying. In fact we were talking about her earlier." He looked so concerned and apologetic that Jane, who was not in the least annoyed, had to smile and assure them that everything was all right and she would look after the children whenever Robyn needed her.

*

Robyn's appointment came through the following week. Jane was drinking her breakfast coffee and puzzling over the final clue in the crossword when her phone rang. At first she couldn't quite make out who it was. Robyn's voice was very faint and dreamy, as if she was not focussed on what she was saying.

"I hope you don't mind but you did say you'd come if we needed you. The GP has arranged for me to see a consultant and I'm afraid Sue's mother has taken another turn for the worse. If you can't manage it I'll try and change my appointment, but they seemed to think it is a bit urgent..." Robyn trailed away. There was a paused, then her voice floated back a little stronger this time. "I'm sure it's nothing. So will you come?"

"Of course. Don't worry, I'll be there." Jane put down the phone and was loading her mug into the dishwasher when she realised what she had let herself in for. Kit and Phoebe would be at school and the only child left at home would be Finn.

He was waiting for her in the hall when she arrived, sitting solidly on the bottom step staring at the front door. As soon as she stepped inside his eyes swivelled away and he directed his glare at the tiles on the floor. Jane's heart sank and plunged even lower as Robyn said with false brightness, "I've told him that Jane is going to look after him and he'll be fine."

She turned to her son. "Won't you darling?"

Finn said nothing and Jane felt a prickle of nerves. This was her first time alone with the child and what would she do if he had one of his screaming fits? Or tried to run out of the door after his mother? She wouldn't be strong enough to hold him. If only Anna could have come with her, or the other children were around to help.

"You'll be late," she told Robyn, who was fluttering around picking up her bag, searching inside it for the front door key, finding it then wandering away in bewilderment at having forgotten what she had done with it.

"Here it is." Jane took charge. "You look fine," she said as Robyn ran her fingers through her hair and smoothed down her skirt. "Go on or you'll be late. Don't worry about Finn. We'll be okay." *I hope.*

"In that case I'll…" Robyn finally made her way through the door.

"Gone. Mum's gone," Finn said.

"Yes, but she'll be back," Jane said as cheerfully as she could manage.

"Peter Rabbit's gone," Finn continued and Jane's unease grew. Was this the start of another outburst? What could she say that Finn would understand?

"I know," she said at last.

"I know. Chair lady." Finn looked hard at her. Jane had no idea what to reply so she nodded. "You sat on the chair and Mum painted you."

"She did." Jane wondered where the conversation was going. Finn nodded slowly and solemnly as he processed this information. When he was sure he knew who she was and how she fitted into his world he walked away down the corridor. In the kitchen he pulled open a cupboard and took out all the saucepans. He put them on the floor in a straight row and picking up a wooden spoon began to bang.

The noise went on and on. Jane sat at the table and wondered if she dare ask him to stop, but that might set off a temper tantrum. Caught up in his drumming Finn was not asking for his mother or talking about his missing rabbit. No wonder the other children kept out of his way. How on earth Robyn managed to stay sane she could not imagine. It was hardly surprising she looked so pale and strained. What she needed was a break. A long holiday somewhere in the sun. Somewhere she could relax and paint. A few weeks of that and she'd be fine. But who would have the children? Phoebe and Kit Jane could manage. It would be like having grandchildren to stay. But Finn. Jane shuddered. For the first time in her life she understood how some children ended up in care. Very few people would be able to cope with a child like Finn.

FIFTEEN

Tracey sat at the bottom of the stairs, her arms over her head in the brace position. The letter lay at her feet, the bold print staring up at her. Repossession. The word was burned on her brain. They were going to take her house away. Her home. Her kids' home. What would they do? Where would they go? This could not be happening. Not to them. She and Eddie had worked so hard. All the overtime and extra shifts they had done to scrape together the deposit, and now they were going to lose everything.

A wet nose thrust itself into her cheek, followed by the oily smell of water spaniel. She tried to push him away but Jake, sensing how miserable she was, began to lick her face. His breath stank of dog food and things she did not want to think about. She had to get away but he was doing his best to climb into her lap. His eyes under his long fringe gazed adoringly at her. "Sit. Now. I mean it." Tracey heaved herself to her feet sending Jake sprawling on the ground. "Don't look at me like that. You know I never wanted you. It was all Eddie's idea."

The dog rolled over onto his back, rubbing himself all over her lovely clean floor. Tracey let out a bellow of rage and looked round for something to throw at him but Jake was already scrambling to his feet and, with a skitter of claws on the laminate, shot into the kitchen.

"Good dog, eh. Who's my good boy?" Eddie, coming

in through the back door, stopped to rumple the dog's curls and tug at his ears. Jake yelped with joy and threw himself panting at his master's feet. "You need a drink, don't you? There." Tracey heard the water pouring into the dog's bowl, and was filled with rage. The first thing Eddie did when he staggered in from the pub was to look after the dog. Not a word to her. No "Hello, I'm back, how have you been?" The bloody dog was more important than she was.

As for the kids, most of the time he seemed to have forgotten they existed, leaving her to deal with them and everything else besides. She was the one who got them dressed and ready for school in the mornings, did the shopping and cleaned the house, as well as going out to work, doing two jobs, not one, so at least they had some money coming in. Not that it was going to do them any good. She could work until she dropped but her miserable wages weren't going to save them. Tracey bent down and scooping up the letter from the building society stormed into the kitchen.

"Look at this," she screamed, shoving the paper into her husband's face. Eddie staggered back. Tail between his legs, Jake slunk into a corner. "It's all over. They're going to take the house. We're losing our home and all you're bothered about is the wretched dog." The colour drained from Eddie's face. Jake began to whimper.

"I'm sorry," Eddie muttered.

"Sorry! Is that all you can say. We're going to be homeless and you're sorry!" In her fury Tracey turned away from him. "We'll be out on the streets and just when I'd got it all so nice." Her voice trembled, the anger gave way to tears and she sank down on a chair and wept.

Eddie stood and watched until at last the sobs subsided. Jake pressed his warm body against his master's leg and Eddie reached down and tangled his fingers in the dog's curls.

"See," Tracey said bitterly. That's all you care about."

"That's not true, Trace, you know that. You and the kids mean everything to me. You always have." His throat choked with tears Eddie faltered to a stop. Somewhere deep down she knew it was true but she was too angry, too upset, and too afraid to listen to him.

"He'll have to go. The dog will have to go. We won't be able to keep him. We can't even afford to feed him."

Eddie pulled gently at a curl and Jake pressed closer. "I'll find somewhere for us, Trace, I promise."

"Oh yeah! And while you're doing that do you think the building society will let us stay here?"

"We could talk to them again."

"Again? I've been there, done that. I've told them about the kids and you losing your job. I said we'll pay back bit by bit what we owe, but even if they'd agreed we couldn't do it. There's no money, Eddie. We're up to our eyes in debt. There's only one thing for it, the kids and me, we'll have to go and stay at Mum's."

Eddie flinched as if she had struck him, but Tracey didn't care. If it wasn't for Eddie they wouldn't be in this mess.

"I'll go to Steve's. I can kip on his sofa for a bit."

"Yeah. Okay. You do that," Tracey said quickly. Without looking at him, she added, "It's for the best. There won't be room for us all at Mum's and in any case you two don't get on."

"That's what I'll do then." Hearing his master's voice Jake butted his thigh. His whip-like tail began to wag.

"That's sorted. We'll sell what we can. It should go okay. It's all new and in good condition. Most of it's hardly been used."

"Yeah," Eddie growled.

"Don't start," Tracey swung round. "Okay, so it was all on the credit cards but I didn't do nothing different from anyone else. How was I to know you were going to lose your job? We were behind before and that was the final straw. What did you want me to do? Get second-hand stuff? Freecycle? Sit on other people's tatty sofas?"

Eddie shook his head. His thrust his hands into his pockets and stared out of the window.

"Go on say something. No? Typical" She snorted when he stayed silent. "That is so you!" Whirling round she slammed out of the room.

*

Eddie listened to Tracey raging around upstairs, stamping about, opening and slamming cupboard doors. The house seethed with anger and he knew that when the children got home they would get the sharp end of her tongue, but if he stayed things would only get worse. Picking up Jake's lead he whistled to the dog and let himself out of the back door.

Man and dog walked along the riverbank, Jake trotting obediently at his master's side. Eddie's face creased with worry as he tried to decide what he was going to do with his beloved pet. Whatever it was he wasn't going to have Jake put down. It would be like killing one of the family.

"I couldn't do that to you, boy. I won't. I promise."
Overcome with emotion he gave the lead a jerk to indicate
that the dog should sit and when Jake did Eddie knelt on
the hot pavement and buried his face in the water
spaniel's neck.

"Are you okay?" Wiping his face on the dog's coat he
looked up. It was the blonde with the three-legged terrier.
"I'm sorry, you looked a bit..." Debbie hesitated.

"Smashed?" Eddie got to his feet.

"Possibly," she said warily.

"Nah." He shook his head. "I've not been drinking."

"Is it the dog? Is he all right?" Debbie's concern shifted
to Jake who was looking curiously at his master. "He's not
sick, is he? It's awful when they are, isn't it? I mean, they
can't tell you what's wrong. You know there's something
but you're not sure what and the vet's so expensive." She
held out her hand to Jake who sniffed it curiously. "I don't
think you need to worry, he looks okay to me. I've had a
bit of experience with animals. My daughter Frankie says
our house is like that *Animal Hospital* on the TV. I can
never turn away an animal in trouble. Which explains
Tigger." She glanced over her shoulder at the white blur
of terrier that was trotting towards them down the
pavement. "There you are, you naughty boy." She pulled
a lead from her pocket. "No one wanted him, not after he
got run over and lost his leg, so I took him in."

Eddie's hand tightened on Jake's lead. "I've got to re-
home him," he blurted out. "If I can't find anyone to take
him—" He stopped, unable to say any more. Debbie's
hand was on his arm.

"Look, Eddie, why don't you come back with me and

163

you can tell me all about it?"

He was going to say no. He hardly knew her. They'd only met once before, but where else was he going to go? He couldn't take Jake to the pub, not in the state he was in. One drink and he'd be blarting all over the bloody dog. They could carry on with their walk but what would that solve? If they walked to the moon and back nothing would change.

"It's not that far, but you don't have to if you don't want to," Debbie said hastily.

She looked so kind and understanding that he made up his mind. "I'd like to. Thanks." Eddie managed a smile though part of him wanted to bury his head on her shoulder and howl.

As if she understood how raw he was feeling, Debbie told Tigger to sit and busied herself with his lead. Then side by side, dogs at heel, they walked away from the river and through the side streets to the row of terraced houses where Debbie lived. "See what I mean." Debbie laughed as she pushed open the gate and they stepped into the small back yard. "Mini-zoo or what?"

"You've certainly got a few animals." Eddie looked at the row of cages set against the wall. Their doors were open, the rabbits were out in their run, which had been set up on a rather bald patch of lawn. There were six of them, all different colours and sizes, munching placidly at the sun-burnt grass.

"I'm going to have to move them tomorrow. With all this hot weather the grass isn't growing. I'll have to start watering it soon."

A black-and-white cat strolled down the path and

wound itself round her legs. Tigger snapped and the cat moved on to stare at the rabbits. Jake seemed indifferent to the cat and rabbits.

"No you don't Smokey-Joe. Rabbit is not for you. Not unless it comes in a tin." Debbie turned to Eddie. "You have to watch him or he'd be in that run and that would be it for the bunnies. Mind you, it's not just cats that are taking them. I saw a post on Freecycle today about a little boy's rabbit being stolen. What makes it worse, is the kid's autistic and can't understand what's happened to his pet. It seems like that bunny was the one thing he could relate to. Then someone takes it and its cage as well. It really makes you wonder about people. How can anyone be so cruel and thoughtless? Even if the kid didn't have a condition, he'd still be upset. Anyway, I've emailed back and told his mum she can have one of Flopsy's last litter. I can't help with the cage as mine are all full but someone else might have one they can give her."

"I can do that," Eddie said.

"You've got a cage? Don't tell me you keep rabbits as well?"

"No. Tracey wouldn't have them. She says a dog's enough. What I meant is, if you've got a rabbit for that kid I can make a cage for it. It's not as if I've got anything else on."

"That would be great," Debbie turned to him. "I'll get straight back to her. She'll be so relieved. She's been having a terrible time with the little boy. Seems he can't understand why his Peter Rabbit's gone missing. You know something, Eddie. That's really kind of you."

"It's nothing." He flushed, embarrassed yet pleased. "It won't take long and it will give me something to do. Shit." He stopped.

"It's okay if you can't do it. It's not as if you know the kid or anything, or me even."

"No that's not it. I'll make the hutch. I want to do it. There will be plenty of bits and pieces of wood hanging about the yard. Milton Corbishly will let me have them if I ask. It's the least he can do after letting me go. The trouble is, I need somewhere to do the work."

Debbie's face lightened. "Oh, that's no problem. You can make it here. There's loads of room. Well—" she looked round the crowded yard and laughed "—sort of. I'm out at work most of the time and Frankie won't get in your way. Not like this brute." She waved her hand at the ginger cat sunning itself on the back doorstep. "Go on, Onions, shift." The cat slowly got to its feet and strolled into the house. Tigger growled unconvincingly after it. "Oh, he's all right," Debbie said. "I know they're supposed to chase cats but Tigger doesn't bother. I think he was after a cat when he ran into the road and got hit by a car. I don't know for sure but I reckon that's why he's all mouth and no trousers. He does a hell of a lot of growling but no chasing. Maybe he's just lazy." She laughed again and for the first time that day Eddie felt some of the misery lift from his shoulders.

"Now that's settled let's get a drink. Do you want tea or a beer, or coffee, or coke, if Frankie's left us any?"

"A cup of tea would be great," Eddie said surprising himself.

"Two sugars I bet," Debbie grinned. "Go on tell me I

guessed right."

"How did you know?"

"You look a two-sugars man, that's all." She led the way into the kitchen, a crowded untidy room with drinking bowls on the tiled floor and herbs growing in pots on the windowsills. There were packets of cat food on the work surface, dog biscuits in a jar on the draining board, and a tea towel draped over the back of a chair.

"You'll have to excuse the mess. I never seem to have time for a proper tidy up. Can you give the dogs some water while I make the tea? Oh, and take Jake off the lead if you like. The garden is pet proof so he'll be all right. Won't you, boy?" The water spaniel wagged his tail furiously, banging it against a unit door. "Hey, be careful, you'll hurt yourself."

"He'll more likely hurt the cupboard. That tail's hard as steel," Eddie said.

"You wouldn't mean to hurt anything, would you," Debbie crooned to the dog. Bending down she stroked his velvety nose. "He's an old softy."

"Soft as butter. Wouldn't hurt a fly. Would you?" Eddie spoke to the dog but in his mind an idea was taking shape.

In the kitchen, dogs at their feet, a cat on the table between them, another asleep on the windowsill, Debbie poured tea. Jake, with an eye on the biscuits she had set out on a saucer, edged closer and closer until his head was resting on her knee. "All right then you can have one, but only one. If that's okay with you?" She looked at Eddie.

Do I dare? he thought. *Would she?* He nodded. "You're good with him," he said. "And he's taken to you."

167

"He knows I think he's gorgeous. There's no need to get jealous. I love you too," she told Tigger who was casting baleful glances at the intruder.

That's it, Eddie decided. *I'm going to ask her. I may as well. I've got nothing to lose. If she says no I'm back where I started. But if she agrees...* He took a deep breath and trying to sound casual said, "You know I'm looking for a home for him."

"Yes." Debbie took a sip of tea and waited for him to go on.

"I don't want him to go but I've got no choice," Eddie's voice trembled. "We're losing the house. Trace and the kids are going to her mum's. There's nowhere at Sheila's for a dog, even if they wanted him."

"Oh," Debbie let out a sigh. "That's terrible. I couldn't bear to lose any of my animals. Silly isn't it, but it's like losing a member of your family. I don't mind if they're going to a good home." She stopped and shook her head. "No, that's not true. It's stupid of me but I do mind even when I know it's for the best. If any of them had to go because I had nowhere for them to live I'd go mad with grief and worry. Poor you." She leaned across the table and took Eddie's hand. "I'm sorry, I really am."

"Thanks." His eyes met hers, then looked away. She was warm and kind and loved her animals like he loved Jake. For one crazy moment he convinced himself that he'd found the answer to one of his problems. Then the familiar feeling of hopelessness and desperation swept over him. He tried to pull his hand away but Debbie's grip tightened.

"I know what you're trying to ask and the answer is

yes. I'll have him. If you'll let me. You'll have to tell me if he needs anything special in the way of food and how to look after his coat. I'd love to have a go at grooming him. I always wanted to do hairdressing but that didn't work out and I bet there's a lot of combing and brushing and trimming with a water spaniel."

"You'll take him? You really will?" Eddie could hardly believe what he was hearing.

"I'd love to. I think he'd be happy here. I mean, he's ignoring the rabbits and cats. If there are any problems or if you're not sure about me I could take him on approval."

"There won't be. Look at him. He's made himself at home already. Debbie, I don't know what to say. I'm going to miss him so much but if I had to leave him with anyone it would be you."

"Mum." A slim dark-haired girl stood in the doorway. "Wow!" she cried when she saw Jake. "Who are you?"

"This is Jake, our new dog," Debbie said.

"Cool," Frankie breathed. "Our very own Rasta dog. He really is something."

Debbie and Eddie looked at each other and smiled.

SIXTEEN

Jodie glanced over her shoulder then back at the display. The earrings, two little studs, glittered enticingly against their black card. The salesgirl at the counter was chewing gum and staring blankly out of the window. The other customers in the shop were busy flicking through display stands crammed with hair bands, earrings, bracelets, fluffy purses, sparkly purses, purses with spots, and ones embellished with black-and-white Scottie dogs. There were hanks of false hair, silky flowers to wind around a ponytail, and scrunchies of every colour. No one would see her. No one would notice the earrings were gone. A single pair of studs would never be missed. Not in Claire's Accessories. Standing as close as she could Jodie slid the packet off the stand. She stood looking at it as if she was trying to make up her mind whether or not to buy the studs and when she was sure no one was looking she slipped them into the pocket of her jeans.

She'd done it. Her heart was beating hard and she felt really hot, but when she caught a look at her face in a mirror she looked the same as usual. Jodie grinned at her reflection and moved on to the scrunchies. A blue one would go with her jeans and a pink one would match her new top. This time she was less careful, not bothering to check if anyone was watching. She folded the card into her palm, looked across the shop and saw the salesgirl's eyes on her. *I know what you're doing,* her eyes seemed to say. *And I don't care. It's a lot more exciting than what I'm doing. Good luck to you if you can get away with it.*

Jodie licked her dry lips. The girl's eyes swivelled to her customers, a mother with a little girl of about four. She leaned forward to take the money the child was holding out to her and as she did so she winked at Jodie. *Yeah!* Jodie wanted to thrust her fist into the air but she still had to be careful. With her hands in her pockets she strolled towards the entrance, stopping once or twice to look at a display to show that she was in no rush to leave.

A few more steps and she'd be back in the Mall and into the Ladies to put on her new earrings before she caught the bus. She had plenty of time. So long as she got home at quarter to four no one would know that she'd skipped school. All she had to do was get out of the shop. She was almost there when someone grabbed her arm. "Where do you think you're going?" The woman came out of nowhere – Jodie hadn't seen her or she'd have legged it.

"Get off me. Leave me alone," she squealed. "Let me go or I'll scream. You're abusing me, that's what you're doing. I want the police." She stopped as she remembered what she was hiding. "Mum!" she wailed.

"Don't worry, we'll be phoning her." The woman's grip tightened. "Before we do why don't you show me what you've got in your pocket?"

"I haven't got nothing," Jodie muttered.

"You know that's not true so give them to me." She held out her hand. Jodie shook her head.

"It's your choice," the woman said. "Let's go

somewhere more private and I'll get your mum and you can tell us why you were leaving the shop without paying for the earrings and the scrunchies."

"I forgot."

"That's what they all say." The woman shook her head. "Why can't you make my day and think of something new?" Holding Jodie's arm she led her through the staff entrance to a small window-less office. "Sit there." She pointed to an orange plastic chair. "Are you going to co-operate and give me your mum's number or shall I call the police?"

*

"They phoned me at work. I lost an afternoon's pay," Tracey said as Eddie walked in through the kitchen door. He looked at her blankly, his mind still saying goodbye to Jake, remembering the puzzled expression on the water spaniel's face when he'd left him with Debbie.

"Well, say something. Your daughter's been caught shop lifting and all you can do is stand there with a gormless expression on your face."

"I didn't know, did I?"

"Too right you didn't. Because where were you when we needed you?"

"I was out. I've found Jake a home."

"There you go again. We've got a week before we've got to get out of the house and you're stressing about the dog."

"I had to find him somewhere."

"Good. I'm glad he's settled. The kids are falling to pieces. Jodie's gone well and truly off the rails. I feel as if my head's bursting but you've found a home for the dog."

"If that's how you're going to be I'm going out."

"Go on. Leave it all to me. As usual," Tracey snarled. Eddie walked out of the kitchen and her glance followed the figure of her husband as he went down the path and out of the back gate. "Gone to the pub," she sniffed, her eyes filling. Angrily she wiped the back of her arm over her face but there was nothing she could do to stop the tears. Fuelled by anger and fear they poured down her cheeks. Her mouth fell open and she began to howl. Terrified the children would hear her, she grabbed a piece of kitchen roll and stuffed it against her lips.

"Eddie," she wailed through soggy paper. "Don't go. I don't want you to go. I need you." Her legs weakened. Her whole body was too heavy to move. Even breathing was an effort. "I'm so tired," she whispered, sitting down at the kitchen table. "If I had my way I'd go to sleep and never wake up again. Oh Eddie!" She rested her head in her hands and stared out of the window, half-wishing he had changed his mind and was about to come back through the garden gate.

She was woken by a hand on her shoulder.

"Mum," Josh mumbled, sleepy and rumpled in his pyjamas.

"What is it love?" Tracey's neck was stiff. Her back ached.

"I don't want to go to Gran's." Josh wriggled himself onto her lap and snuggled his head against her shoulder. "I want to stay here."

"So do I."

"I want to be with you and Dad. Why can't Dad come with us?"

173

"Cos he can't." Abruptly she stood up tipping him onto his feet. "Go back to bed. I've got things to sort. Go on. Now," she ordered as he hesitated. Part of her wanted to scoop him into her arms but another harder part wanted him to feel as bad as she did.

*

The day they moved out of Benbow Close was one of the worst of Tracey's life. Her brother Ryan drove over in the car he was currently working on. They loaded it with the boxes that held the few possessions they were taking.

Makes us look like we're doing a moonlight flit. Except it's broad daylight, Tracey thought. *Go on, gawp,* she addressed the neighbours she knew were watching from behind their blinds and curtains. *Spread the news. Tell everyone. Just don't think it couldn't happen to you.* Determined to leave with her head held high she kept a firm grip on Milly's hand and walked out of the road without a backward glance.

The heat of the day beat down on their heads. Milly's hand was hot and sweaty. The little girl wriggled and complained but holding on to her child was the only thing keeping Tracey sane. If she let go of Milly she would throw herself screaming into the river.

"I want to go to school. Why can't I go to school?" Milly wailed.

"I told you why. I said I wasn't sure what time Ryan was coming to get our things. If he'd been late I couldn't come and pick you up."

"But I wanted to go." Milly stuck out her lower lip. Tracey knew that the change of routine had scared her littlest one. Josh was scared too but he was swaggering along the pavement as if he didn't care, while Jodie was walking on the other side of the road as if the rest of the family were nothing to do with her.

When they arrived in Drake Road, Sheila was out. Using the key her mum had reluctantly given her Tracey felt as if she was ten years old and sneaking home from school with a warning letter in her bag. The kitchen smelled of lemon cleanser, there was a bunch of blue and yellow silk flowers on the windowsill, and every surface was sparkling clean. Everything was in its place and she knew exactly where to find the coffee and tea. Right now it wasn't tea or coffee she wanted but a large gin, possibly even without the tonic.

"Here we are," she said brightly. The children looked at her, their expressions hard and stubborn.

"I told you I didn't want to go to Gran's. Gran's is shit." Josh kicked the leg of a chair.

"Stop it." Losing whatever remnants of control she had left Tracey swung out and cuffed the side of his head. "What have I told you about swearing?"

"That's child abuse," Jodie said coldly. "Dad's lost his job. We're homeless, and now you're abusing us."

"I'm sorry. I'm sorry. I didn't mean to hurt you but you've got to mind what you say," Tracey said.

Josh averted his glance. Jodie glared at her younger brother and sister. "If she carries on like this we'll be taken into care."

"I don't want to go in care," Milly shrieked. She flung her arms around Tracey's waist and buried her face in her mother's chest, squeezing so hard that Tracey could barely breathe.

"No one's taking you away from me," Tracey gasped, stroking Milly's hair. "None of you," she added looking pointedly at Jodie. *Not even if you're doing my head in. No social services are going to snatch you away from me.* "I'm your Mum and I won't let them. Whatever happens we're staying together."

Jodie snorted loudly. Josh kicked another chair. Tracey felt terrible. What Jodie had said had jolted her out of her rage and made her realise that if she was scared her children were even more frightened. Seeing their mum out of control was going to make them feel worse so from now on she would do her best not to shout or scream at them. Whatever they said or did she would stay calm and positive. "Let's go and see where we're all sleeping," she suggested.

"Don't want to," Josh muttered.

"I'm not sharing a room." Jodie said in shocked disbelief.

"It's only till we get our new place," Tracey wheedled as Jodie pulled a face. "There's only three bedrooms in this house. So let's make the best of it. We're lucky to have somewhere like Gran's to go to."

"Yeah. So," Jodie snarled.

Tracey said nothing. She knew how her daughter must feel about having to give up her lovely room and losing much of her stuff. The thought of having to go back to sharing a bathroom with the whole family made her skin crawl, and sharing a bed with Milly wasn't going to be easy. Eddie might snore but she could kick him in the back to make him stop. Her youngest ground her teeth in her sleep. She did it when she was anxious and given their

176

situation there was nothing Tracey could do to make her feel better.

"I want to see my new bedroom. I want to sleep with Mum." Milly tugged her hand and with a sigh Tracey let her lead the way up the stairs. The pink carpet was new. It ran along the landing to the main bedroom, the door of which stood open showing off the wide king-sized bed covered in a scarlet satin spread and piled high with silky cushions. The walls had been painted a light brown colour, and velvet curtains hung at the windows where white blinds were drawn against the sun. A wide-screen television stood on a white chest of drawers and there were matching lamps on tables on either side of the bed. It was obvious that no money had been spared here, unlike the small single room, which used to be hers and was now temporarily going to be her brother's.

It was pretty and feminine with blue and pink flowered wallpaper. Ryan's boots stood in the middle of the room and his leather jacket hung over the back of the delicate little chair in front of the dressing table. In spite of her mum's air fresheners the air smelled heavy and greasy, like the garage where Ryan worked.

"Your Uncle Ryan's letting us have his room so he's having this one," Tracey told Milly. "There's more space for the four of us in the big bedroom."

"I don't want to sleep with Josh." Milly's bottom lip quivered.

You think I do? The words trembled on Tracey's lips but she held them back. Milly's face crumpled and to stop her crying Tracey pushed open the door of the back bedroom. "Go on," she said harshly. To her surprise Milly let go of her hand and ran in. Dodging past the single bed and the put-u-up that was obviously intended for Josh she scrambled onto the big old-fashioned double bed and began bouncing up and down. The springs sighed and squeaked.

"Get down," Tracey snapped.

"Uncle Ryan lets us," Milly said defiantly.

"He might, but your Gran won't like it."

Milly bounced harder. "Uncle Ryan says not to tell," she said.

"Great," Tracey muttered. She would have to keep the peace between her mum and her brother as well as trying to keep the kids under control. It was doing her head in. The dreary room with the old-fashioned furniture, scarred and scraped from when her brothers had jumped and fought all over it, was enough to drive anyone to despair. There was no room for any of her things and she had no idea where she was going to put the kids' stuff. Hopefully there was some space in the loft to store their spare clothes and toys. She plonked her bag down on the chest of drawers and turned her eyes away from the poster of a huge motorbike pinned to the wall.

"Trace," Ryan yelled. "Get your fat backside down here and give us a hand. I haven't got all day."

Together they unloaded the car, stacking boxes up against the bedroom wall, while Milly shrieking with excitement bounced up and down on the bed. Josh kicked a football relentlessly against the back wall and Jodie sat on the kitchen doorstep, plugged into her music. Tracey's arms felt as if they had been pulled from their sockets and sweat dripped down her face stinging her eyes like unshed tears. At last the final box was balanced precariously on the top of the pile in their bedroom.

"That's done so I'll be getting off. I need a drink." Ryan wiped his face with the back of his arm. See you, little one." He grinned at Milly, who giggled and grinned back.

What about me? Tracey wanted to say. *I'm gagging for something long and cool but who's going to be left looking after the kids? Me, that's who. Like it always is.*

"Bye Uncle Ryan!" Milly sprung as high as she could and waved her arms in the air.

"Stop it," Tracey snapped, her resolution to be kinder to the children melting away. "If you don't want a slap you can get down now. I mean it."

Milly gave a final exhausted whoop and tumbled onto the pillows. Eyes brimming with tears, she stuck her thumb in her mouth and turned her back on her mother. *That's right, make me feel bad. As if today wasn't bad enough.* She looked down at the exhausted child. Her little girl's face was flushed and streaked with tears. Tracey was reaching out to stroke the hair from Milly's forehead when the front door opened. There was the click of high heels on the hall floor. Sheila was back.

Wearily Tracey heaved herself off the bed. Her face in the dressing table mirror was pasty and heavy. Her throat was parched and her skin grainy with dirt. *I'd kill for a shower,* she thought as she forced herself down the stairs. *A shower and a pint of gin and tonic would do me.* "Hi Mum," she said, trying to smile.

"Tracey. Look at the state of you."

"We've been moving our stuff." Was it too much to hope that her mum might realise how gut wrenching it was to lose your home and offer a little bit of sympathy? But showing tact and understanding was not Sheila's way.

"Your hair could do with a good cut and blow dry and you need to get rid of those jeans. They are not doing you any favours."

"I know Mum." Tracey was too tired to argue. While she looked and felt about a hundred years old, her mum was crisp and smart in a white skirt and navy top. Sheila's blonde hair shone, her makeup was intact in spite of the heat, and her nails were painted scarlet to match her lipstick.

"Put the kettle on for us. I'm knackered." Sheila sank down on a chair. "This heat does you in."

Tell me about it, Tracey muttered as she moved obediently to the sink. Looking through the window she could see Josh slamming his football against the brickwork. Bang thump, bang thump, over and over again, like a headache that wouldn't go away.

"Boys, bless!" Sheila sighed, following her glance.

They always were your favourites. Tracey craned her neck for a glimpse of Jodie. She was sure she'd left both the older children in the garden. So where was her daughter? She couldn't, she wouldn't, have gone out without telling her? Only a few months ago she would have been certain that Jodie wouldn't do anything as stupid as that. Basically she was a good girl who in spite of the odd flare up did what she was told. Then everything had changed, and all Tracey could hope for was that her eldest wasn't out there getting herself into more trouble, like she had done over those earrings.

"They need their dad," Sheila remarked. "Boys," she added pointedly.

Lost in her worries, Tracey scarcely registered what her mum was saying. She moved to the side to get a wider view out of the window and saw her eldest daughter huddled on the kitchen step. Head bent, Jodie was frantically texting. Swamped with relief Tracey flung tea bags into the pot, poured on boiling water, and mashed them down hard with a spoon.

"That's enough," Sheila said. "I like it strong but not so as you can strip paint."

"Sorry," Tracey muttered.

"Use the blue mugs. The ones with the flowers on. You know I like to drink my tea out of proper china. George laughs at me but he's got no idea, bless him. He's a coffee man, like your dad was." Sheila measured sweetener into her cup and continued: "Your dad would have been devastated if he'd been here to see you lose your house. It would have killed him seeing his grandchildren homeless."

"It's not much fun for me either," Tracey said sharply.

Sheila ignored her. "You'd have done better to marry someone with a trade. After all, what's Eddie? A lorry driver!" There were years of contempt and dislike in Sheila's voice. "If he'd been a plumber he could have been making a fortune. Driving around in Ferraris and Mercedes, they are. And when you need something doing you can't get one for love or money, or so I'm told. It's a good thing George is handy or I don't know where I'd be. He and Ryan fitted the bathroom and the new kitchen for me. Your brother Steve offered to help too, but he's been so busy with their new house I didn't want to impose." She looked meaningfully at Tracey. "The boys have always been good to me. Once they'd left home they never asked for anything."

Not like me. Always needing a babysitter or someone to leave the kids with when I'm at work. "I thought you liked looking after the kids," Tracey said a little desperately.

"Of course I do." Sheila smiled a genuine open smile and Tracey remembered how proud and delighted her mum had been when Jodie was born. She was the first granddaughter, so pretty and so special. Sheila had kept the baby's picture in her purse and was always pulling it out to show people. Her mum put down her cup and looking beyond Tracey so she could avoid her daughter's eyes said, "I love the children but I've done all that. I had years of looking after you and your brothers. Now I have my own life to lead. It's not that we won't help but you've got to learn to stand on your own two feet."

"I'm doing my best, Mum. I've got two jobs. I don't know what else I can do."

"It's not you I'm talking about, Tracey. It's that Eddie of yours. All right, he's lost his job. He's not the only one it's happened to and I'm not saying it's easy, but what I want to know is what he's doing about it. After all he's got you and the kids to think about."

Tracey couldn't speak. If she did she'd cry and she wasn't going to cry in front of her mum. It was true that her husband could appear as if he wasn't bothered, but that was Eddie. He might seem all laid back on the surface, but not having a job was eating him up. Her mum, however, wouldn't see that. She never liked Eddie.

She never thought he was good enough for her daughter. Taking an instant dislike to her son-in-law because she thought him common, Sheila had never taken the time to get to know him.

It was easy for her mum to judge but if any of her precious sons lost their jobs would they manage any better? Would Marc, Steve, Paul or Ryan pick themselves right up and go on to get better lives than the ones they had before? No way. That sort of thing only happened in cheesy films.

"Eddie will find something. He's a good dad." Tracey looked defiantly at Sheila, who raised a disbelieving eyebrow. "He is," she said more strongly and somewhere beneath the cold panic something warm and loving stirred.

SEVENTEEN

Robyn stood at the front gate watching sunlight filter through the trees that lined the river. The light threw interesting patterns on the water; in some places the river sparkled, in others it ran dark and grey-green, almost oily, thick and viscous, concealing what lay beneath its unbroken surface. She glanced longingly at the window of her studio. Was there time to run upstairs and fetch her sketch book? It wouldn't take long and if she was very quiet Finn might not even hear her. Robyn turned round. The purple front door glowed in the sunlight, rich and sensuous as an emperor's cloak. This too needed to be drawn. If she stood at this angle she could suggest a glimpse of what lay inside, showing the contrast between the heat of the day and the cool shadowy interior.

"No you don't." David's hand closed round her elbow.

"But," Robyn protested faintly, "I need…"

"You need to get to the hospital," her brother said. "You have an appointment, remember."

She spread out her hands in a gesture of defeat. There was nothing to say. After the initial blood test and the urgent summons to see the consultant David and Jane had arranged everything. Like a leaf floating downstream she seemed to have no choice but to do as they said. Obediently, she let her brother help her into his van. The front seat gave her a good view of the river and she noted every ripple and change in colour and texture until the road veered towards the suburbs. Away from the water she focussed on how sunlight bounced off the on-coming traffic and dust shrouded the sides of parked cars, its powdery film turning bright metal dull and lifeless.

In the hospital car park David lifted her down and she breathed in the smell of hot tarmac.

"It reminds me of France."

"What?" David threw her a startled glance.

"I was thinking of the holidays we used to go on. Do you remember that summer in the Dordogne?" Her voice was stronger now and he relaxed a little, his fingers loosening their grip so that the keys to the van were no longer pressing into his palm. "We stayed at that camp site in the hills, the one with the swimming pool. There was that incredible thunderstorm. The air quivered with electricity and everyone else ran for shelter but we stayed in the pool and the water was cool and silky and a sort of green." Robyn frowned trying to recall the exact shade. "The sky was grey and dark. The raindrops huge. They were slapping against the water so hard that you wanted to dive under the surface to escape from them." She laughed a little wildly. "I'd like to go back there but I don't think I could do the drive with the kids. It would be too difficult. Poor things, they've hardly been anywhere. It seems so unfair."

"Come on sis, there will be plenty of time for travelling and holidays abroad. They're still young and we didn't do any of that till we were in our teens." David slid his keys into the pocket of his jeans. "You can take them when they're older."

Shit, he thought. *Not the best choice of words in the circumstances.* It had got to her, he could see, by the way she gave him a half-glance, then let her hair fall over her face so that he couldn't read her expression. The fear of not being there for her children must be with her night and day. He tried to think of something he could say to make it better but there were no words for what his sister was facing. While he was still searching, Robyn raised her head and smiled a painted-on smile like a good girl doing the right thing.

"Let's get it over with." Her skirt floating around her she led the way towards the reception area. She was so pale and thin that in her blue-green dress, her hair tumbling around her shoulders, she was like some otherworldly creature, a water nymph or tree spirit. An entity glanced briefly before it disappeared like a shadow on the grass.

The doors hissed open and they were met by the smell of hospital: disinfectant, polish, and something indefinable but inexorably linked to sickness and decay. David flinched inwardly but he said, "Are you sure you don't want me to come in with you?"

"I'm sure." Robyn rested her hand on his arm. Her skin was almost translucent, a single bruise vivid on her knuckle. "Really. I don't need you."

"All right. I'll wait."

"Where? In the van? You'll boil." She laughed, a tinkling, brittle laugh.

"Don't worry, I'll find somewhere cooler. I'm not going to leave you here." He frowned, running his fingers through his hair. "You shouldn't have to do this on your own. Jane would have come if we'd asked her and I could have stayed with the kids."

"Jane? Why would I want Jane?"

"I thought maybe, well, she's a woman, so perhaps you'd prefer her."

"What? Rather than you? That's crazy. I hardly know her and you're my brother. Even so, that doesn't mean I want you to come in with me. I don't." Her eyes wandered towards the sign indicating the way to the oncology department. "You know me." She shrugged and her voice had a faint faraway quality. "I deal with my demons myself."

"This isn't demons, this is…" David began, but Robyn was already moving away from him down the corridor. "Damn and fuck," he swore quietly. Why wouldn't she let him be there for her? Why wouldn't she let anyone help her without the most horrendous battle? He sighed and thrusting his hands into his pockets jangled his keys. His sister had always been like that. Right from when she was little, Robyn had done things her own way. She might seem fey and vague at times but that was when she was lost in her own world. Once she had made a decision there was no deflecting her from the path she had chosen.

Having Finn, then that bastard of a husband walking out on her, had made her more stubborn. Because it was so difficult for her to ask for help, or to find anyone that could cope with Finn, she'd stopped asking and managed as well as she could on her own. She had carved out a way of life that made it possible to do her painting and look after her children, which was fine so long as she was okay. But what if she wasn't? *That*, David told himself, *isn't going to happen.* His little sister might look fragile but she was strong. She'd always been. Mentally as well as physically. Whatever was wrong with her the doctors would sort out. Treatment was so good now and they were developing new drugs all the time.

Never trouble Trouble till Trouble troubles you. Nanny's voice sounded in his ear. *And don't make mountains out of molehills or you'll never get to where you want to go.*

Right Nanny, I've got the message. He bought a coffee and a newspaper and tried to read. Keeping still proved to be impossible. The headlines meant nothing and after flicking through the rest of the paper he got up and wandered off to the door where the smokers hung out, defiantly puffing at their cigarettes. What he could do with was a spliff to calm him down and make the waiting bearable, but there was little chance of sourcing one in the hospital, nor would getting out of his head help the situation. With a wry grin he moved back to his seat and made an attempt at the crossword.

*

The consultant had a face like a hawk. A beaked nose and hooded eyes. Were they kind or cruel? While Robyn was trying to decide, Dr Bland's mouth moved and words came out. Cancer of the blood, leukaemia. The words floated around the room somewhere above her where she couldn't quite catch them. They were important, that was why she was here. But what was more important was how the man in front of her held his head. Was he a bird about to strike or an eagle brooding on a crag? *The wrinkled sea beneath him crawls.* The line from Tennyson came into her brain and gave rise to a series of images:

188

dark waters crashing against rocks, blue-green depths where colourless fish feasted on dead men's eyes.

"There are a number of different approaches. Chemotherapy will be one and we would like to start that as soon as possible. Mrs Latimer-Jones?" The consultant noticed that his patient appeared not to be listening. He tapped his pen on the desk dragging her back from a sunless sea.

"Latimer. I'm Robyn Latimer. I dropped the Jones. Except for the children. They use it because of their father."

Dr Bland cleared his throat. "Is there anything you want to ask me?" He leaned forward. "This sort of diagnosis often comes as a shock but let me assure you there is a lot we can do." Robyn wondered whether his hands were claws or pieces of branch. "The nurse will book you in for your first treatment. She will also give you some literature which will explain what is going to happen." He nodded encouragingly at her and Robyn nodded back.

"It isn't good," she said.

"I do understand that is how you feel. It will take some time for you to adjust. There will be plenty of people to help you with the process." He glanced at his screen. "You will attend Dr Gilling's clinic." His smile stretched his thin face. "She will be able to answer any questions you might have. You will find her very accessible."

What kind of bird is she? Robyn wanted to ask but the nurse came in and took her away to a small cubicle where she was given things to read and sign, and another nurse explained what they were going to do to her. *Will I get*

189

better? That was the important thing to know but she dare not ask because what would she do if they said no?

"We'll see you next week." The nurse was smiling as she showed her to the door. "Try not to worry. I know that's easy for me to say but our oncology team is one of the best in the country. Dr Bland—" *did she blush as she said his name?* "—is the top consultant in his field. I'm lucky to be working under him, and Dr Gilling is very nice."

Will all these nice people be able to stop the nasty things that are gnawing at me, making me so tired I can hardly move? Swamped by a wave of weariness Robyn swayed and had to put her hand on the wall to stop herself from crumpling to the ground. She rested against the slush grey surface, her breath sticking in her chest, her head spinning. Half-closing her eyes she concentrated on the door at the end of the corridor where a faint ray of sun spilled in from the glass-roofed atrium. If she could reach the light all would be well.

Taking a breath steadied her. Walking back to the reception area she made herself focus on the smallest of details, the slap of her sandals on the vinyl, the swish of her skirt against her legs. Then David was at her side. He put his hand on her elbow and she looked up at her big brother. His face was anxious but he was trying so hard to look positive and not to ask the questions she could feel trembling on his lips.

"I'm okay," she said.

"Robyn," he said reproachfully, sounding like Nanny catching one of her charges out in a lie. He pulled her close and she leaned against him, breathing in his clean healthy smell. He was so firm and solid. Nothing inside him was destroying his blood. With David holding her she felt so safe. If she closed her eyes she could blot everything out and when she opened them maybe it would all have gone away.

"Do you want a drink? Shall I get you some tea? Or coffee? It's fairly foul but it packs a certain kick. Or shall we find a pub? There are some good places by the river."

"I want to sleep."

"Poor old sis, you're worn out. Shall I take you home?"

Home. Robyn thought of Coombe Magna with its scruffy furniture and dusty curtains, ancient dogs flopping along stone-flagged corridors, and Nanny waiting in the nursery. If only she could put her head on Nanny's breast and cry and cry until there were no more tears. More than anything she wanted her old nurse to stroke her hair and tell her that it was going to be all right. Only then could she believe that it might be, that she would have the treatment and she would get better and life would go on as it had before.

Nanny was long gone. Her gravestone was gathering lichen in the village churchyard. Home now meant a tall narrow house with bare floorboards and echoing rooms. There was nowhere to lie in peace and quiet, no secret room where she could escape her children. Phoebe whining and demanding, Kit like some nervous thoroughbred shying at every shadow, his eyes dark with fear, his shoulders hunched under the strain of being responsible for them all. And Finn, who drained the very life blood from her, sucking away her energy leaving nothing but this dried out husk.

"Robyn?" David prompted. He was waiting for her to

say something but she was too tired to know what she wanted. She had been too tired for what felt like centuries, ever since Finn was born and had looked at her with cold eyes and screamed when she'd tried to cuddle him.

"I can't," she said and miraculously he understood.

"Okay. We'll go for a drive. I'll take you up to The Downs. We'll go to the Sea Walls and sit on a bench overlooking the gorge like a couple of tourists. If you're very lucky I might even buy you an ice cream before I take you home and tuck you up in bed." He slipped his arm around her waist and supported her as they made their way to the van.

EIGHTEEN

Phoebe leaned her forearms on the table. The classroom was hot and the plastic surface was sticky against her bare skin. She lifted one arm then the other and examined the patches of dampness they left. The windows were wide open but there was no breeze, and she could smell the fumes of the traffic that purred relentlessly along the road outside Clifton Park Primary. Her dress felt tight and the edge of her chair dug into the backs of her legs.

How much longer before it was time to go home? Phoebe wriggled uncomfortably and her arm caught the side of the table sending Chloe Frazer's pencil case tumbling to the ground. Made of bright shiny plastic, it spewed out a slew of pink, purple and sparkly pens followed by a cascade of silver and lilac pencils. Among them was one with feathers on the top, like fairy wings, that Phoebe wanted more than anything in the world. Girly pink was forbidden by Robyn who said it was a vulgar colour and utterly sexist. But Mum wasn't here so she need never know.

Phoebe bent down and reached out for the pink feathers. All she wanted was to hold the pencil, stroke it and maybe, without really meaning to, accidentally slip it into her bag.

"Phoebe Latimer-Jones what do you think you're doing?" said Mrs Greene.

"She's got my pencil, Miss," Chloe whined.

"Have you Phoebe?" Mrs Greene's voice was cold.

"I was only picking it up," Phoebe mumbled, her face flaming scarlet at the lie.

"That's not true, Miss. She threw it on the floor on purpose," Chloe's best friend Jenna said.

"She did. I saw her," Daniella chimed in.

Phoebe wanted to crawl away and hide. They were all getting at her. None of the girls in class liked her. They laughed at the things she said, the way she did her hair, even the sandwiches she ate. However hard she tried she couldn't be like them. Mostly she didn't care but sometimes, like today, she wished passionately that she belonged.

Mrs Greene told her sharply to pick up the pens and pencils and say sorry to Chloe. Phoebe turned even redder. Her mouth went dry and her throat closed over the words so they came out in a scratchy whisper.

"I can't hear her, Miss," Callum Taylor shouted. He liked to get other pupils into trouble and Phoebe hated him.

"She's too quiet," his friend added.

There was a ripple of agreement from the rest of the class. They were hot and tired and anything that distracted their teacher was welcome. Mrs Green, however, was too experienced to be caught out. "I heard her and so did you, Chloe, and that is all that matters."

Chloe did not dare contradict a teacher so she nodded, but as soon as Mrs Green had turned her back she pulled a face at Phoebe and her friends did the same. They wrinkled their noses and stuck out their tongues, switching on their smiles when Mrs Green looked back at them. Phoebe's eyes filled with tears but there was nothing she could do. If she told on the girls they would hate her even more. If she cried they would wait for her after school and call her names. She stared out of the window and wished the lesson would end.

At last the bell rang for the end of the day and Phoebe bounced to her feet, to be told that because of her behaviour her table would have to wait until last to be dismissed. When their turn came, Chloe, Jenna and Daniella flounced past making a point of not looking at her as they left, whispering and giggling, which made Phoebe feel worse than ever. She picked up her bag, heaved it onto her shoulder, and trailed miserably into the playground. Apart from a few older boys kicking a football about it was empty.

"Hurry up folks. It's time to go home and I want to lock the gates," Mrs Clarke the deputy head called. One of the boys aimed a final shot at their makeshift goal, another picked up the ball, and laughing and joshing about, the group made their way into the street. Phoebe looked around anxiously. Where was Kit? And Sue? She was sure it was the babysitter's turn to fetch them.

"Is everything all right?" Mrs Clarke asked.

"Yes, Miss," Phoebe whispered and at that moment Kit came running towards her.

"Where were you? We've been waiting ages. Come on." He grabbed her arm and pulled her to where Sue was waiting with Finn, keeping their little brother as far as possible from the noise and bustle of departing children.

"It's all right, Kit. I'm sure Phoebe didn't mean to be

late. Now you're here let's get you all home as quick as we can."

"Did Mrs Green keep you in?" Kit said as they hurried along the pavement.

"No," Phoebe lied. "It wasn't my fault. It was nothing to do with me."

Head down, Phoebe set off at a run, desperate to get as far from Clifton Park Primary as she could.

*

Frankie wandered along the High Street deep in thought. She wanted to find something really special as a thank you present. It couldn't be expensive – she didn't have much money. She had thought of flowers or chocolates but these were too ordinary and she wanted something unique and personal for Jane. The Freecycle rules said you couldn't pay anyone for what they'd given you but without Jane there would have been no dress, and with no dress Frankie wouldn't be going to the prom. She smiled dreamily as she thought of how well it fitted. It could have been made for her, and the colour was perfect. Emma and Amy were going to have a big surprise when they saw her. Designer dress or what. She'd show them.

The late-afternoon sun blazed down. The awning had been set up at Lucy's and under its shade the outdoor tables were full. Mothers were treating their children to homemade ice cream or frozen yoghurt. Friends were gossiping over coffee and cakes.

Across the road Frankie saw Robert; she waved and he stopped and waved back. Brought to a halt in front of the bakery, she had a brilliant idea. Weaving her way through the chattering customers she went into the shop. Even in this hot weather the scent of vanilla and cinnamon was enticing, but she was on a mission to find the perfect present. As well as bread and cakes Lucy's sold handmade gifts. A pair of silver earrings hung in the jewellery cabinet. Shaped like pear drops, they were both elegant and simple and not too expensive. Frankie could afford them and there would be enough left over for a card.

When the earrings had been wrapped in tissue paper and slipped into a sophisticated little bag with the shop's logo printed on it, she found Robert outside sitting at one of the tables.

"Do you want a drink?" he asked.

She hesitated for a split second then said, "And how."

"I'm going to have a lemon spritzer. What about you."

"I'll have the same. Whatever it is."

"Lemon juice, sugar, soda and ice. It's good when it's hot."

"Sounds great. Thanks."

As Robert ordered and paid for their drinks Frankie wondered what she was doing sitting in a café with such a definitely un-cool guy, but Robert seemed so in control, as if he sat in pavement cafes all the time that she decided she might be wrong about him. Perhaps he was more cool than everyone else because he didn't go on about things like they did. In his place Emma would be boasting about being in the South of France or somewhere more exotic with her mum and stepdad. Then Amy would chip in about Florida and all the other places she'd been to, even though they both knew full well that Frankie had never been anywhere.

Frankie took a long sip of her drink. The first mouthful took her breath away. The lemon spritzer was cold and sharp, searing her throat then soothing it as the sweetness kicked in. "Wow!" She raised her head and grinned at Robert. "That is something."

"It is good," he said in his plain almost old-fashioned way. "It's the mix of sweet and sour that does it. It's a shock each time."

"So you come here a lot? Oh!" Clapping her hand over her mouth, Frankie giggled. "That was such an un-cool thing to say."

"What's wrong with 'do you come here often'?" Robert's face was totally expressionless and for a terrible moment Frankie thought he was suffering from a terminal lack of humour and she would have to grab her bag and run. Then he began to laugh and with the laughter any awkwardness between them vanished. They sat and chatted and Frankie showed Robert the earrings she had bought for Jane.

"She fixed my prom dress for me. I was really gutted when I thought I couldn't go."

"Why?" He looked at her genuinely puzzled.

"Well, everyone else is going."

"I'm not."

Frankie frowned then realised that she was not surprised. Somehow, she couldn't see the prom being his sort of thing.

"It's not that important," he continued. "And I don't like most people in our year."

"I don't either." Frankie laughed. "What's weird is that I've been doing my head in about going for weeks and I don't even like most of the people that'll be there." She slapped her forehead with the palm of her hand. "So what am I going for?" They looked at each other half in astonishment, half in understanding. "It'll be nice to dress up though and the prom only happens once in your life," she ventured finally.

"That's why you're doing it."

"Yeah," she said slowly. "I guess it is." She glanced at him, glad that she hadn't gone down in his estimation for going along with the crowd.

"The disco's okay. Even the limo's bearable. I don't like the dressing up bit," Robert said. "Though if I'd known you were going, well if you'd..."

"It would have been good," Frankie said quickly.

"Another time then?"

"Yeah." She nodded, her heart racing. "Bet you're a mean dancer," she said, thinking of his slim hips and the easy way he moved.

"You'll have to wait and see." He looked at her and grinned.

They walked together along the riverbank. Not quite touching, not yet holding hands, they were so wrapped up in each other that Frankie didn't see the little girl trundling along the pavement, her bag bouncing on her back, her face streaked with tears, until Phoebe cannoned straight into her. Gasping for breath, Frankie caught hold of her arm. "Watch it. You nearly had me over."

Phoebe's lips trembled. Her mouth opened and she began to wail. A long heartrending desperate cry that reminded Frankie of a sick animal.

"Whatever is it? What's the matter? What's wrong?"

Forgetting her own shock, Frankie crouched down and put her hands on the little girl's shoulders. Phoebe was sobbing so hard that she couldn't speak. "We won't hurt you," Frankie continued. "Honest. Tell us where you live and we'll walk you home." Phoebe gulped but said nothing. "Are you hurt?" Frankie persisted. She reached for her bag but Robert had already got his phone out.

"Do you want me to phone your mum?"

The top of Phoebe's dress was soaked with tears. She wanted her mum, but Mum wasn't feeling well. She'd not got out of bed that morning because she said she had a headache, and Sue said they had to let her rest.

"Don't you want to go home? Is that what's wrong?" Robert said.

"No," Phoebe managed between sobs.

"Then what is it?" Frankie glanced quickly at Robert and an idea struck her. "Is it school?" The expression on Phoebe's face showed she was right. "School's pants, isn't it?"

"It is," Robert agreed. "I never liked it." He pretended to look away. "I always wanted my mum and dad to let me study at home," he said to Frankie.

"That would be cool." Frankie straightened up but she kept a hand on the little girl's shoulder. "My mum wouldn't let me. She had all our animals to look after. There's Tigger, our dog, he's only got three legs. Onions the marmalade cat, Smokey-Joe and Fluff…" As she ran through the list naming all the cats and dogs Phoebe's sobs subsided.

"All those animals, wow!" Robert whistled.

"That's not counting the rabbits," Frankie began.

200

"There's Mops and Blackie and—"

"We had a rabbit. He was called Peter. Someone stole him," Phoebe interrupted.

"That is not good." Robert ignored Frankie's warning glance. She didn't want to start the child crying again but Phoebe seemed to be recovering.

"I hate school," she confided. "I hate Chloe and Daniella and Jenna. They're mean and horrid and they don't like me."

"No one likes us either," Robert said.

"Why not?" Phoebe's interest was captured.

"I think it's because we're not the same as them," Frankie said.

"But we don't care. We're us and that's all that matters. Isn't it?" Robert turned to Frankie, who nodded.

"So it's okay," she smiled encouragingly. "Anyway, why would you want mean people to like you?"

"I don't." Phoebe stopped and pointed across the road. "That's my house. The one with the purple door."

"And that's Jane! She did the hem on my dress for me," Frankie cried as a slim elegant woman climbed up the steps and took a key out of her bag.

"She's coming to make tea for us and she's bringing cakes. But—" Phoebe glanced over her shoulder "—I'd better wait for Sue and Kit."

"Quite right too," Robert said as a boy came running towards them followed by a woman with another boy in tow. "Are you all right now?" Phoebe nodded but they waited until the others had caught up with her before they walked away.

"That is weird." Frankie gave Phoebe a final wave. "I

was telling you about Jane and there she was."

"It's synchronicity."

"Um?" Frankie tried to look as if she understood then gave up and asked him what the word meant.

"Things coming together," Robert explained.

"You mean like Fate?"

"No. I don't believe in Fate."

"Then what?"

"Some people think…" he began. They were still talking an hour later when they arrived at Frankie's back garden gate.

"Do you want to come in?"

"I'm sorry, I can't. I've got a cello lesson in—" he took out his phone and pulled a face "—five minutes ago." Pausing only to enter her number in his phone he was off down the road.

Cello lessons, synchronicity, discos. How could anyone have so many different sides to them? Let alone a lad? In Frankie's experience, boys were only interested in football, sex and cars, and she and Robert had spent all this time together and she didn't even know if he was a Rovers or a City fan. Frankie's mind whirled. There was so much to think about and at the same time she was full of a lovely bubbly fizzy feeling. She gave herself a quick hug and pushed open the gate to be greeted by a yelp of joy from Tigger who charged lopsidedly at her, his stumpy tail wagging furiously.

"At last, Frankie. I was getting worried." Debbie sounded not the least bit concerned. She was sitting on the back doorstep with Jake at her feet, a glass of wine in her hand, watching Eddie hammer the last nail into a new rabbit hutch.

"What do you think?" he asked as he stepped back to inspect his handiwork.

"It's ace. It's a palace for rabbits." Frankie put her hand on the roof, feeling the rough wood beneath her fingers. "A proper Buck House." She glanced at her mum but Debbie didn't get the joke as Frankie knew she wouldn't. Robert would though. She'd have to tell him tomorrow.

"You look as if you've had a good day." Debbie winked at Eddie.

"Yeah, kind of," Frankie said dreamily.

"Do you want to tell us about it?"

But Frankie was already drifting upstairs to her bedroom where she could sit and mull over the deliciousness of her afternoon.

*

"Hello," Jane called as she walked into the hall. There was no reply. She was wondering what to do next when the front door opened and a somewhat flustered Sue ushered the children into the house. "Is everything all right? I thought you'd be home by now."

"It's fine but I've got to run," Sue said. "Finn, you go and play in the garden. Kit, Phoebe you get changed out of your school uniform. Be good for Jane and I'll see you all tomorrow."

"It was Phoebe's fault," Kit said, when Sue had gone.

"No it wasn't."

"Yes it was. You made us late. Then you ran off and started talking to that girl and boy."

"What boy and girl?" Jane's heart caught under her ribs in a way it had not done since Anna was little. "You know you mustn't talk to strangers."

"Stranger danger," Phoebe recited. "I know that but they weren't strangers. You know them. The girl said she'd been to your flat."

"That could be Frankie. Yes, I know her and her mum, Debbie. She's all right, but all the same Phoebe, you should be careful. Why didn't you walk with Sue?"

Phoebe's mouth turned down and she muttered, "Don't know. Didn't want to." She was obviously upset.

Not being sure whether the little girl would want to confide in her, Jane said, "Never mind. Would you like me to pick you up tomorrow?"

Phoebe's face reddened and for a horrible moment Jane thought she was angry then with a huge sniff she said, "I'd like that lots." To deflect any more questions she walked into the kitchen. "I'm hungry. Can we have a snack?"

"Of course, don't you always?"

"Is there cake?"

"It's in my bag. Kit, do you want some, and what about Finn?" Jane looked out into the garden where Fin was sitting staring at the space where the hutch used to stand.

"He's missing Peter Rabbit," Phoebe said.

"Do you think he'd like a new rabbit?"

"Don't know. Finn doesn't like new things." Phoebe stopped then said, "He liked you though. He said you were the chair lady."

"If I asked him about a new rabbit do you think he might say yes?"

"Don't know," Phoebe repeated. She was beginning to lose interest but Jane was not ready to give up so easily.

Maybe if she were the one to make the suggestion, rather than anyone in the family, Finn might agree. Bracing herself against a possible temper tantrum she went into the garden.

Unlike any other child Finn did not look up as she approached. Careful to keep her distance she squatted down beside him. "Peter's gone," she said. Finn said nothing. "He's got a new home." There was still no response but at least he wasn't shouting and screaming. "And I know another rabbit who could come and live here instead."

"Peter Rabbit," Finn said stubbornly.

"No." Jane was determined not to lie. "Not Peter. A different rabbit."

"Mopsy, Flopsy and Cottontail," Finn said, his gaze still fixed on the back wall.

Which one? Jane thought desperately. *Which one shall I choose? Or maybe it doesn't matter.* "Cottontail," she said at last.

"Cottontail," Finn repeated. Jane's heart thumped. She held her breath. "All right," he said as if it did not matter in the least. "Cottontail." And turning around he smiled.

NINETEEN

Frankie lay in the bath, luxuriating in the silky feel of the bath oil on her skin. A few more minutes and she would get out but for now she was going to relax. Sliding deeper into the water she closed her eyes. It was the day of the prom and she had been going to spend the whole time getting ready but meeting Robert at Lucy's was more important than spending hours waxing her legs and giving herself a facial. Her mum had done her nails for her when Debbie got home from work, and was going to help her with her hair when she was ready.

"Frankie," Debbie's voice floated up the stairs. "Are you out of the bath yet? It's getting late."

"Not yet. I'll let you know when I'm ready." Almost reluctantly Frankie got out of the water. Trailing wet footprints she padded across the landing to her bedroom where she took her time drying herself, smoothing on body lotion, then deodorant, and finally spraying herself with perfume.

*

Sitting in the kitchen, Debbie had to stop herself from rushing up the stairs. "I'd be less nervous if it was me going to the prom," she told the dogs, glancing once again at the clock on the cooker. How much longer was Frankie going to take? Sensing her anxiety, Jake put his head on her knee. She ran her fingers through his fringe and

Tigger, in a fit of jealousy, started butting her leg. The cats, draped sleepily over chairs and cupboards, didn't flick a whisker.

"Mum," Frankie called at last. "Can you come up and do my hair?"

Debbie was about to race up the stairs when she heard a van pulling up outside. *Great timing. What's the matter with the lot of you? Frankie's had all day to get ready and just when she needs me Eddie arrives.* "I'll be up in a minute," she called. "Stay," she told the dogs who were frantically wagging their tails and falling over each other to get to the door. Jake sat down but Tigger took no notice. "Out of the way, you stupid creature," she scolded, pushing him gently aside to let Eddie in.

"Sorry we're late. Steve here had some trouble with the van." Eddie was followed by a tall Jamaican who grinned and raised a hand in greeting.

"Yeah. Hi," Debbie said, as Jake bounded past her; leaping up at his previous master he started to lick his face. The water spaniel's tail whipped from side to side forcing Debbie to flatten herself against the wall to avoid being beaten black and blue, while at the same time she had to hang on to Tigger's collar in case he did a runner down the road. Steve showed no sign of getting a move on and it was getting later and later. There was the rabbit to be got into the hutch and then manoeuvred it through the gate and into the van before Dan arrived with the Aston Martin to take Frankie to the prom. Most important of all, she had to fix her daughter's hair.

"Hello, Mrs Murray." To add to the chaos Robert arrived on the doorstep. "I've brought my camera and I'm going to take some pictures. You did say it was okay."

"Sure," Debbie smiled. In her panic she had completely forgotten. "You'd better all come in."

"Mum!" Frankie was sounding panicky now. "Where are you?"

"Beer's in the fridge. Help yourselves." Debbie pushed aside the tide of dogs and ran to help her daughter.

Frankie sat down in front of the mirror and Debbie set to work, twisting her daughter's hair onto the top of her head, fastening it with a single silk flower before teasing out some tendrils to wisp around her face.

"Do you want some hair spray on it?" Choking down the lump in her throat, Debbie could hardly get the words out. Her baby looked so grown up and sophisticated.

Frankie shook her head. "I want to keep it looking natural."

"Right then, time for the dress." Debbie took the blue-green silk off the hanger and held it so that Frankie could step into it. Then very carefully she zipped her up.

"Is it okay?" Frankie twisted and turned, trying to see herself in the mirror.

Debbie's eyes filled. "You look lovely," she gulped. "Come on, Robert's here to take your photo. If you don't hurry up there won't be enough time." Debbie leaned over the banisters and called, "She's on her way."

Holding her dress up carefully, Frankie made her way down the stairs to where Robert was waiting. "Hold it," he said as she was halfway down and took a picture.

Frankie giggled. "I feel like I've won an Oscar or something."

"You look like you've won an Oscar." He took another

and another. "Now I want to take some shots outside."

"Wow!" Eddie said as Frankie walked through the kitchen. Steve put down his can of lager and gave a long low whistle. Frankie blushed and bit her lip but their honest appreciation made her feel wonderful.

In the back yard it was hard to find somewhere without any cages, or animals. "It'll have to be in front of the gate or the back door," Robert said when he'd dismissed every other possibility. "Or do we have time to go down to the river? With the trees and the water I could get some great shots."

"Yeah, why not? It wouldn't take that long," Frankie agreed then looked at her dress and shoes. Robert followed her glance and they both shook their heads.

"Take the pictures here. I don't mind about the animals," Frankie said. "If I'm going to be a vet, animals are going to be part of my life like they already are. With me and Mum it's kind of love us, love our animals." Her hand went to her mouth and she flushed as she realised what she had said but Robert didn't seem to notice.

"Okay, stand there. No. A little to the right will be better." Lining up his shot he took hold of her arm. As his fingers touched her skin Frankie swayed towards him.

"I wish you were coming with me," she whispered.

Robert nodded and swallowed. "Me too," he murmured.

"Have you two finished?" Debbie appeared at the back door. "Dan should be here any minute."

"Mum, don't fuss."

"I'm not but you can't keep him waiting, not when he's doing us such a big favour." Debbie frowned. "It's not even as if we know him or anything. Oh—" She hadn't meant to say it but the thought had been at the back of her mind ever since she had come home from work. Seeing Frankie all dressed up and looking so beautiful and grown up, she couldn't help wondering how any man could resist her. But it was too late. Whatever her concerns Debbie couldn't stop her going. She'd have to hope and pray that Dan was as decent as Tracey said he was. After all, perverts and paedophiles didn't use Freecycle. Did they?

It showed, yet again, what a bad mother she was. How could she be so irresponsible as to let her daughter drive away beautifully dressed and with a man she didn't know? And in a fast car! In spite of herself a groan escaped Debbie's lips. Luckily, Frankie and Robert were completely lost in each other's gaze and neither noticed. "It's a shame you're not both going," Debbie said.

"Mum!" Frankie managed to break away. "It's going to be okay." Her face as she turned back to Robert was radiant.

"Sorry." Debbie was close to tears. Not for the world did she want to spoil Frankie's night. She had to stay calm which was proving very difficult. She heard a car drawing up outside the house.

"Eddie, have you left space for Dan to park?" Debbie went back into the kitchen, her hand on her chest as she foresaw another problem.

"No problem," Steve drawled. "Eddie here, he warned me to leave plenty of room for the princess. I just wish I was the lucky guy escorting her to the ball. But I reckon my van can't compete with that piece of motor out there."

He grinned at Frankie who had followed her mother into the kitchen, and she blushed and smiled back.

A car door opened and shut. "I'm thinking someone should be lettin' in the chauffeur," Steve said.

"Oh!" Debbie's hands flew to her face. No one moved.

"I'll do it," Robert said. He came back, followed by a tall blonde man. He was wearing a dinner jacket and looked absolutely gorgeous. Debbie gulped.

The stranger held out his hand and looking directly at her said, "Hi, I'm Dan. The driver for tonight." His grip was firm, his expression reassuring. "I know we've not met before but we both know Tracey. She works for me and she's ordered me to tell you that you are not to worry about anything. I'm going to take good care of your daughter."

"Thank you so much. This is really good of you." Debbie breathed a silent thanks to Tracey who once again was saving the day.

"Think nothing of it. I'm glad to be able to help." He turned to Frankie. "If you are ready, your carriage awaits." Debbie saw Frankie shoot a look at Robert who raised an eyebrow and the weight fell from her shoulders. Dan might look like something out of a Bond movie; he might drive a car worth more than her whole house; but Frankie still thought of him as an oldie. With a light heart Debbie followed them out to the street to wave goodbye.

The Aston Martin gleamed silver in the evening sun and half the neighbourhood had turned out to see what was going on. Some of the lads were looking at the car but quite a few had their eyes on Frankie. A couple of older women, heads together, cast meaningful glances in her direction and were obviously wondering what Debbie's daughter was doing with such a glamourous older man. Debbie was tempted to tell them straight that he was only the chauffeur, driving her to the school prom, but there wasn't any need. Although Dan handed her into the car, taking care to check that her skirt was safely in before he shut the door, it was Robert that Frankie was looking at. It was Robert, not her mum, that she blew a kiss to. Robert who stood looking down the road long after Dan had swept Frankie off to Ashton Court.

After all the trouble she'd gone to, after all the tears and agony, there wasn't even a wave. Feeling a little hurt, Debbie went back inside and was about to shut the door when Robert came up the path.

"I've got the number of his car on my phone," he said. "In case."

Resisting the urge to hug him, Debbie said, "Do you want to come in and wait for her?"

"No. Thanks. I'll get home. I'll text her later."

He'll be texting her all evening, Debbie thought, and she was smiling as she went into the yard to help Eddie and Steve with the rabbit and the hutch. "Be good to the little boy," Debbie whispered to the grey rabbit before settling it gently on a pile of sweet-smelling hay. "Tell them I've put in some food but she'll need her water bottle filled up tonight," she said as the men lifted the hutch into the back of the van.

"Why don't you come with us and tell them yourself?" Eddie said. "Then we can all go for a drink. It'll be better than sitting at home wondering how Frankie's getting on."

"Count me out for the drink," Steve added. "I've got other business tonight. You go and enjoy yourselves. And don' be back too late, man." He winked suggestively at Eddie and they all laughed.

*

It was a glorious summer evening. The air was sweet as honey, the sunlight golden, glittering on the river as the Aston Martin crossed the bridge and swept up the hill into the grounds of Ashton Court. Acres of smooth green lawns lay on either side of the tree-lined drive. The house stood at the bottom of a slight dip, its windows glowing with light. Dan drew up at the main entrance. Not quite believing that she'd actually made the prom, Frankie drank it all in. Then she stretched out her hand to open the door.

"No. Let me." Dan got out of the driver's seat and went round to the passenger side to help her out. The air was filled with the scent of new-mown grass; music came pouring out of the open doors. Mrs Hayden, head of year eleven, was waiting at the top of the steps to welcome her students. She looked very elegant in a strapless black dress, her hair up and with long dangling earrings. Frankie's heart gave a nervous flutter. She was moving into a different more sophisticated world than the one she knew and, since Amy and Emma had let her down, she was going to have to navigate it all on her own.

"You look lovely. Have a great night," Dan said. "Go and enjoy yourself. I'll be back for you at midnight, and you can always call before if you need a quick exit. You've got my number."

"I'll be fine." The thought that she wouldn't be trapped

if things went wrong made Frankie feel better. Whatever happened she was determined to enjoy herself. Mrs Hayden gave her a welcoming smile, and as Frankie was about to climb the steps a pink limo drew up. The doors opened – music blared; there were shrieks and giggles – and Amy clambered out followed by Emma, Simon and Toby.

"Frankie!" Amy shrieked, waving her arms. "Hiya."

"Come and have your picture taken with us," Emma called.

For a fraction of a second Frankie hesitated then she thought why not. She, Emma and Amy had gone around together most of the time they were at school, so she may as well have a picture or two to remind her. And if she didn't want to remember she could delete them. The girls draped their arms around each other and Simon took a picture on each of their phones. Then it was Simon and Toby with Amy and Emma taken by Frankie. She was about to slip her phone back into her bag when Toby said, "What about one with us?"

"All five of us?" Frankie asked in surprise.

"No. You and me and—" he grinned wickedly "—Simon."

Emma's face fell. Amy started to protest but the boys took Frankie by the arm and swept her over to a huge old tree. They handed their phones to a group of year elevens. Simon and Toby stood on either side of her and they didn't pull faces or clown about to make fools of themselves, or her.

"We look pretty good," Toby said looking at his screen. "See." He held up his phone and there they were, Frankie

Murray with two of the coolest boys in the whole year. That was too much for Amy who came charging across the grass and grabbed Simon by the arm.

"Come on. I want one on the steps," Amy said. As she led him away he looked back at Frankie as if to say "look what she's making me do."

"I want one too. It's so romantic." Emma fastened herself onto Toby who shrugged his shoulders but did as she said.

Frankie didn't watch them go. It no longer mattered what they did. She knew what they were like and she was finished with them. To her surprise, other people in her year wanted her to be in their pictures and she was soon busy fitting into group shots and taking some herself.

When the photos had been taken the year elevens made their way into the house where there were speeches by the Head and Mrs Haydon to be sat through. These was the usual boring stuff about not missing out on opportunities, about the rest of your life being in front of you. Though when Frankie thought about it, she had to admit that most of it was true.

How sad am I? she thought. *I sound like my mum. Or Robert.* He had this really weird way of looking at things. Sometimes it was like being with an adult while at other times he was like a child. He could be silly and funny or serious and thoughtful, asking deep questions to determine what really mattered in his life – and hers. *He's the first person who's truly interested in where I'm coming from.* Frankie sighed happily and smiled.

The speeches were over and the buffet was declared open. Everyone hovered around the table not wanting to be the first to start on the food. Frankie, who had been too excited to eat anything all day, was starving. She looked around and decided that it was all too stupid and she was going to help herself. Once she started the others joined in. At first it was mostly the lads while the girls hung back, pretending that they were on a diet and shrieking that they didn't do wheat, or dairy, or meat.

Returning to her seat with a plate piled high with delicious food, Frankie was surrounded by a group of lads she had dismissed as being too boring and sporty to bother with. They soon proved her wrong and when the disco began they swept her onto the dance floor and kept her laughing and dancing all night.

As the evening drew to a close the music slowed. Not wanting to hurt anyone by turning them down, Frankie pretended she needed the Ladies and slipped out into the grounds. A golden moon hung low over the trees. The air was soft and warm. The lights from the house spilled out across the dark lawns. *Magic,* Frankie thought. *There's only one thing missing to make it perfect.* Taking out her phone she checked her messages.

I hope you're having a good time, she read.

Great, thanks, she texted back. Can't wait to tell you all about it. F x

TWENTY

Robyn breathed in the stale smell of her unwashed body. Her hair, lank and thick with grease, hung around her shoulders. Her nightdress, soaked by her night sweats, was rank. She should get up and shower to wash away the outward signs of her sickness. But what was the point? It would only cover up what was happening inside her. Since her white blood cells had gone on the rampage, her body was rotting and she might as well lie still and wait to die. There was no hope and she hadn't the energy to do anything. Moving, thinking, or even feeling took too much effort.

Framed by the window, plump white clouds floated slowly across a blue sky. Shepherded by the breeze, the soft round shapes elongated and unravelled like threads of cotton. Robyn's fingers curled as if holding a paint brush. A wash of blue layered with a build-up of whites, each one a slightly different shade. Would she use watercolours or should it be a collage? Her hand fell open. There wasn't going to be a picture. Not now, not ever again.

A key turned in the lock followed by the sound of footsteps as someone came into the house. For a moment she wondered who it might be. Not that it mattered, nothing mattered. Not even her children. Someone, most likely Sue, was looking after them. It was probably for the best that their mother couldn't see to them now for they would soon have to manage without her. A sliver of pain slid under her ribs then faded as she shut her eyes and listened to her own breathing, so loud and so insistent in the quiet room.

*

"Hello," Jane called as she walked in through the front door. "Robyn?"

"She's still in bed." Sue came into the hall, wiping her hands on her overall. She looked flushed and hot, her grey hair sticking out in wisps. "Finn's in the garden watching the new rabbit. I've got him to wear his hat and he let me put some sun cream on his arms and legs."

"That's good," Jane said flatly. She meant to sound more positive but she was worried. It was half past two and Robyn had still not got up. Yesterday, coming home from the hospital, she had seemed more ethereal than ever. Her responses were vague, her glance skittering all over the place as if unable to take in where she was or what had happened. Eventually she had drifted upstairs leaving Jane and David to deal with the children. It wasn't until the end of the day, when the children were finally in bed, that David had told her about Robyn's diagnosis.

I can't go through all that again, had been her first selfish thought and hard as she tried to banish it, the image of Hugh, gaunt and grey, sitting in his chair, came flooding back. The memory was so vivid she could almost touch his hand, the fingers skeletal, the skin covered in bruises from all the needles they'd stuck into him. She caught her breath against the remembered smell of sickness. Whatever she did, opening windows, bringing in flowers, washing and washing and washing bedding and flesh, she could never quite get rid of it. It was always there and even though no one else seemed to smell it she could.

It had taken all her courage and resolution to go to Robyn's the next day and having got there it looked as if she was going to have to deal with yet another crisis.

"Are you all right?" Sue asked. "We can't be doing with another invalid."

"I'm fine." Jane managed a smile. "It's the heat. It's another scorcher out there."

"That's right. Terrible it is. Saps your strength 'specially if you're not feeling too good to start with." Sue spread out her hands and raised her eyes to the ceiling.

"It's not the heat," Jane said.

"I know." Sue turned away and went back to the kitchen.

Another one who can't talk about it, Jane thought despairingly. *Just when we need everyone to be strong for Robyn and the children. I'm on a loop with Hugh when I should be thinking of the kids. They're the ones that need attention. Kit picks up every vibe, and so does Phoebe in her own way. Their mum's not getting out of bed so they must have realised something's wrong.* The sharp shrill of her phone interrupted her thoughts; she glanced at the screen and saw it was Anna.

"Mum, you haven't forgotten about tonight, have you?"

"No," Jane lied. In her concern for the Latimers her own life had taken second place and the arrangement with her daughter had slipped from her mind.

"Mum," Anna said in a tone of voice that showed she

knew perfectly well that Jane wasn't telling the truth. "I'll collect you from Robyn's after work and we'll go for a meal at the Tobacco Factory."

"Are you sure? I can easily throw something together. There's plenty in the freezer, or I can stop off at the deli on the way home."

"Mum," Anna said warningly. "You're not cooking. You and I are going out for a meal. You're looking tired and you've lost too much weight recently."

Look who's talking, Jane wanted to say. *You're as thin as a rake.* She said nothing. There was something odd but very comforting about being looked after by her daughter. For the first time since Hugh had died Jane felt truly loved and cared for.

"Goodness only knows what you've been doing," Anna continued sternly. "Whatever it is, you need a break."

"You're right," Jane agreed. She was not as young and as fit as she once was and the situation with Robyn and her children had been constantly on her mind. Even now her attention was split between the conversation with Anna and listening out for Finn and what was going on upstairs. "We'll go out to eat."

"Great."

Jane ended the call almost before Anna had finished speaking. Having put things right with her daughter she should go and check on Robyn. But what if she wanted to be left alone, did Jane have the right to go barging in? On the other hand, after the devastating news she'd received yesterday Robyn might be in need of comfort and support. Apart from David and Sue, who had enough troubles of her own, there was no one but Jane. *I can do this*, she told herself, but the further up the stairs she went the more slowly she climbed. The memory of Hugh's illness was too vivid and her whole body rebelled against being put through another round of shock, hope, despair and grief.

Outside the bedroom she hesitated then knocked quickly. There was no reply and although she had not expected one Jane was assailed by a fear that while she was talking to Anna something terrible had happened in that shuttered room.

Jane Poynton, stop this at once. Calm yourself down and get a sense of perspective. She pressed her hand against her temples to steady herself. *You were like this with Hugh, always expecting the worst, and did it work out as you'd imagined? Of course not. These things never do. The end when it came was peaceful and in a strange way, wonderful. Besides, every case is different and Robyn is much younger and hopefully stronger. So push the door and go in.*

The air was thick and stale, the figure on the bed motionless. "Robyn?" Jane whispered through dry lips. There was a faint answering sigh and she was swamped with relief. Coming closer to the bed she said, "Are you in pain?"

There was another pause before Robyn said, "I don't feel anything. Nothing at all."

"So you're staying in bed because you are tired," Jane prompted. She glanced at her watch. With a bit of luck there would be time to get Robyn up and dressed before Jane went to collect Kit and Phoebe from school. The new regime had delighted the children and given Sue a break from dragging a reluctant Finn to and from Clifton Park Primary.

"Yes," Robyn breathed. "I'm tired. Too tired for anything."

"Have you had something to eat?"

"I'm not hungry." Robyn's thin chest rose and fell, her hand fluttered and lay limp.

She's given up, Jane thought.

"I'm dying." Robyn shut her eyes against the afternoon light.

"No." The word burst from Jane's lips before she could stop it and she flushed with anger and embarrassment at her crassness. When Hugh was ill she had hated people telling her that, however bad things might seem, medicine could perform wonders; new drugs were always coming on stream, and if they did not work there were alternative therapies that could be tried.

"I know you are very ill." Jane sat down on the edge of the bed and tried to look Robyn in the eye. "But from what David has told me there are things that can be done and, as far as I know, no one has said that you're going to die. The treatment can be horrible but it works." Jane crossed her fingers. "In more cases than not it is successful. You've got to believe that. You must."

"I'm not having any treatment."

"Why not?" In spite of her effort to stay calm, Jane's voice rose.

"Because there's no point in going through it all. I'm too tired and I don't care what happens to me. All I want is to be left alone." Robyn rolled over on her side and turned her back on Jane.

Oh no you don't. Jane's mind was racing. *You're not doing this. You've got to think of your children. What would Kit and Phoebe and Finn do without you? You simply can't do this to them. You cannot give up without a fight.* The thought of those children without their mother sent a shiver up her back. She leaned over and put her hand on Robyn's forehead, the way she used to with Anna when she was little. Robyn's skin was hot and clammy. "Come on, let's make you more comfortable." She slipped her arm under Robyn's shoulders and helped her to sit up against the pillows. "I'll get you some water or would you prefer herbal tea? Before I do that, I'll sponge your hands and face and then we'll get you changed."

It was like dealing with a sick child. Working slowly and gently, she got Robyn into a clean nightdress and persuaded her to drink some rosehip tea while she found clean sheets and remade the bed. Then it was time to rush off to school.

When they got back Finn was lying at the bottom of the stairs and a flustered Sue was trying to persuade him to move.

"No. Mustn't go up. Mum upstairs," he said. Jane's hands itched to pick him up and forcibly remove him to the kitchen but if she tried to touch him he would work himself up into a huge tantrum.

"Mum," Phoebe wailed. I want to see Mum."

"You can't." Kit was white, his lips thin with anger. He glanced furiously from Sue to Jane as if they were two more adults who were going to let him down. Then he shrugged and walked away. They heard him opening the fridge and pouring some lemonade. No one moved.

"Why don't you show me your rabbit?" Jane said.

"No," Finn said.

"I want to show Mum my picture. I did it for her," Phoebe waved her bag. "I'm going now."

"No." Jane swooped catching hold of her arm. "Not now, poppet. Mum's having a rest. You can go up in a little while." *When hopefully Robyn will be more herself. As for Finn, if we leave him maybe he'll follow us. A normal child would but who's to say what Finn will do.*

"I brought it home specially." Phoebe's voice wobbled.

Jane pulled the distraught little girl close. Phoebe buried her face in her shoulder and began to cry. "There, there, it's been a long day and it's hot." Stroking the child's back she murmured meaningless phrases, until finally Phoebe stopped crying. "That's better. Shall we go and see if there's any ice cream left in the freezer? Or have you eaten it all?"

"I didn't," Phoebe said indignantly.

"Am I supposed to believe that? Are you sure you're not telling me porky pies?" Jane teased.

"I'm not and I'll show you." Phoebe stamped off to the kitchen.

Ignoring any pretence at healthy eating, when Sue had gone home Jane fed the children chocolate and toffee ice cream, encouraging them to make as much noise as they could with their bowls and spoons and deliberately keeping the door ajar to tempt Finn. Her ploy didn't work. He lay on the bottom step like a dog guarding its mistress.

When Kit and Phoebe had eaten their tea Jane supervised their homework and checked what they were watching on television. She was starting to clear up in the kitchen when Phoebe came in to collect her schoolbag, which she had left hanging on the back of a chair. "Finn's gone," Phoebe said. Jane's heart lurched as she was struck by a nightmare vision of the little boy unlocking the front door and wandering out into the street. "He's gone upstairs to see Mum. He's lying on her bed." Phoebe pulled a disapproving face.

Thank God. Jane hadn't lost him. Maybe his sneaking in to be with Robyn would convince his mother that she had to get well, if not for her own sake, for the sake of her children. On the other hand it might harden her resolve to let the disease take its course because Finn was part of the problem.

Why is it all so difficult? Jane thought as she went to tell Kit and Phoebe to get ready for bed. She would leave Finn with his mother for a little while longer then, when they were all asleep, she would go home to gather her strength. Maybe Anna would join her and they could sit and watch the sunset.

"Oh no!" Jane groaned. She had completely forgotten they were going out together.

When she got upstairs, the three children were in their rooms. Kit was reading, Phoebe was playing with her dolls, and Finn was in bed sitting bolt upright dressed in his pyjamas. She was so grateful she didn't ask how he'd got there or whether he had cleaned his teeth.

Finally they were all settled and Anna was at the door.

"I'm sorry. I was looking forward to tonight, but I can't leave the children. Robyn's completely withdrawn into herself so there's no functioning adult in the house, and

Kit is too young to be in charge."

Anna said nothing and Jane braced herself for an outburst, but her daughter smiled and shrugged. "You're right. If things are as bad as you say we can't walk out on them, not tonight."

"I'm sorry. I've ruined your evening. You go. I'll stay here and try to work out what to do for the best."

"Your evening's ruined too," Anna pointed out. "There's nothing we can do about that. Tell you what, I'll send out for a takeaway. What do you fancy, pizza, Chinese or Indian?"

"A large white wine."

"That can be arranged," Anna smiled. "First decide on the food, then I'll pop into the minimart and we'll be all set. Not quite what I had in mind, but hey." She gave her mother a quick hug.

Later, sitting in Robyn's kitchen eating Chinese food and drinking wine, Anna leaned her elbows on the table and said, "We've got to sort this out."

Jane nodded. "If Sue can get here a bit earlier in the morning and stays a little longer in the afternoon, I can cope with tea and bedtime."

"Their bedtime or yours?"

"What do you mean?"

"Who is going to be here at night if Robyn is too ill to get out of bed?"

"I suppose I could stay…"

"For a night or two, but that's hardly a long-term solution. What we have to look at is the bigger picture. What's going to happen in the future? Who is going to be responsible for the children full time? Don't look at me like that, Mum. It can't be you. You can't be on call twenty-four/seven. You look exhausted as it is."

"I didn't sleep very well, that's all."

"Maybe." Anna wasn't convinced. "In any case, to be brutal, you don't have the energy to cope with Finn day in, day out. There's got to be someone else who can help out, or we'll have to get in touch with Social Services."

Jane was opening her mouth to protest when the door opened and Kit came in. His eyes were glazed as if he had just woken up.

"Anna!" his face lit up.

"Kit!" To Jane's surprise her daughter got to her feet and gave the boy a hug, rumpling his hair and pulling him close to her side. "How's things?"

"Okay," he muttered.

He looked at the dishes on the table and Jane was about to say that he'd already had his tea when Anna put out another plate. "Help yourself. We're stuffed, aren't we Mum?" She refilled their glasses and they let Kit eat until he said he was full.

"Are you sure? Quite, quite sure? You ate so much I thought you had hollow legs," Anna teased. Just as Hugh had teased her when she was little, Jane remembered, which was how family sayings were passed down from parent to child.

"He's very fond of you," Jane said, when Kit had finally gone to bed.

"That's what makes it so much harder and why we're going to have to find someone to help look after them. There's got to be some family somewhere."

"They've got an Uncle David. He's Robyn's brother.

227

But I've no idea where he is."

"No problem. I'll find him and we'll go from there."

Jane looked at her daughter. Anna held her gaze and without a word being spoken they agreed that whatever the future held for the Latimer children, mother and daughter would deal with it together.

TWENTY-ONE

Debbie and Eddie sat under the trellis in the Green Man, he with a pint, she with a vodka and orange.

"He seems a nice lad, that Robert," Eddie said. Debbie nodded, glancing at her mobile. "Frankie won't be texting you. She'll be having a good time."

"I know and I can't help wishing he'd gone to the prom with her. She looked so lovely."

"Yes she did. She's got class, your Frankie," Eddie paused and for a moment Debbie thought he was going to say *like her mum,* but instead he took a long drink of his beer.

"Maybe it's a good thing they didn't go together," Debbie mused. "You don't want things to be too easy, not right from the start. If you can get through the bad times, you'll make it in the long term." She stopped as she realised what she had said. "Oops, sorry, I wasn't being personal. I wasn't thinking about you and Tracey."

Eddie shook his head as if to say it was okay but she could see the hurt in his eyes and hurried to explain. "I was thinking about Lamar, Frankie's dad. He was drop-dead gorgeous, with the cutest little bum, and he could sweet talk his way into anything and out of it again. When he was with you he made you feel so special like you were the only person in the world for him. Which you were till he moved on to his next baby-mother. That was the problem with him, as soon as things got a bit difficult or real life kicked in, Lamar was off."

"Leaving you holding the baby."

"I don't regret that bit. Frankie's more than I deserve. I just wish I was a better mum to her."

"You're a great mum. Look how you sorted her out for the prom. And—" Eddie hesitated "—a great friend. Taking on Jake like that."

"That's nothing. I love him to bits. Now, I think it's time I went home. The animals will want feeding and watering and I want to be ready for when Frankie gets in."

"I'll walk you back." Eddie finished his drink and got to his feet.

"There's no need. It's only round the corner and it's not properly dark yet. I'll be all right. Besides mine is in the opposite direction to Steve's."

Eddie shook his head. "I'm not going there tonight. He's got some mates coming up from the country. There won't be room, so I said I'll find somewhere else."

"Haven't you left it a bit late?" Debbie looked at the gathering shadows and the moon hanging low over the river.

Eddie shrugged. "There's people I can ask."

"At this time of night?"

"I can always stay out. It's a lovely warm night and I'll have my sofa back tomorrow. I should've sorted it out before, like I told Steve I would."

"You've been sleeping on Steve's sofa?"

"Yes. What's wrong with that?"

"Well nothing, except I've got a spare room going

begging, so you could come and stay at ours."

"I couldn't."

"I don't see why not. It would only be temporary cos I know you're doing your best to get a job and get back with your family. All I'm doing is giving you somewhere to stay until things work out for you. I wish I'd known before then you could have moved in with Jake."

"Only till I've got a place of my own."

"Sure. I'm not asking you to move in with me, to be my partner or anything." *Though that stupid Tracey doesn't know what she's throwing away. A lovely kind dependable bloke like you.*

"I'll pay my way."

"Sure. When you can. I'm not going to be charging you rent for tonight. You'd better go and get your stuff from Steve's. Then you can sit up and wait for Frankie with me. Mind you, when she gets in and the gossip gets a bit girly you're off to your room."

"Thanks," Eddie said slowly. He flushed. "I can't tell you how much this means to me, first Jake and now this…"

"Then don't try. Make sure you're back with your stuff in time to take the dogs for their evening run."

*

In her mum's kitchen, Tracey sat at the table nursing a large gin. The back door was open, but there was no breeze and the air reeked of the lemon-scented air freshener that Sheila used and which left a bitter chemical taste in the back of the throat. Or was it the gin or the letter from school that was making her feel so bad?

Dear Mrs Brown,

I have been trying to reach you for some time without success, which is why I am writing to ask you to come in to school to discuss Josh's progress. There have been a number of incidents in the schoolyard recently and his behaviour in the classroom is also giving cause for concern. Please ring the office at your earliest convenience to make an appointment.

Yours sincerely,
Ellen Ferns.

What's he done now? And why hasn't he told me he's been in trouble. Tracey groaned. She should have told the school as soon as they'd lost the house. She had put it off because once the news got out the other children would look down on hers and everyone would be talking behind her back. What would that pretty Miss Ferns think of her then? Josh adored her. He was always trying to find ways of impressing her and, although like his mum and dad he wasn't much for schoolwork, he had been doing so well in her class. Until they had moved to his gran's.

It was all such a mess, but there was no point in getting upset. Not here where there was no one to comfort her. No one who would understand. She had no idea where Eddie was. Her mum and George had gone out. Not that Sheila would care. The one good thing about this evening was that the children had finally gone to bed.

At the thought of that cramped and crowded room,

Tracey shuddered. It was hot and stuffy and smelled of sleeping children. Even if she kept the window open all night it still smelled. Besides, the noise of the traffic would keep her awake and, if that didn't, she didn't get much sleep with Milly tossing and turning beside her, Josh flinging his covers about, and Jodie sighing loudly and pointedly whenever she thought her mum might be listening.

Then there were the nights when Ryan came roaring up on his motorbike in the early hours of the morning and woke them all up. No wonder she was so tired could scarcely think.

Tracey yawned and attempted to get to her feet. Her legs were too heavy and her head felt like a concrete block, unbalancing her whole body. It would be easier to sit a bit longer and doze. Her eyes closed, she dreamed she was lying curled up next to Eddie, his arm around her keeping her close, making her feel safe. The sound of the front door opening and closing woke her.

"Ooh George," her mother squealed.

Tracey pursed her lips. Sheila had been drinking; they both had by the sound of it and if they didn't keep the noise down they were going to wake the kids. Wearily, she pushed back her chair then sat down again. She could hardly tell her mum what to do in her own house.

"Are you still up?" Sheila came into the kitchen. She lurched against the door and gestured to George to go upstairs. "Maybe it's for the best." She felt her way to the table and collapsed onto a chair. She smelled of alcohol and sweat and her heavy musky perfume. "George and I have been talking." Her words slurred and she rested her hand on her chin. "For God's sake, Tracey, make us a cuppa. Yes, we've been talking," she continued as Tracey filled the kettle. "We've come to the conclusion that it's no good. This isn't working. There isn't enough room for all of us. I know I said you could come and stay but that was only temporary. Only temporary," she repeated her voice rising.

Please don't let her wake the kids, Tracey thought.

"I love my grandchildren. I love them to bits, you know that, Tracey. Everyone knows that. I'd do anything for my family, but—"

Tracey went cold. "You want us to go."

"I don't want it. I wouldn't say it, not if we had enough room. You know that. But children, well they take up so much space. And Ryan can't get to use the shower in the mornings."

"Ryan's complained? He's not said anything to me."

"Well, he wouldn't, would he? This being my house he goes along with what I want. Bless him." Sheila smiled and nodded, then sitting up straighter said, "No, I think it's best for all of us if you find a place of your own, or you get that husband of yours to find something. That's if he's not run off somewhere."

Another dig. You can't resist it can you? You've never liked Eddie. Always said he was common. "I'll get us a place. You won't need to bother about us much longer. I'll try the council tomorrow."

"That's all right then. Some of those flats are ever so nice. We should have thought of that in the first place. It would have saved us all this bother. Come on, where's that tea? I'm parched."

234

Lying in bed beside Milly, Tracey planned her next move. She knew that Sheila wouldn't throw them out on the street but there was no way was Tracey staying where she and her children weren't wanted. What really hurt was that their own grandmother could do this to them. Anyone else would try to understand what they were going through, would see that they weren't bad kids, they were just having a rough time.

Josh turned over and muttered something in his sleep, Jodie sighed and Milly threw out her arms, just avoiding hitting her mum on the nose. "Hey, mind what you're doing." Tracey moved Milly's arm along the pillow. She looked at her little girl, her baby, and was flooded with love for all three of her children. "I'd do anything for you," she whispered. "Anything." Not like her own mother. Sheila didn't care and possibly never had, Tracey thought bitterly. If her dad was still alive it would be different, she was sure of it. Her eyes filled with tears. Milly turned and jammed her knees into her mother's side. Wincing from the pain Tracey buried her face in the pillow.

Was this night ever going to end? As soon as it was morning she was going to whisk the children in and out of that bathroom like greased lightning. That would put an end to Ryan's whinging. Then she'd get herself over to the council offices and see what they could do.

*

"I'm sorry Mrs Brown but we have no properties available at the moment."

Tracey stared at the woman across the desk. "But

we've lost our house."

The woman glanced at her notes. "You say you're living with your mother."

"Yes, but there's no room. It's overcrowded. I'm sharing a bedroom with my kids. A boy and two girls."

"How old is your son?"

"Josh is eight. Why?"

"He's still a child. There are lots of families on our lists whose living conditions are far worse. If you were to be homeless we could arrange for bed and breakfast accommodation."

"You must be joking." Tracey got to her feet. "I've heard about those places on the TV. Rotting, damp, filled with rats. I wouldn't put my dog in one of those, thank you."

That's telling them, she thought as she swept out into the bright afternoon sunlight. For a moment she felt really proud of herself – then it hit her. If the council couldn't re-house her, she had nowhere to go, nowhere to take the children. When she went back to Drake Road tonight she'd have to tell Sheila that they were staying until she found a privately rented flat. And how on earth was she going to afford one of those on her wages?

Feeling sick and desperate Tracey bought a copy of the local paper and tucked it into her shoulder bag. She'd look at the property-to-let pages later when she stopped for a break in cleaning Dan's flat.

*

The first thing that Tracey noticed as she stepped into the apartment was how cool it was. The air conditioning was on which made her think that Dan was working from home. She called out, but no one answered.

He must have left it on for me, she decided. *That's so like him. He's so considerate and helpful. You've only got to ask and he does things like giving Debbie's daughter a lift to her prom. He treats people like they matter. Even me, even the cleaner.* She rubbed the back of her hand over her face. Dan cared for her more than her own mum.

"No," she said out loud. "You're not going to cry, not again. Any more tears and you'll be dehydrated." She looked in her bag for a tissue, wiped her eyes and blew her nose. She had to keep it together. There was too much to do and someone had to stay strong for the children.

Tracey took out her cleaning things and started on the kitchen. Working in the airconditioned flat made it easy to get round. She finished what she needed to do and decided there was time for a cup of coffee before starting on the ironing. Since coming to work for Dan she'd developed a taste for good coffee and looked forward to her break.

Sometimes she brought a couple of cakes or cookies from Lucy's, in case he was there to share them. She loved it when they sat and talked. Dan was so interesting; he'd travelled all over the world and knew such a lot about everything. If he wasn't home she'd give herself a treat by letting herself imagine that this was her own apartment, although it was lovely the way Dan had it, it was a bit too masculine for her taste. She'd sit and dream about the new furniture and fittings she'd have and what colours she'd choose for what room.

Today there was no time for daydreams. With her mug of coffee in front of her, Tracey took out the Evening Post and spread it on the table. "Garden flat, Lower Clifton. Two bedrooms, living room, kitchen and bath," she read. Possible. If the worst came to the worst she could sleep on the sofa. Then she saw the rent. There was no way she could possibly manage that. Taking a gulp of coffee she went down the column. There were plenty of houses, flats and apartments, but none even remotely close to anything she could afford. Tracey balled her hands into fists and struck her forehead over and over again. There had to be something she could do. There must.

"Tracey. Are you alright?"

She'd been so wrapped up in her worries that she hadn't noticed Dan coming in. Now his hand was on her shoulder, warm, firm and comforting. Tracey screwed up her eyes and swallowed hard.

"What's wrong? It's not one of the kids, is it?"

She shook her head. She couldn't speak. Despite all her efforts, tears streamed down her cheeks.

"If you feel you can, tell me. I'm a good listener." Dan moved away and without thinking Tracey put her hand on her shoulder where his had been. He sat down opposite her. "You don't have to if you don't want to."

"I do want to," Tracey sobbed. "But I can't stop crying."

"That's all right. I can wait till you're ready. All night if that's what it takes." Dan smiled and Tracey managed a watery grin in return. "That's better," he said. "Where do you want to start?"

"I don't know. There's so much going on. My mum doesn't want us and we've got nowhere to live," she began and, bit by bit, out came the whole sorry tale of how in the space of a few weeks she'd lost everything, her house, her husband, and a future for her children.

When she had finished, Dan didn't say anything. He came round to her side of the table and pulling her to her feet gave her a hug. Wrapped in his arms Tracey wanted nothing more than to lean her head against his chest, close her eyes, and stay there forever.

As if he knew what she was thinking Dan released her gently. He poured them both coffee, sat down at the table and said, "I can see the problem. The question is, what can be done about it?"

"I don't know."

"Let's look at the practicalities. The first thing you need is a place of your own."

"There are no council houses, not even any flats." Tracey could feel the tears starting again.

"So?"

"I can't afford anything else."

"Not on the open market, you can't, that's true. However, there are other alternatives."

"Like?" Tracey let her head fall on her hands.

"Housing Associations, for a start. They help families in your position and there are other avenues we can explore. But I've got a better idea."

"You have?" Tracey was almost too tired to care. The conversation with Dan had worn her out. Talking was supposed to help but saying it all out loud had made her feel worse.

"What I have in mind would solve your current problem. I've recently bought a property on High Street, which I'm having refurbished as another branch of my business. The flat above is empty and it's yours if you want it."

"You're going to let us live there?"

"Yes, but there are conditions attached."

"I don't care. I'll take it." Tracey raised her head.

"You should be asking me what I want you to do for it."

"I know I can trust you." Tracey looked into his eyes.

"You can but you should be careful. There will always be people who will try to take advantage of a woman when she's vulnerable. Okay?" Tracey nodded. "Lecture over, you'll want to know more about the flat. There are three bedrooms, four if you count the little storeroom. The place comes rent free until you get your benefits sorted out. In return I want it kept clean and you can supervise any jobs that need to be done, like the painting and decorating, laying carpets, that sort of thing. Okay?"

"Okay! I feel as if I've died and gone to heaven. You are an angel, Dan, you really are." Tracey leaned across, took his hand and raised it to her lips. "Thank you," she said quietly. "I think you've just saved my life."

TWENTY-TWO

Anna looked up from the laptop. "I've found David Latimer."

"Well done." Jane put her hand on her daughter's shoulder. Leaning forward she read what Anna had brought up on the screen. Gullswing? What sort of a name is that for a group?"

"Sad sixties tribute band, if you ask me," Anna said crisply. She sat back letting her mother's arm rub against her cheek. "You've met him, haven't you, Mum? What's he like?"

"He seems nice enough and very concerned about Robyn. He's the one who insisted she went to the doctor and he went with her to see the consultant."

"Then why didn't he stick around to see if she was all right?"

"Robyn probably told him she could cope. You know how she is."

"Stupid and selfish."

"Anna!"

"I'm sorry, I didn't really mean that. I suppose it's got to me. There she is, with great kids, an amazing talent, and everything to live for, and what does she do? She crawls under her duvet and gives up. Honestly, Mum, there are people out there who are fighting every inch of the way to survive."

"She's got cancer and she's depressed."

"I know." Anna's tone was softer now. "I don't mean to sound hard and unsympathetic but I keep thinking about Kit and how this is all going to affect him."

"I don't suppose she's told him."

"No," Anna said. "I don't suppose that even Robyn could be that irresponsible. Her brother sounds a prat but he's our best hope. Let's see." She turned her attention back to the computer. "Gullswing are on tour and their next performance is…" She gasped. "This is weird, Mum. They're on tonight at The Place in Gloucester.

"Oh good. David's bound to come and see his sister."

"I wouldn't be too sure about that." Anna was studying Gullswing's website. "The band is booked for a gig in Newcastle later in the week, so my guess is he won't bother with a family visit. You did say he's not around much."

"That's true. So what do we do?"

"I could phone The Place and leave a message but there's no guarantee that they'll pass it on. In which case there's only one thing for it. I'll have to go and see him. It's years since I went to that sort of thing. I don't even know what to wear."

"Don't ask me." Jane laughed. "I'm stuck back in the summer of love, remember."

"Which could be horribly relevant if theirs is the sort of music I think it is, but even if I'm right I'm not going dressed as an aging hippy." Anna shook her head and laughed with her mother. "I'll have to find something that will do. Jeans and a floaty top probably. It's going to be hot and sticky in that club."

Later that evening, suitably dressed, Anna drove down the A38 with the car windows open and music blaring in an attempt to put her in the mood for the rest of the night. She hadn't had time to download anything by Gullswing so she put on a CD she thought might be similar. It was not a good choice. The music irritated her. She felt stupid and old and wished she could drive straight back to her apartment, have a cool drink and an early night. Sitting through hours of pounding music in a darkened room was not something she was looking forward to.

When she arrived in the city the setting sun was throwing long shadows over the pavements and the sky glowed scarlet behind the dark bulk of the cathedral. There was still time to scrawl a quick note, hand it to the doorman, and drive home, but Anna could not bring herself to take the easy option. The thought of Kit's white face, the way he hunched his shoulders as if waiting for the next blow life was going to deal him, made her pay her entrance money and stumble down the dark stairway into The Place.

The basement room was hot and crowded. It smelled of alcohol and the faintest haybarn whiff of a joint. There was a stage at one end of the room and to Anna's relief a small bar at the other. As she threaded her way through the audience she was glad to see that she was not totally out of place. Gullswing obviously appealed to a variety of age groups. She asked for a mineral water, heavy on the ice, and settled down to wait. Voices buzzed around her, there was the clink of glasses, and she was beginning to feel drowsy from the lack of ventilation and the concentrated effect of the drugs in the air, when a sudden squeaking of mics jolted her back to wakefulness.

A beam of light arced across the stage and the group came on. In spite of her misgivings Anna enjoyed the music. Gullswing played a strange blend of ethereal New Age and pounding rock. They finished their set with "Lady of the Lake", a haunting mysterious song that reminded Anna of Robyn. As the last notes faded away and the group left the stage there was a spatter of applause and the stage lights went out.

Anna waited for an encore but the gig was over; the audience was moving towards the bar, talking, laughing, ordering drinks. The noise grew so loud she could scarcely hear herself think.

"Where can I find the band?" she asked the guy behind the bar.

"The Ladies is over there." He waved towards an illuminated sign.

"No," Anna yelled. "I want to see David Latimer, the lead singer." The barman shrugged and turned to his next customer. Cursing inwardly Anna pushed her way towards the stage and out through the door she had seen the band use.

"Hey, you can't come in here." A hand seized her elbow.

"Tough." Anna wrenched herself free and blinking in the sudden light looked into a pair of hazel eyes in a thin intelligent face. He was tall and slim and instantly recognisable with his shock of auburn hair. "You're Robyn's brother."

"Yeah!" He looked at her in surprise. "Although that's

not my only claim to fame."

"Kit's uncle." Anna knew she was rambling but she couldn't help herself. The whole situation was so strange.

"And you love my music." He was laughing at her now but she didn't care. She'd found him and that was enough.

"Actually it's not bad." She pulled herself together.

"Thanks. Though I take it that's not why you came to see me."

Anna shook her head. "I've got to talk to you about your sister and the kids."

"And you are?"

"Sorry. I'm Anna Poynton, Jane's daughter. You know my mum."

The bored somewhat sardonic expression on his face vanished and instantly he was all concern. "Did Jane ask you to come? Has something happened? Is the chemo not working? Is that what you've come to tell me?"

"No, not exactly. Is there anywhere quiet where we can talk?"

"Sure." He led her through a maze of passageways and out into a small back yard. The night was warm and still with a smattering of stars far above the city glow and a faint hum of traffic from the bypass.

"Well?" David said harshly.

Anna's mouth went dry. She brushed a tendril of hair away from her forehead. "Robyn won't go for her treatment. We've, that is Mum and me, have done everything we can to persuade her but nothing works. She won't even get out of bed most days. If she goes on like this it will be too late."

David nodded briefly. "Wait here," he said and disappeared inside. He returned within minutes. "Where's your car?"

"About a five-minute walk from here."

"Good. Let's go." She stared at him. "I need a lift back to Bristol," he said impatiently.

"You're going now?"

"I'm not waiting till morning. If things are as bad as you say I need to be there."

They drove back in silence. Anna concentrating on staying awake; David staring intently through the windscreen as if willing the journey to be over.

They arrived in Bristol at three in the morning. Turning into Coronation Road Anna said, "Where do you want to go? You can stay at mine for the rest of the night," she offered reluctantly.

"No, I'll go straight to Robyn's." David rummaged in the pocket of his jeans. "I've got a key somewhere."

"So have I." Pulling up in front of the Latimer's house, Anna took the front-door key out of her bag. "Robyn gave my mum one when she started coming round to look after the kids. We thought it was because it was easier that way, but I think it was so Robyn didn't have to come downstairs to let her in." She slid the key in the lock and pushed the door open as quietly as she could.

"Anna, is that you?" Jane's sleepy voice came from the kitchen.

"Oh Mum, you haven't been waiting up?"

"No," Jane yawned as she came out to greet them. "I wasn't planning to. I was going to go to bed when you left but I must have fallen asleep." She rubbed her eyes.

"David, you've come. I didn't expect you to be here tonight."

He shrugged and held out his hands. "What else could I do? I told the guys we might have to cancel the rest of the tour and they were cool about it. They're a great bunch."

"We could do with some coffee," Anna spoke quietly keeping one ear open for any sound from the children.

"They're fast asleep," Jane assured her. "I checked on them a couple of hours ago. She glanced upwards as she spoke and, in the eerie light of the hall lamp, caught a glimmer of white on the landing. In her long nightdress, her hair tumbling over her shoulders, Robyn was as pale and transparent as a ghost. David leapt up the stairs two at a time. He put his arms around his sister and she fell against him. Her face alight as she wound her arms around his neck. He picked her up and carried her into the bedroom. "Now you listen to me…" they heard him say before the door closed behind them.

Jane turned to Anna. "Thank goodness you found him." She sounded so relieved and concerned that her daughter had to suppress a tiny dart of envy. Jane cared so much. David was prepared to put his whole career on hold. Would anyone ever feel like that about her? she wondered guiltily. Not wanting to delve any deeper into her emotions, she said, "Can we go home now?"

"We can, but you're coming back to mine," her mother said and Anna was too tired to argue.

*

The following morning Jane woke at seven. She looked in on Anna and seeing that her daughter was still asleep left a message at Anna's office saying she was not well enough to come in. Then she waited until midday before waking her.

"Mum how could you?" Anna sat up, her hair all over the place, her makeup smudged. Jane smiled and handed her a cup of tea.

"You were exhausted. I thought you could do with the sleep."

"I was and I did. Thanks." Anna touched Jane's hand. "If it had been left to me I'd have struggled in and tried to cope but you're right, taking the day off is the right thing to do. I feel as if I've been emotionally chewed up and spat out. That and trampled by a herd of elephants." She put down her cup. "Do you think now that David's here Robyn will do the sensible thing?"

"I think she will. I only hope it's not too late."

When Anna went downstairs to her apartment to have a shower Jane took a cup of tea onto her balcony. She looked out over the city and thought how strangely sometimes life turned out. After all their problems, she and Anna were getting on better than they had ever done, and all because a woman they scarcely knew was desperately ill. Watching the river water leap and sparkle in the sun she prayed that they were not too late and Robyn would get better.

Towards the end of the afternoon David rang. "I'm sorry to break into your day but I've got a favour to ask. If there was anyone else I'd try them first, but … well, there isn't. School breaks up the week after next." There were shouts of joy from Kit and Phoebe in the background. "Cut it out, you two," David called before apologising for the interruption.

"It's all right," Jane assured him. "It's good to hear them behaving like ordinary kids for once. What do you want me to do?"

"Some babysitting, if you could. Sue will be here part of the time but once I get Robyn's appointments sorted I'm going to be taking her to the hospital – and the kids really get on with you. Kit in particular seems to have fallen for Anna."

"Of course I'll do it. Anything to help out and I'm sure Anna will too." Jane smiled to herself. How ironic that she had finally been proved right. Her daughter did have a maternal streak in her. Jane had always known it. It was a shame Anna had found it too late.

"Hey, leave off," David yelped as Kit thumped him on the back. "I'm not making it up. You do have a thing about Anna and I don't blame you mate, she's a fit bird."

"Ugh." Kit made retching noises.

"Okay, a cool chick." The noises grew louder and more graphic. "Jane, I don't know how to thank you," David said, his voice receding as he held his phone at arm's length. "Stop it Kit, you're not having the phone. Sorry, got to go."

"Who was that?" Anna asked coming into the apartment.

"Your fan club," Jane teased and explained what David had wanted.

Anna gazed out at the hot afternoon sky. "I've been thinking. Since Alistair and I have broken up I've not booked a holiday abroad and I'm due some time off, so how about I help you with the kids?"

*

Tracey put on her slimmest pair of jeans and a fairly new top. She wished she'd had her hair cut but when there wasn't much money coming in she couldn't spend it on herself. Instead, she bundled her hair up into a denim cap, which didn't look at all bad. She was so scared she'd be late for Dan that she ended up being early and spent ten minutes wandering up and down the High Street until she realised it was time and she had to race back to the shop. She was squinting through the blacked-out window trying to see what was going on inside when she heard footsteps behind her.

"The flat has its own front door, in case you're wondering," Dan said.

"You walked over." Secretly Tracey was a little disappointed that no one would see him driving up in his Aston Martin.

"That car is an ecological disaster," Dan smiled ruefully. "I'm trying to give it up but I haven't managed yet. Hence, I use it as little as I can, which is kind of crazy but it's my way of dealing with my conscience."

"Mm." Tracey wasn't interested in his scruples, she wanted to get in to the flat.

"Here." Dan handed her the key and stood aside as she unlocked the front door. "It's totally empty, I'm afraid," he said as he followed her up the wooden staircase. "There's a cooker and a fridge, but that's about it. I don't suppose you have any furniture of your own?"

"No we don't. It all had to go. We owed on everything. I don't care, anything's better than being at Mum's. All this empty space, it's like … full of possibilities."

"You'll need something to sleep on."

"I think Mum would give us our beds if it means getting rid of us, but before it comes to that I'll try Freecycle."

"I'll put a wanted message up for you when I get home, if you like," Dan said. "As soon as you've got some stuff you can move in. I have to get back to work but you take your time and have a good look round."

After he'd left Tracey allowed herself a few minutes to wander through the echoing rooms with their tall windows and bare floorboards. After all her worry and panic, she had finally got somewhere to live and it was so much better than anything she could have expected.

Back at Sheila's, her mum and George were sitting, cuddling on the huge sofa in front of the television.

"I've got a flat," Tracey announced triumphantly.

"That's all right then." Sheila scarcely looked in her direction.

"When will you be off?" George asked.

"As soon as we've got something to sleep on, if not sooner," Tracey said and swept out of the room.

*

Tracey has guts, Dan thought as he typed, Wanted: Furniture for family moving into empty flat due to repossession.

Pressing send, he realised what it was he admired about her. It was her courage. She could have been devastated by what had happened, but not only did she admit responsibility for the disaster, she'd picked herself up and was ready to start again. She deserved all the help she could get. He had some odd bits and pieces he could

251

let her have. Ex stock that had either not sold or had been damaged in transit. He'd offer her those and see what the community of Freecyclers came up with. Scrolling down the list of incoming emails he saw that people had already responded. On Tracey's behalf he accepted a double and a single bed and bunks for the children. Feeling good about humanity in general he poured himself a glass of wine and went out on the balcony to watch the sun set behind the Dundry Hills.

*

When Tracey got home from work the next day she told the children that they were leaving their gran's."

"Right now?" Jodie said.

"As soon as we've got our things together. So get packing."

"We're moving!" Josh threw his arms into the air. "Will there be a garden?"

"Will we have our old house back?" Milly wanted to know.

Jodie narrowed her eyes. "Where exactly are we going?" she said scathingly. "We're not going to be living on a council estate, are we?"

"No we're not. Though there are a lot worse places to be than that."

"Like Gran's," Josh muttered. Fearing for the windows George had taken his football away.

"Gran's been very kind," Tracey forced herself to say. There was no point in turning the children against their gran and she needed Sheila to look after Milly when she was working. "I've got us a flat in the High Street."

"Will I have my own room?" Jodie demanded.

"You'll all have rooms of your own," Tracey told them.

"Yeah" Josh yelled.

"Great!" Jodie joined him. Only Milly said nothing. She stuck her thumb in her mouth and stared at the carpet.

"What's wrong, love?" Tracey knelt down beside her.

"Is Dad coming too?" Milly whispered.

Tracey's eyes burned, but whether the tears were of anger or hurt she didn't know. Eddie had been round a couple of times to see the children. He'd taken them to the park where, Jodie told her, he had played football with Josh while she had to look after Milly. "It isn't fair, Mum," Jodie's voice had been full of hurt, and Tracey had promised that she would say something to Eddie on his next visit, but she hadn't had the chance.

At pick-up and drop-off time he was off before she could say anything, and despite her promise to Jodie, Tracey had been relieved. Seeing Eddie was too complicated. She didn't know anymore how she felt about not being with him. In some ways she missed him – but in others? She was coping fine on her own, wasn't she? Who'd got them somewhere to live? It wasn't Eddie. If there was one thing she'd learned since she and Eddie split up, it was that the only person she could rely on was Dan.

"I don't think so," she told Milly who promptly burst into tears. "We'll have to see," she added a little helplessly. After all, it wasn't only up to her. If she hadn't exactly been keen to see Eddie, he hadn't made much effort either. He was probably having too much of a good time hanging out with Steve and his mates. Still, she couldn't go off without letting him know where she was taking his kids. That wouldn't be right. Not for the children, nor for him. As for her, what did she matter? So long as her kids were okay that would have to be enough.

Outside the house Ryan thumped his fist on the horn.

"Are you going or what?" Sheila called from the bottom of the stairs. "Our Ryan's going to drive us round the bend with that noise."

"Give us a minute," Tracey shouted back. "Come on you lot, get a move on. Jodie take that case. Josh you can carry a box and Milly you're in charge of this bag. It's special so you have to be careful. Can you do that?" Milly nodded tearfully. "There's a good girl." Tracey gave her a quick hug.

The other two clattered down the stairs, loaded their things into the car and hurried back for more. It seemed as if they couldn't get out of that house quick enough. Even George came to help. *Shows how much he wants to get rid of us.* Tracey cast a final look around the room to make sure they hadn't left anything behind. She didn't want any barbed comments from Sheila about her messy badly brought-up children.

There was one last thing to do before she left. Holding the scrap of paper in front of her like a weapon she went into the lounge where Sheila had one eye on some daytime soap, the other on what was going on in the street.

"This is where we'll be," she told her mother. "When you see Eddie can you let him know?" Sheila took the address between two manicured fingers, her lips pursed as if handling a dirty tissue. "You promise you will, won't you Mum?" Tracey persisted.

"I don't see why you can't tell him yourself. After all, he is your husband."

Tracey sighed. "Mum, I don't have time for this. I can't ring him, cos I don't have enough money on my phone, nor does he. So when he comes round for the kids will you tell him? It's not too much to ask, is it?"

Sheila looked as if she was going to snap back at her, then changed her mind and smiled. "Don't you worry about it. You've got enough going on in your life. You leave that husband of yours to me."

TWENTY-THREE

Eddie walked slowly up the path to Sheila's front door. Usually he could see Josh's face pressed up against the front room window, or his son would be sitting on the low wall waiting for his dad. Today there was no sign of either him or his sisters. Where were they? Had something bad happened to one of the children and Tracey hadn't told him? Or had he simply got the day wrong? Eddie frowned. He saw the children most Fridays but maybe Tracey had to change the arrangement and he'd got muddled, which was easy enough to do as they never really talked. The one time in the week he saw her, his wife was too busy getting the children ready to go out, and he never wanted to stay long around Sheila.

The thought of his mother-in-law brought him out in a cold sweat and it took all his courage to ring the doorbell. As always she made him wait. Standing on the doorstep worrying, half-tempted to run away like a naughty schoolboy, the only thing that kept him there was the thought of how disappointed his kids would be if their dad hadn't turned up. He was wondering whether to go round to the back when the door finally opened. Holding it ajar, Sheila gave him the sort of look she usually reserved for door-to-door canvassers, or Jehovah's Witnesses.

"Yes?"

Eddie's throat clamped shut. His mouth went dry and he had to force himself to say, "I've come to see the kids."

"Oh." Sheila raised one plucked and painted eyebrow. "They're not here."

"What's wrong? What's happened?"

"Nothing. They've moved out, that's all."

"Where have they gone?"

"I can't tell you that. Tracey told me she doesn't want to see you anymore."

"But the kids," Eddie said desperately.

Sheila shrugged. "You'll have to sort that out between you," she said coldly and shut the door in his face.

I'll kill her. I'll bloody kill her. The thought spun in his brain but whether it was Sheila or Tracey he wanted to kill, he didn't know. He felt like putting his fist through the door, breaking it down, charging through the house and trampling everything in his path. "Cow!" he yelled raising his arm but before he could bring it crashing down a hand grabbed his elbow.

"Leave it." Ryan's voice brought him to his senses. "Go on get lost. If our Tracey doesn't want to see you that's it, mate."

"She told you that did she? Did she?" Eddie tried to get free but his brother-in-law twisted his arm behind his back and shoved him out of the gate so hard that Eddie staggered across the pavement and into the road.

Horns blared. Drivers swore. Somehow, he made it to the other side where he sank down on a garden wall and put his head in his hands, desperate that no one should see his tears. What he had always feared was true. Tracey didn't love him. She probably never had. He'd tried so hard but in spite of everything he'd done he'd failed his wife and kids and now he was paying the price.

The shadows lengthened. People began coming home from work. The road became clogged with cars, the residents competing with each other to be the first to slip into a vacant parking space. When a car drew up in front of him Eddie knew he had to leave. His head felt as heavy as if he'd been on an all-night drinking binge; his legs like water as he heaved himself to his feet and walked slowly away.

Don't look back, he told himself. *Keep going.* Looking down at the pavement, shuffling along like an old man, he was almost knocked off balance by a furry brown body. Jake leapt at him, joyfully licking his hands as Eddie tried to wrestle himself free.

"Stop it," Debbie cried tugging at the lead.

"It's okay." Eddie buried his fingers in the dog's curly coat. "Good boy. There's a good lad," he murmured.

Debbie saw the slumped shoulders, the sadness in his eyes and took his arm. "You know what, I could do with a drink," she said, steering man and dog along the road towards The Green Man.

*

"Jodie, give us a hand with the washing up," Tracey called from the kitchen. There was no reply. Sighing she went out into the hall. "Jodie," she yelled again.

"I'm doing my hair." Jodie managed to sound angry and whiney at the same time. "Why can't Josh do it?"

Tracey popped her head round the living room door and ducked as a ball shot in her direction. Because there was so little furniture Josh seemed to think he could use the room for football training. A proper ball had been banned but he was allowed to use a foam one. After all, the child had to do something when all they had was one small television.

"Goal!" Josh threw his arms in the air. Tracey lobbed the ball back to him. He made a half-hearted attempt at intercepting then let it roll into an empty corner.

"Where's Dad?"

"He won't be long," she said, trying to sound convincing. It was getting late and Eddie should have been here by now. It wasn't that far from her mum's to the new flat.

"When's he going to be here?" Josh hacked at the floorboards with the toe of his boot. "It's gonna be dark soon."

"Not quite yet. There's still time for a game in the park." Tracey glanced towards the window where Milly stood, her face pressed against the glass looking down into the street. She was sucking her thumb and twirling her finger in her hair as she used to when she was a toddler. "It's all right love," she said going over to give her youngest a cuddle. Milly said nothing but leaned against her mum and wound an arm tight around her waist. "Hey, let me breathe." Tracey tried to laugh.

"He's not coming," Josh shouted. "He's not bloody well coming!"

"Josh," Tracey cried. "Don't swear."

"He's not though," Josh ignored her. "I hate him," he snarled and thumped the ball hard against the wall.

"Is Dad not here yet?" Jodie sauntered in. Her jeans were skintight, her top skimpy, showing too much skin.

You're not wearing that, Tracey wanted to snap but said nothing. In an attempt to get her dad's attention Jodie had spent hours getting ready and if Eddie didn't get here soon there would be no point in going out.

"He's not coming, is he?" Jodie said and when her mother did not reply she added, "I'm going out."

"No, you're not," Tracey said wearily.

"I am," Jodie countered. "I'm not waiting around. I'm going to Jade's."

Tracey sighed in defeat. "Be back by half nine," she called after Jodie as she clattered down the uncarpeted stairs and slammed the front door behind her.

"I'm going down the park with Noah," Josh said.

"No you're not. You're staying in."

"But I want to."

"I said, no."

"It's not fair. You let Jodie go."

"Jodie's older than you."

"It's still not fair."

No, it's not. Tracey thought. *I tried. I tried really hard with your dad. I thought he was the one I was going to spend the rest of my life with and what does he do? He breaks my heart and yours too and I'll never forgive him for what he's done. Never.* Still in the shelter of her mother's arm, Milly began to cry.

Later that night, unable to sleep, Tracey sat on the sofa. It was a strange construction of leather and wood, and oddly comfortable. It was part of the shop-soiled stock that Dan had given her but if you didn't know what it was meant to look like you'd never know there was anything wrong with it.

The room was filled with the orange glow of

streetlights. The children were asleep, each in their own room. Even Milly had finally settled and Jodie, to Tracey's surprise, had come home on time. When she had gone to kiss Josh he turned his back on her, but she'd bent and kissed him anyway and he hadn't pushed her away, which was something.

Looking back over the past few weeks, Tracey realised that her marriage was over. Her mum was right. Eddie was no good. Not for her or the children. From now on she was going to have to face life without him.

*

"Is Mum going to die?" Dressed in her pyjamas, Phoebe wandered into the kitchen.

"No, of course not." Anna dropped the sheet she was about to load into the washing machine. Gathering it up again, she turned her attention to the little girl. "Whatever made you think that?"

"She keeps going to the hospital and you and Jane are here all the time."

"The hospital is making her better and we're here to look after you while that's happening."

"Can I have a biscuit? With chocolate on?"

"Anything you like, poppet." Anna hurried to the biscuit tin and gave Phoebe not one but two of her favourites. "You'll have to clean your teeth again afterwards. Then it's back to bed with you."

"Will you come and read me a story?"

"If it will help you sleep, I will." *But it will have to be a short one because I've the kitchen to tidy up and supper to get ready for your Uncle David. And I could do with sitting down for a minute or two.*

Dealing with the children after a day at work was exhausting but nowhere near as boring as Anna had expected. She was enjoying the everyday tasks involved in getting the children clean, fed and entertained, although that was where David came in. He was always ready to play a game with Kit or Phoebe, and had an uncanny knack of dealing with Finn.

Later that evening, sitting over the remains of supper, she and David talked over how the children had been and how they were coping with the way their lives had changed. "I think they're getting used to the new regime but Kit's still very withdrawn, and Phoebe's constantly on the lookout for distractions. If I keep on giving in to her need for chocolate she's going to be as round as a little barrel," was Anna's assessment.

"Does it matter?"

"I suppose not in the short term but I wouldn't want her to get into the habit of using food as an emotional crutch."

"Better that than boiling bunnies."

"Not Phoebe. She'd never do anything like that. Finn on the other hand is becoming obsessed with Cottontail."

"It's a family trait. Look at his mum. Look at me. Once we get into something we're lost. Craziness runs in the Latimer clan. There's a long line of madwomen and madmen," he said hastily in response to the reproving look that Anna gave him. "In their time they have all been shut up in various parts of the ancestral pile. There's a folly in the grounds which is supposed to have been built for some particularly mad eighteenth century mother-in-law. Apparently, she was so jealous of the new bride that her brain curdled. Or maybe the newly marrieds needed an excuse for getting rid of her. Who knows?"

"You can't talk about Finn like that," Anna objected. "Nor all those other people. He's not mad and maybe they weren't either."

"On the other hand who's to say they weren't?" David challenged. "In those days they didn't have labels like autistic or bi-polar to hang around people's necks. They'd call someone mad when they didn't conform to normal expectations. You know what, Anna, you're hung up on political correctness. Never call a spade a spade if you can call it a gardening implement. Let's face it, Finn's brain doesn't work in the same way as ours. There's nothing wrong in saying so. In fact I think it's the healthier option."

"Like your five a day," Anna suggested slyly, diffusing the argument.

"Okay. Let's go for healthy." David grinned. "God alone knows, it's what this house needs," he added softly, his face so sad that Anna almost went over and put her arms around him to comfort him as she would one of the children. Instead she got up and began to clear away the dishes, resisting the temptation to rest her hand on his shoulder when she caught him glancing upwards towards the room where Robyn lay.

"Shall I take her some supper?" she asked.

"She says she's not hungry. The treatment makes her sick."

"She should still eat or at least try to. How about something very plain? Toast maybe, or a piece of fruit?" *Grief, I sound like my mum.* When she had been ill as a little girl, Jane had always insisted, once any sickness passed, that Anna had to eat to get her strength back. Anna remembered strawberries dipped in chocolate after mumps, and the delicious homemade raspberry ice cream that followed a throat infection.

"What we need is Nanny Herbert," David said. "She never stood for any nonsense from any of us. "Sorry." He pushed back his chair and wandered over to the window where he stood out of the light so that she could not see the expression on his face. "This is so bloody hard."

"What do the doctors say?"

"Nothing. They won't know how things are going until the chemo kicks in."

"And Robyn? Is she beginning to feel more positive?"

"Who knows? She's still inside herself but hey, that's the way she's always been. Never one to share her deepest feelings. Stiff upper lip and all that jazz. A true Latimer to the end."

No, Anna thought. *Not the end.* But what if it was? A cold shudder of premonition slid over her. "She's going to be all right," she said firmly. To her horror she realised she had crossed her fingers.

"Sure," David said equally firmly. "No doubt about it, whatsoever." He squared his shoulders. "I'm going upstairs to check on her."

"And I'll finish off here." Anna turned her attention to the saucepans, scrubbing furiously until he left the room. When he'd gone she let her hands fall limply into the water and stared blindly out of the window at the gathering darkness. What was to be done? What was the best way of helping Robyn and her children?

I could do with some input, Anna thought as she was walking home later that evening. *Mum might have some useful suggestions.* She took out her phone and texted, *Can you do early breakfast tomorrow before I go to Robyn's?*

The next morning she hurried upstairs to Jane's apartment to be greeted by the smell of freshly brewed coffee and an offer of toast or croissants. Having chosen toast, then promptly changing her mind, Anna sat down to a plate of pastries oozing with butter and apricot jam.

"Mum, I don't know what to do."

"About?" Jane prompted.

"What happens when Robyn—" Anna stopped.

"*If* Robyn dies," Jane corrected. "Nothing is certain. But you're right, we have to face the possibility. We can't expect David to take the children on even if they were all…"

"Normal," Anna supplied. "However well he manages Finn, that kid is a fulltime job."

"In term time he could cope, I suppose. It's in the holidays when the problems start. I'm surprised there isn't some sort of provision for children like Finn during the summer to give their mothers a little respite. You'd think there would be something in a city this size."

"If there is, it will be full, I should imagine. You'd probably have to put the kid's name down before it's even born." Anna attempted to make light of a terrible situation. "There might be private play schemes, or summer schools for autistic children he could go to, but I don't think Robyn could afford it. To be honest Mum, I don't know how much money either of them have. They talk about the family manor house in the country and it sounds as if they had a pretty comfortable childhood, but by the look of things David isn't making vast amounts. As for Robyn, well you've only got to see the state of the house to realise that there's no spare money."

"That isn't necessarily true. She might be spending it on other things."

"Like what?"

"I don't know. The things she needs for her work?"

"I wish you were right but I'm pretty certain that's not the case. In any event she's not been earning anything since she got ill."

For a while both women were silent then Jane said, "What about their father, doesn't he contribute?"

"I suppose he must, but he's never mentioned. Except Kit did say something … what was it?" Anna frowned as she thought back to that first meeting outside her mother's apartment. "Something about their dad leaving them after Finn was born, that's it. So at least there was a dad who had stayed around for a while. It wasn't a case of one-night stands and never knowing who the father was."

"Robyn isn't like that," Jane said.

"I know that," Anna admitted. "But she definitely doesn't live her life by the same rules as the rest of us so I thought maybe—"

"Don't go down that path. Robyn is a caring mother who's done her best in an extremely difficult situation. How would either of us have coped with Finn? Or with a partner that left at the first opportunity? We don't know what we would have done. To be honest, I think I'd have found it next to impossible."

"You're right, Mum. It's easy from the outside looking in to say what Robyn should or shouldn't do when actually the kid can be murder. So what do we do?"

"I think someone should let the children's father know what's going on," Jane said slowly. "It doesn't have to be you. But one of us has to broach it with David. Even if he wants to look after them himself, though like you I don't see how he could manage it, there must be legal implications if their mother dies. Custody issues for example. Do we know if Robyn and the children's father are divorced? Or if they were ever married? In either case he may have the right to have them live with him."

No way, was Anna's reaction. *That's not going to happen. If Robyn dies those kids are going to be devastated. They can't go off and live with a stranger who's had nothing to do with bringing them up.* "I don't think that's likely. He ran out on them once and I can't see him wanting them after all this time," she said.

"I agree, but he has to be told. Then we'll know that avenue is closed."

"I'll talk to David. He may already have sorted something out. You never know."

Having steeled herself for what she feared would be a harrowing conversation, Anna set off for Robyn's. It was a beautiful late summer morning, cool but with the promise of heat, the sort of heat that made you lazy and slightly careless, as if reality itself was wrapped up in its haze. She drifted along the High Street as if she had all the time in the world, gazing into shop windows as she passed until she reached Lucy's where she stopped under the dark-green awning. She and David had slipped into the habit of having something sweet with their morning coffee, and cakes from Lucy's were always special.

I'll be getting fat if I'm not careful, she thought. *But what does it matter? Why not enjoy life when you have it? And I am. It's crazy, sick almost, but it's good being able to help out Mum and David with the kids. Much better than being in the office.*

She went into the shop and ordered half-a-dozen Florentines glowing with cherries and glossy with chocolate so thick that she could almost taste it. As Vee packed them carefully into a box Anna was tempted to ask her to leave one out for her to eat with a coffee. It would be so pleasant to sit outside with an Americano and watch the world go by. The longer she stayed the longer she could delay talking to David. What was she going to say to him? How could she bring up the subject? If only there were some alternative. But if the worst came to the worst the children might need their father and she had no idea how to contact him. If she asked Kit or Phoebe, they were clever enough to work out why she wanted to know and Anna wished to spare them the truth for as long as possible.

If she were totally honest, the children weren't the only people she wanted to protect. Clutching the box of cakes, Anna made herself walk faster. She and David were both adults and he, like her, would have to deal with the situation as it unfolded, but the thought of witnessing his pain was almost more than she could bear.

TWENTY-FOUR

The sun cast shadows on the grass as Frankie and Robert walked hand in hand through the park. Sometimes he stopped to kiss her; sometimes she stopped to kiss him. In between kisses they talked about how things were going at college, where they were both studying chemistry, physics and biology.

"If we were in the same group I could copy all your notes," Frankie teased.

"Or I could copy yours, or we could—" Robert broke off as a football came careering towards them. He sidestepped, quickly steering Frankie out of trouble, then whirling round he kicked the ball back to the tousled-haired boy who was racing towards them.

*

"Yo mate!" Josh regained control of the ball and holding it steady under one foot gave Robert the thumbs up. The rest of his team was waiting and as he was lining up to kick the ball back into play he saw his dad on the other side of the pitch. Eddie had Jake with him and standing beside them was a woman Josh had never seen before. She had a small dog on a lead and she and his dad were talking like they were really good friends.

Something cold and hard landed in Josh's stomach. His legs turned to stone and when he kicked the ball it only rolled miserably a little way then stopped. He tried to run forward and get possession, but he couldn't take his eyes off his dad even though he didn't want Eddie to see him. Josh wished he could make himself vanish, or get whirled up in the air and swept off to the other side of the park like a character in a cartoon. Instead, he kicked at the ground and pretended to watch the small cloud of dust that rose into the air.

Had his dad noticed? Did his dad care? He hadn't been to see them, not once since they'd moved to the new flat, so why should he bother to come over now? Especially since he was with that woman. Josh rubbed a hot, sweaty arm over his face. His skin tasted salty. He wasn't crying. He'd never cry over his dad. His nose was running he told himself, and sniffed miserably.

A large brown curly haired dog bounded over the grass. Ears flying, tail wagging furiously it skidded to a halt in front of Josh. It gently butted its head against the boy's side until Josh lowered his arm and stroked its head. "Good boy, Jake," he murmured.

"That's right. He is a good boy. He's found you for me." Eddie swept his son into a great big bear hug.

Josh fought to free himself but Eddie held fast and after a moment Josh gave in. Leaning against his dad, his legs felt all wobbly and he breathed in Eddie's familiar smell as he rested against his solidness. For the first time since they'd been rushed out of the house in Benbow Close he felt safe. Then he remembered and his stomach churned with anger. "Dad, where have you been? Why didn't you come and see us?" he demanded, pushing Eddie away.

"I wanted to but the last time I came round to your gran's she said Mum didn't want to see me anymore. She wouldn't tell me where you were. I missed you all like crazy — but I wondered if it was probably for the best."

"It wasn't. It wasn't." Furiously Josh thumped his dad.

"I'm sorry." Eddie stood passively under the blows until a furry head butted Josh's arm out of the way. Jake gave a low warning growl. "It's okay," Eddie said, and Josh thinking his dad was talking to him burst into tears.

Desperate not to let his friends see, he let Eddie take his arm and walk him to the park gates. Halfway there he turned and gave the team a quick wave to make them think his exit was planned. At the same time Eddie gestured to Debbie to come and take Jake.

"This is my boy Josh," he said proudly, rumpling his son's hair as Debbie took the water spaniel's lead.

"Nice to meet you Josh."

"And you," Josh muttered after a long pause. His dad's new lady looked nice. She had a kind face and she didn't fuss, so he supposed she was all right.

*

Back in the flat, Tracey stood in front of the mirror and tugged at the waistband of her jeans. Size twelve and they were falling off her. At this rate she'd have to buy another pair. She hadn't been this slim since before she had Jodie. Another few more pounds and she would fit into that turquoise silk dress she'd freecycled. She turned sideways and studied her outline. Better not lose too much more or she'd have no boobs left, which wouldn't be good because most men liked a bit up front. She thrust out her chest and smiled. She'd do. Her hair was newly highlighted with blonde streaks. Not being able to afford the hairdresser's she'd done it herself and it had turned out even better than she'd hoped. Now all she had to do was to put on her makeup and she was ready.

Once that was done she picked up her bag and checked the flat. Jodie had gone to a friend's after school. Milly was with her gran; in spite of everything Tracey still needed Sheila's help with childcare. Josh was out playing football with strict orders to come straight home after the game. The older two had keys and she'd be back from Dan's before they got in.

Because none of the children had been at home she had plenty of time to herself. The washing was hanging up in the bathroom and she'd hoovered round and tidied up everywhere, apart from Milly's room which was a disgrace; there was nowhere to put her toys. A few shelves built into the alcove, like in the old house, would help. Tracey suppressed a twinge of sadness. Eddie had put the shelves up for Milly's books. She had used them for her dolls too, the ones that she didn't have room for on her bed.

Don't do that, don't go there, she told herself as she tried not to think of the pretty pink bedroom with the pink carpet and white curtains. Those days were over and she should count her blessings instead of moping over the past. She was very lucky to have the flat. Anything, she shuddered, was better than living with Sheila and George. And there were other compensations.

For a start she was never lonely. With the shop downstairs full of workmen she soon got used to the radio blaring and the guys joshing each other. They were all young and fit. In the heat they stripped to the waist, and those muscles were something else. Sometimes she'd go down with a tray of tea, always strong, brown and full of sugar, and have a bit of a chat and a giggle and a look round to see how things were going, because she owed it to Dan to keep an eye on the renovations. Which, truth to tell, appeared to have come to a bit of a stop. They were waiting for some part or other to arrive, the foreman had told her. Tracey couldn't remember quite what it was but it wasn't really any of her business. It was strange, though, that none of them had been at work today. She shrugged and was about to go downstairs when the front door burst open.

"Mum," Josh cried excitedly. "Dad's here."

"Oh!" Tracey gasped. Then Eddie appeared standing in the narrow hallway, looking the same as he always did except for a worried expression she didn't remember. Or did she? Was that how he'd looked when she'd told him they were going to her mum's and there was no room for him at Sheila's?

Tracey clutched hold of the bannister trying to make sense of the thoughts whirling through her brain. When she got downstairs she found herself holding out her hand then snatching it back again as Eddie said, "You're looking good."

"Thanks." *Perhaps now you can see what you walked out on.*

"Dad was in the park with Jake and it was Jake that found me. Dad says he's been looking for us everywhere."

Tracey turned to Eddie. "You didn't think to go to Mum's and ask?" How dare Eddie let Josh believe that their dad had missed them when he hadn't even bothered

273

to come round to see if they were all right?

"He did and Gran didn't tell him. Why didn't she Mum? She knows where we are."

"She didn't tell you?" Tracey's voice rose.

"No." Eddie glanced meaningfully at Josh.

Cow! Tracey thought. *How dare she decide what's best for me or the kids? It's all right for her, she's got George. She's not a single mum coping with three kids and two jobs.*

"I'm sure she had her reasons," Eddie continued.

"Yes," Tracey said flatly. *Go on,* she willed him. *Tell me how much you've missed me. How you want to see me again.*

"Now I'm here I thought I might start taking the kids out on a regular basis."

"That depends," Tracey said coldly, determined to keep the quiver out of her voice. "I mean once it starts getting colder you won't be able to take them to the park." *And you can't afford to take them anywhere else. Not unless you've got a job you haven't told me about.*

"Dad says we can go to Debbie's. She's got lots of animals. Rabbits and all sorts. Has she got a snake, Dad? I like snakes."

"No snakes as yet but I wouldn't put it past her if one wriggled up needing a home." Eddie laughed self-consciously.

Tracey glared at him. "You're living with this Debbie then? That was quick."

"I'm lodging at hers."

"Paying rent?" There was an edge to Tracey's voice.

"When I can afford it. Yes. In the meantime I do jobs for her."

I bet you do, the words balanced on the tip of her tongue

274

but one glance at Josh stopped her. All the joy had gone from the little boy's face. "That's all right then. I'm glad you've found somewhere." Tracey forced a smile. "I'm on my way out but it's okay for you to stay and to see the kids. You and Josh can sort out when and how. Bye love." Dropping a swift kiss on the top of her son's head Tracey slung her bag over her shoulder and left without looking back.

Eddie had found himself someone else. He said he hadn't but why should she believe him? He was a nice good-looking guy. Why shouldn't some man-hungry slapper pick him up? Tracey didn't care. The marriage was over and she was moving on. So why was there this pain beneath her ribs? It was probably because she was walking too fast. There was no need to hurry. She had plenty of time and she'd better slow down if she didn't want to be all hot and bothered when she got to Dan's.

Now there was someone she could really go for. Not that she would. He was way out of her league. But he was so considerate and so kind and always ready to listen. He'd done so much for her and the children and he'd never disappear then turn up without a word of warning. Not like Eddie who was like that wretched dog of his, blundering in where he wasn't wanted.

No. That wasn't right. Tracey stopped so suddenly that the woman behind her had to veer across the pavement to avoid careering into her. Eddie still had a place in her life. He was the father of her children and he and she had a history together. Apart from the past few months there were so many good memories, like when she told him she was pregnant with Jodie. She caught her breath as she remembered the wonder in his eyes, the tentative way he stretched out to touch her stomach though nothing showed as yet. After he'd lost his parents, Eddie had been brought up partly in care, partly in a foster home. Because of that he'd always said that having a family was the most important thing in his life. If that was what he really believed why had he gone off to live with someone else? It was like he had switched off from her and the children the moment things got tough. And yet…

It was so confusing. If Dan was in she would talk it through with him while they were having coffee. He had this knack of seeing things clearly and it would help her get it straight in her own mind.

Going up in the lift she ran her fingers through her hair, then checked that she wasn't looking too hot and flushed. A quick spray of perfume and she was ready. Tracey slipped the key into the lock and braced herself for disappointment. With her luck, today was going to be one of those days when Dan was working late. Pushing open the door she stepped into a cool air-conditioned space. Ears straining anxiously she stood and listened. Nothing. Then the door to the bedroom opened and Dan came out talking on his phone. He gave her a quick wave and carried on with his conversation.

"You're sure about that? But we agreed. It says in the contract…" Frowning, he walked over to the window and Tracey lost the rest of the conversation until he turned towards her. "In that case I'll wait to hear from you tomorrow. Blast!" He thumped the wall with his fist.

"Trouble?"

"Workmen!"

Tracey took a cloth from the cleaning cupboard and started on the kitchen. Dan paced up and down staring moodily at his phone. "Were the builders there when you left?"

"No one turned up at all this morning," she replied. A warm feeling settled under her ribs; talking like this was like being married and having a life together. "I thought it was strange," Tracey continued then was swept by a sudden feeling of guilt. "I'm sorry. Should I have let you know?"

"It wouldn't have made any difference." From somewhere beneath his obvious frustration Dan managed to dredge up a smile. "I can't blame you for the contractors letting me down."

"Is it serious?"

"It means that unless I can get someone else to finish the job the shop won't be ready for the opening, which makes life difficult as all the publicity and advertising is scheduled around that date."

Tracey put down her cloth. She was thinking hard. She really shouldn't let what she felt about Dan get in the way of Eddie earning some money. If they got divorced they'd need as much as they could because bringing up children was expensive at the best of times, and it would get worse as they got older. "What exactly needs doing?"

"That's the most infuriating part. The majority of the work is done. It's the finishing off I'm waiting for. There's a bit of woodwork, some decorating, the sort of things a skilled DIY guy could do, or even one of those old-fashioned handymen you used to be able to get, but not anymore. People like that seem to have vanished off the

277

face of the earth," Dan finished gloomily.

Tracey took a deep breath. "I think I might know someone."

TWENTY-FIVE

"Two ounces of butter and two ounces of sugar," Phoebe read from the Ladybird Book of Cakes. "What's an ounce?"

"Oh my goodness! I'd forgotten the measurements wouldn't be in metric." Jane pulled a rueful face at the book she had bought many years ago for Anna and had kept for the grandchildren that had never arrived. "Never mind. We'll use four hundred grams. You can measure it out."

Phoebe, almost swamped by one of Jane's old aprons, stuck her tongue out in concentration as she cut a block from the butter and set it carefully on the cast iron scales.

"Next you can cream the butter and sugar and break in the egg," Jane said.

"What are you doing?" Kit wandered into the kitchen.

"Cooking," Phoebe said importantly. "I'm making fairy cakes for Mum." She stirred vigorously with her wooden spoon, pounding crystals of sugar into the creamy butter. "Jane says I can lick the bowl when I've finished."

"Can I have some?" Kit asked. Phoebe added the egg and looked at Jane.

"We'll let him, shall we?" Jane said, handing her the flour.

"He didn't do the cooking," Phoebe objected.

"No. But cooks always let friends and family have a lick to see if it tastes all right," Jane improvised. Everything was going so well she didn't want any scraps between the children.

"Finn can have some too," Phoebe decided.

"Finn as well," Jane agreed, glancing into the garden where Finn was sitting in his usual place in front of Cottontail's hutch.

"When's Anna coming?" Kit said.

"She's had to go to work but she said she'd call round when she's finished. In fact I think that might be her now."

Kit raced out into the hall leaving Phoebe to ladle dollops of cake mixture into the paper cases.

"That looks lovely." Jane slipped the baking tray into the Aga then looked in the mixing bowl. "Can I have a taste?" Phoebe solemnly offered her the wooden spoon. "Thank you, but we have to use our own spoons so as not to share each other's germs."

"Mum mustn't have germs," Phoebe murmured, her eyes filling with tears.

"No she mustn't. That's why she has to have the cakes when they've been baked. The rest of us can have a taste of the mixture before it goes into the oven."

"That looks good." Anna came in with Kit.

"You can have some and so can Finn," Phoebe said with the air of a duchess granting favours. "Don't touch anything. Wait till I come back." She took off her apron and went to fetch her little brother.

"You used to do this when you were little," Jane said as the children scraped out the mixing bowl.

"I remember." Anna smiled. She filled the kettle and made tea. "I was planning to take Kit and Phoebe to mine tomorrow but I don't think I could compete with this."

"Is that cake? It smells fantastic."

"Uncle David!" Phoebe cried. Her face fell. "There's no scrapings left. We cleaned it all up."

"But there will be cakes in about—" Jane consulted the kitchen clock "—twenty minutes."

"But they'll still be too warm." Anna shook her head, laughing at their impatience.

"All right, in about half an hour. The cakes will have cooled by then. In the meantime we'll wash up and put everything away." Jane organised the children at the sink while Anna poured tea for the adults.

"Where are we taking them tomorrow?" David asked.

"I was thinking of my apartment and organising some games, but because the weather is so gorgeous I wondered about a trip on the river. We could take them to see the SS Great Britain. I don't think they've ever been and Bristol children ought to know about Brunel's great iron ship."

"Sounds good," David said.

"You can't take Finn on the river," Jane objected. "You know he doesn't like change and all the noise and bustle could really upset him." Anna and David's faces dropped. They looked so like a pair of disappointed children that she had to hide her smile. "I tell you what. Why don't I keep him here with me and you take the other two?"

"We can't do that," Anna lowered her voice. "The idea is to keep them all out of the way."

"Finn will spend most of his time in the garden with Cottontail."

"Until he decides he needs his mum and throws a tantrum because he can't be with her," Anna said in her usual no nonsense way. Jane sighed in defeat but David was grinning.

"Boats are out but how do you fancy going to the seaside?" he asked the delighted children.

"In the van. We're going in the van," Finn said.

"Like you did before," his uncle told him.

"Is Anna coming too?" Kit said.

"I couldn't leave her behind if I wanted to," David assured him.

"And Jane?" Phoebe slid a sticky hand into Jane's and she had to resist the impulse to give her a hug.

"I'm afraid I can't. I have to stay here with your mum. Don't worry," she said, seeing the child's-stricken expression, "I'll come with you another time."

"Promise," Phoebe insisted.

"I promise," Jane said.

The next day she saw them off into a crisp bright autumn morning that was perfect for a day in Weston. David brought the van round to the front of the house and Kit and Phoebe scrambled aboard while Anna handed Finn to David to strap into his seat. Standing on the front doorstep waving them goodbye, it was like watching her family going off for the day. With a brisk slam Jane shut the door on that thought. The children weren't hers. This was not her family. She and Anna were helping out a friend and today her task was to be there for Robyn in case she needed her support.

Robyn was upstairs in her studio, where she had spent the past few days working with a passionate intensity from first thing in the morning until the children were in bed. Was this a final burst of creativity before an inevitable decline, Jane wondered. Or was it Robyn's way of showing that she was determined to live and would not be beaten by cancer?

From time to time she emerged, paint splattered and vague, to grab a quick sandwich, but it was obvious that her mind was still on her work. The children had learned to stay out of her way, even Finn wouldn't disturb his mother – instead he would sit with his cheek pressed against the studio door, arms around his knees, seemingly content just to be there.

Jane tidied up the breakfast things and set about a thorough clean of the kitchen. It was not something she usually did but she had to distract herself from the phone call that Robyn should be making.

Once the subject had been broached, she, Anna and David had each volunteered to ring Philip Jones. Robyn's reaction was to thank them but to insist that it was her responsibility. Philip was the father of her children and he had to know how ill she was in case the treatment did not work and her condition was terminal. She would speak to him at the weekend when David and Anna could keep the children out of the way. Not wanting to leave her totally alone Jane had volunteered to stay and to her surprise Robyn had agreed.

After the floor had been mopped and all the surfaces were gleaming Jane decided that she had given Robyn enough time. *Either she's called him by now or she hasn't. If she has, she might need a shoulder to cry on. If she hasn't, I might have to give her a gentle nudge,* she told herself as she made coffee and brewed a pot of green tea for Robyn. Setting the cups on a tray she carried it up the stairs to the studio.

Robyn was sitting in Hugh's old chair, her head resting against one of the wings, hands in her lap, one still holding the phone. She looked exhausted and barely reacted when Jane came in.

"I thought you might like some tea."

Robyn's grip on her phone loosened and Jane had to move quickly to save it from sliding to the floor. Staring at the trees that lined the river, Robyn said, "I told him."

"And?"

"He's not going to do anything. He says it's so long since he's seen the children that his new family has to be his priority." Robyn paused. "Apparently it wouldn't be fair to disrupt them."

Yet he could walk out on Kit and Phoebe when they were little. They could be hurt and upset because as far as he's concerned they don't matter. You're a total shit, Philip Jones. And I could happily dismember you and feed the pieces to the gulls, Jane thought.

"And then Finn is a special case and no one could be expected to cope with him," Robyn said.

"Yes, Finn is special, but that's no reason for his father to shirk his responsibilities."

"Except I was the one that insisted on sole custody. And see where it's got me." Robyn gave a weak smile.

"You did what you thought was right at the time."

Robyn sighed and half-closed her eyes. "Yes, but I'm

all they have."

"No, you're not." Jane leaned over and put her hand on Robyn's shoulder. "Don't forget Anna and me. We're here for you too."

"Whatever happens?" Robyn reached up and caught hold of her hand.

"Whatever happens," Jane said firmly.

TWENTY-SIX

The email took Dan by surprise. Hi! Will be in Bangkok at the end of September. Any chance of meeting up? Ciao, Paola.

Frowning slightly at the screen, he tried to remember whether it was two years or eighteen months since they'd last met. It had been in northern Thailand. Paola was on her way to a photographic assignment in the Golden Triangle; he was on the search for one-off pieces to sell in his shops. In Chang Mei they had strolled through the markets, ate at local restaurants, drank Singha beer, talked and, in her case smoked, deep into the night.

Paola's penchant for cigarettes was her only drawback. He loved her dry cynical humour, her courage and her determination to do exactly what she wanted, and devil take the consequences, which matched something similar in his own nature. Added to which, she was very attractive although too many years of being out in the wilds had carved lines into her face. Her dark hair was wild and flecked with grey and her deep-brown eyes sparkled with fun and mockery. She took nothing seriously except her job, her friendships, and her daughter Raphaella. Utterly in love with her child, she had named her after an archangel and had been delighted when she grew up with the same devilish temperament as her mother.

Raphaella's father had been a war correspondent who

had been killed when she was six months old. Since then there had been no permanent man in Paola's life and she was happy to keep it that way. When she and Dan had first met in their early twenties they had been lovers, a relationship that had deepened into a lasting friendship that had withstood his marriage to Antonia. So why had he left it so long to see her again?

Hi Paola, he typed. Good to hear from you. Let's make it my treat. The Hilton, 23 September, eight o'clock? Or would you prefer that little place round the corner? Dan grinned as he pressed send. The day was filled with promise and he was humming as he scrolled through the rest of his correspondence.

*

Tracey ran her fingers through her hair and looked critically at herself in the mirror. The colour was good. Not too much blonde and the jagged cut suited her face now that she'd lost weight. But did it make her look older? From one angle maybe, but face on with the fringe softening the lines on her forehead she could pass for a good few years younger, especially wearing skinny jeans and a T-shirt, which had a habit of slipping seductively off one shoulder. Pursing her lips she drew liner around her eyes, curled mascara onto her lashes and applied her lipstick.

From Milly's room came the sound of sawing as Eddie finished off the shelves. The place would be full of dust but at least her youngest would have somewhere to put her toys. "I'm off to work," she called, putting her head around the door. "I won't be late."

Eddie looked up from what he was doing. "No

problem. I'll still be here. I'd like to finish this off today, if it's all right with you." He wiped the sweat from his forehead and she was struck with how muscled and strong he'd become since he'd been doing up the shop.

"No problem. You can keep an eye on the kids, if that's okay?"

"I'll do that and get Milly ready for bed."

"Thanks." Tracey smiled at him. "Oh, I nearly forgot, will you tell her that she'll have to share with Jodie tonight? I won't have time to clear up in her bedroom when I get back."

"You won't have to." Eddie looked quite shocked. "I can easily run the hoover round."

"But you're…" It was Tracey's turn to be surprised.

"A bloke?

And a fit one too. What on earth was wrong with her? Why was she even thinking about him like that let alone sneaking glances at his great shape? It must be her hormones jumping. If she checked she'd find it was that time of the month … or something.

"Blokes can clean. You get off or you'll be late."

She gave him a quick wave and clattered down the stairs eager to get to Dan's apartment. She'd left it a bit late because Dan was often home by this time and she was looking forward to a chat over coffee. She wanted to fill him in on how the shop and the flat were coming on, and he was always interested in what was going on in her life.

Stepping out of the lift, Tracey allowed herself a brief moment with her favourite fantasy. She wouldn't admit it to anyone, but she loved to pretend that this was her apartment and she was coming home after a day at her glamorous but demanding job. Something in television maybe. She would ride up in the lift and Dan would be waiting for her with that lean and hungry look he sometimes had. Tracey gave a little shiver of pleasure. There would be a glass of wine on the kitchen counter. He would ask her about her day she would ask him about his, and their lips would meet—

Get a grip, she told herself as she scrabbled in her bag for the key. Beyond that point she must not go. She liked Dan. Well to be honest, she fancied him to bits and she was sure he liked her too, but so far there had been no more to it than that. Now that she had lost weight and had her hair done she sometimes caught him looking at her in a certain way, but he had never said anything and neither had she. Whatever was going to happen between them, and she was more and more certain there would be something, was going to take time. Sucking in her stomach, she slid the key into the lock.

He was there working on his laptop. Still caught up in her dream, her heart lurched. She felt her colour rise and made a great fuss of turning away and putting down her bag in case he caught sight of her face. "Hi," she said when she felt more in control. "I didn't think you'd be back this early."

"Hi." Dan kept his eyes on the screen. "I wanted a bit of peace to organise my trip."

"You're going away?"

"At the end of the week. I'm off to Thailand on a buying trip." He leaned back in his chair and turned towards her, his face shining as if he had some good news; his expression made it obvious that this was the end of her stupid fantasies. "I'm meeting up with an old friend. Paola and I go back years. We've known each other for so long that I can't remember where we met. I think it was Wendy, my sister-in-law, who introduced us before she and Peter were married, or it might have been a chance meeting in a hotel in the Far East. We keep in touch on and off. Those are her pictures." He gestured towards the display of black and white photographs that lined the walls.

Tracey had never liked those pictures of ragged children, harrowed women, old men with sad eyes, and young boys posing with machine guns. She had wondered why Dan had stuck images of war and misery on his walls. Now she knew.

"So you won't be needing me," she said stiffly.

"What?" Dan seemed to be having difficulty focussing on her, his thoughts obviously with Paola.

"When you're away," Tracey said, "you won't need me to come in."

"I don't see why not. The apartment will still need cleaning and it won't be for long. I'll be away for a week at the most. Then I'll be back with, I hope, lots of new stock for the shops and in plenty of time for the grand opening of the latest branch. Which reminds me, I called in earlier. The place is looking good. Your Eddie has done a grand job."

Only he's not my Eddie anymore. He's living with that Debbie. Dan is seeing someone. And what have I got? Nothing. Serves me right for even imagining I could have anything like this. How could I have been so stupid? Tracey berated herself as she furiously wiped and polished every available surface. When Dan suggested coffee she told him that she hadn't the time, that she had to finish early to get back to the children. They were all she had left now.

Climbing the stairs to the flat she could hear the television coming from the living room. Poking her head through the door she saw that Milly and Josh were watching some nature programme with their dad. They were sitting either side of him on the sofa, Josh half-leaning against Eddie's shoulder, Milly, bathed and in her pyjamas, cuddled up in the crook of his arm. Even Jodie, music plugged into her ears, was sprawled on the far end. It was as if he'd never left. They looked so contented, so right together, that the tears rose to her eyes.

"Hi," she said clearing her throat and instantly the atmosphere in the room changed. Jodie said nothing but her face darkened. Milly refused to look at her mum and snuggled closer to her dad. When Eddie gently disentangled himself she began to cry. If she'd screamed and yelled Tracey could have stood it, but those tears were so quiet and desperate they tore at her heart.

"Dad do you have to go? Does he, Mum?" Josh drew out her name making her feel as if it was all her fault that Eddie was leaving.

"I'll be back tomorrow." Eddie rumpled his son's hair. "If it's okay with your mum," he continued throwing her a swift glance.

"It's fine by me," Tracey said sharply.

"And we'll play football, won't we Dad?" Josh flung his arms round Eddie making her feel even worse.

"You bet. Right kids, I'll be off," Eddie hesitated. For one crazy moment Tracey wondered what would happen if she asked him to stay. Then she remembered that he had that Debbie to get back to and nodding curtly went into the kitchen to find some paracetamol for the headache that was thundering behind her eyes.

*

Josh sat on the chair outside the head teacher's office and waited for Mrs Priestly to finish talking. She was ringing his mum. He was going to be sent home. Excluded from school for two days.

"Fighting in the corridors is a very serious breach of the rules," Mrs. Priestly had told him. "It's not how we behave here at Clifton Park. You know that don't you?" Josh nodded miserably. He knew he shouldn't have thumped Brett, but Brett shouldn't have pushed him and called him names. Ever since they had moved out of their old house Brett had gone on and on about all the stuff he was doing with his dad and what his mum was going to buy him at the weekend.

Thanks to Brett and his showing off, Josh was in trouble at school and with his mum. When they got home she was going to shout and scream at him to go to his room because she couldn't cope with him anymore, then she'd cry and that was the worst bit of all. Josh stared at the door until, after what felt like forever, it opened and Mrs Priestly came out. She usually had a kind face and a nice smile but today she looked so stern that Josh wished he could crawl under the chair.

"Your dad's coming to fetch you. He and I will have a talk when he gets here and after that he'll take you home. While you are out of school for those two days, I want you to think very carefully about what you have done."

"Yes Miss," Josh's voice trembled. "Sorry Miss."

"I'm sure you are," Mrs. Priestly said. "You're not a bad boy Josh, but you've not made a very good start to the year, so you are going to think about what you've done and make sure it never happens again. Now sit there and wait for your dad."

Why was his dad coming and not his mum? Josh didn't know if that was better or worse. What if Eddie was so angry with him that he went away again? It would be his fault. Jodie would find out and she and Milly would hate him for ever. Josh stared straight in front of him and tried not to cry.

When his dad finally arrived he was still in his work clothes. Looking flushed and awkward he knocked at the office door without looking at his son.

"I came as quick as I could," Josh heard him say.

"I appreciate that," Mrs Priestly replied, then the door shut and Josh was left waiting outside.

Abandoned, Josh scuffed his feet on the floor. *I didn't do nothing. Brett started it.* The words went round and round in his head. He knew he had broken one of the most important rules in the school but his dad had always said he should stand up for himself. *That's what I'll tell him,* Josh decided. *It'll be okay,* he tried to reassure himself as the meeting with the headmistress went on and on. When it was over and Eddie came out, he looked so angry that Josh didn't dare say anything. They walked home in silence, Josh sniffing to hold back the tears as he stumbled after Eddie.

Eddie didn't intend to be cruel but he didn't know what to say to Josh. Going into school and seeing the head teacher had made him feel awkward and stupid, as if he'd been the one who had been caught fighting. He had to be honest, if someone had said anything to him when he had been at school he'd have thumped them too. Probably a lot harder than Josh had done. So how was he supposed to tell him off? Besides, the child had been punished enough. He was so upset and ashamed that Eddie longed to reassure him that whatever he did his dad still loved him. The instinct to comfort a distressed child fought with the need to be a responsible parent. Josh had to learn that his actions had consequences, not only for himself but for the rest of the family.

"You know you've let your mum down," was the first thing Eddie said when they got back to the flat.

"I didn't mean to." Josh stared at the floor making his dad feel worse than ever.

"She works really hard for you and this is how you pay her back," Eddie went on.

Josh swallowed hard. "I know," he whispered and flinging himself at his dad broke into wild sobs.

*

Ever since the phone call had come from Mrs Priestly, Tracey had been worrying about Josh. Racing up the stairs to the flat, with Milly trailing behind her, she rehearsed the worst-case scenario only to find when she burst into the living room that Josh was curled up on the sofa, his thumb in his mouth, with Eddie sitting beside him, an arm around his shoulders. "What did the school say?" Tracey demanded.

Josh winced. Eddie shook his head, gently disentangled himself and got to his feet. "Mrs Priestly wasn't happy but we've sorted it, haven't we son?"

"And?"

Eddie looked at Josh, then at the door. "Not here," he mouthed.

It's that bad, is it? Oh well, another thing I'll have to cope with. "How long is he off for?" she hissed as she followed Eddie into the corridor. "You know they won't give me time off work for something like this."

"They won't need to. I'll still be around for the next couple of days. It'll be good to spend some time with Josh while I finish off one or two things here."

And then you'll be gone again. "Okay. Thanks." *Though I don't see why I should be thanking you for helping out with your own kids.* Tracey rubbed a hand over her eyes.

"You look tired," Eddie said.

"It's the stress. I don't think I can stand anything else going wrong. Sometimes it feels like, like I don't know…" She hesitated.

"Like you've got the whole world on your shoulders," Eddie supplied.

"The whole world and some."

"That's because you're doing too much."

Too right and whose fault is that?

"You need a break." Eddie glanced into the living room where Milly had settled herself next to her brother. "How about going out for a drink? Jodie can keep an eye on the other two and we'd only be round the corner."

A drink. Not a riverside apartment and a life of travel to exotic places, but a quick one down the local. Still it was better than nothing. "Won't your Debbie mind?"

"She's not my Debbie,"

"You're living with her."

"I'm not sleeping with her, if that's what you mean. I told you, she let me stay when I hadn't anywhere else to go."

"And I'm supposed to believe that?"

"That's up to you." Eddie shrugged. "Looks like that drink's off, so I'll say goodbye to the kids and then I'll go."

"Back to Debbie's."

"Oh for God's sake, Trace, give it a rest. Can't you get it into your head that it's never been me and her? If you really want to know, it's you. It's always been you … and the kids."

"It has?"

"No one else. Ever. It broke my heart to go and I was hoping … oh forget it."

"Hoping what?"

"That you still felt something for me."

"Oh," Tracey whispered. "Oh," she repeated as everything became clear. "I've been so stupid, haven't I? I was so angry when we lost the house I had to blame someone. I couldn't face the fact that it was all my fault."

"No it wasn't. Not all of it. I'm as much to blame when it came to the credit cards. And I was the one who lost my job."

"That wasn't your fault. People are losing their jobs all over the place. I'm sorry. I've been a total cow."

"Well…"

"Don't make excuses for me. I've treated you badly but that doesn't mean I don't—" Tracey stopped.

"You don't what? You don't care?"

"I love you." Tracey's voice wobbled as she finally

managed to say the words. "What I felt about you was there all the time, buried under the rest of that stuff. I love you. The kids need you. So how about that drink?" She moved closer and suddenly she was in his arms. He held her close and she shut her eyes and snuggled up against him. She could hear his heart beating, feel the warmth of his hands on her back, then a small body threw itself at them almost knocking them off their feet.

"Me too!" Milly cried, wriggling her way in between them.

"And me." Josh was there beside his sister followed a split second later by Jodie.

They hugged and kissed and there was no drink at The Green Man, but it didn't matter. Squashed up on the sofa with her family, eating takeaway pizza, Tracey didn't care. Eddie had told them over and over again that he wasn't going to leave them, that he and Tracey weren't getting a divorce. Not now or ever, and she knew that however difficult it was going to be they would get through it together as a family.

*

Mellow autumn light spilled into the studio. Robyn stood in front of her easel watching how the sun, moving across the canvas, brought out all the delicate gradations of colour in the grey and white abstract. Along the wall behind her hung the rest of the series. The first was a dark grey canvas. She'd painted it using her hands and a palette knife. The twisted shapes were slashed with black gashes, oozing trails of scarlet and magenta. Following this she had moved on to dull pewter shapes. The brush strokes were still rough, the edges thick and dark, but some of the later pictures were lanced by streaks of dove grey. Gradually the paintings grew lighter. Her latest piece was almost silver merging into shades of cream and white. Caught by the sun, it gleamed like sunlight on water. *Summer at Coombe Magna. The lake glittering in the heat of the day.* Brush in hand, Robyn realised the dreams of drowning had gone. Her feelings of utter helplessness had been replaced by a sense of purpose.

Kit and Phoebe were at school, as was Finn. With special help and one-to-one support they were hoping he might be able to stay with his brother and sister in mainstream education. David was touring with his band again, while downstairs Sue was doing whatever she did to keep the house clean and the children fed, and Jane was at the computer doing the admin that came with being a successful artist. Since painting *Woman in a Chair* Robyn had become a celebrity. There were invitations to exhibit, requests for interviews and articles. Everyone wanted a piece of her, even more so as she was reluctant to talk to anyone. Shying away from publicity seemed to have had the opposite effect, as Anna had shrewdly predicted.

Jane was staring at the screen but she was thinking about her daughter. Both Robyn and David could do with an efficient manager and who better than Anna? When she had suggested it, Anna had replied that she already had a job, thank you, but Jane could see from the expression on her face that she hadn't completely dismissed her mother's idea. *She's turning it over in her mind. I know she is. Especially since it would involve spending more time with David.*

"What are you thinking about?" Startled, Jane turned

to find Robyn standing behind her.

"Things," she said vaguely and pressed save.

"So it's nothing that can't wait. Good. I want your hands."

"What?"

"I want to paint them. That's what comes next. Hands. And they must be yours, Jane. You are my muse. You came into my life and inspired me." Bending forward, Robyn kissed her lightly on the cheek.

"And it was all thanks to Hugh's chair," Jane said. "Who could have imagined that one post on Freecycle would have changed our lives in so many ways?"

In the studio both women looked at the chair standing in the bay window. "I think," Robyn said softly, "it was meant to be."

Maybe. Jane didn't believe in fate but she was glad that she hadn't done what she had promised herself all those years ago and thrown the chair out at the first possible opportunity. She had a sudden vivid image of a pair of students pushing a wing chair up St Michael's Hill and wrestling it up the stairs to their flat.

You were right to buy it, she told Hugh. And she smiled.

*

Debbie ran the comb gently through Jake's fringe and stepped back to admire her handiwork. The freshly groomed water spaniel looked wonderful. His coat was thick and curly. His bare tail wagged happily and from somewhere under his fringe his brown eyes were fixed devotedly on his new mistress.

It was a month since Eddie had moved back with Tracey and, as there was no place for a dog in a flat with no garden, he'd left Jake with Debbie.

The back gate opened. "Hey man that is some Rasta dog," Steve drawled.

"He's my beauty, aren't you Jake? You know what, I'm going to start showing this dog. He's real quality and I think I might do well with him."

"You sure will," Steve grinned.

"Yeah man," Debbie teased.

"Hey Mum, I can't find the crisps." Frankie wandered out into the backyard followed by Robert. They had been upstairs working on some college project though Debbie strongly suspected that wasn't all they had been doing. But you were only young once and Robert was a nice lad who made her lovely Frankie feel good about herself.

"I think you had the last of them yesterday. While you're down here, can you put the kettle on?" Debbie turned to Steve. "Do you fancy a cuppa or would you rather have a beer?"

"Now there's a question."

"I'll get the beer."

"Now there's an answer."

The backyard trapped the last of the day's warmth. Sitting on the step with Steve beside her, a hopeful dog at her feet, and a beer in hand, Debbie felt ridiculously happy.

*

The weather sharpened, the nights drew in. A huge orange pumpkin glowed in the kitchen window, another stood sentry in the front room where Anna was supervising a dozen excited children as they bobbed for apples, stuck the tail on the witch's cat and dined on giant's fingers, frog's eyes and dinosaur droppings. Phoebe, Kit and even Finn had invited one or two children from their class, and so far everything was going well.

"This is the best party ever!" Phoebe screeched, cheeks blazing, toffee apple in one hand, a plastic goblet of lemonade in another.

"It's good," Finn said solemnly and Anna and Jane exchanged delighted glances.

The doorbell rang and the first of the parents arrived to collect their offspring. To a chorus of "thank you for having us", happy and sticky children were bundled into their coats and hurried out into the frosty air.

"Cool," Kit said when the last of their guests had left. "That was cool, Anna."

"I'm glad you enjoyed it because I'm shattered. Come on you three. Take the paper plates into the kitchen and put them in the bin. Then it's bath time for you, young Finn. Your mum will be waiting to make sure you're clean from top to toe."

"From toe to top." Finn said solemnly as he made his way upstairs.

*

"How on earth did you manage when I was little? You did a Halloween party for me and my friends every year all on your own," Anna asked Jane when Finn was safely tucked up in bed.

"I didn't do it all on my own. Your dad used to help when he got home from work."

"You miss him, don't you?"

"Yes I do. It's a sadness that never quite goes away but

that doesn't mean to say I don't enjoy things, and I've got you which makes all the difference."

"And us." With a swish of silky skirts Robyn joined them. "Jane and Anna, you're part of our family. Without you two I—"

"Don't say it," Anna interrupted.

"Why not? What I was going to say, and I will so don't stop me, is that without you I wouldn't be working so well, or feeling so good. I'm even getting to be a success in my middle age."

"It's no more than you deserve," Jane said, breaking off as the front door opened and something growled and howled in the hall.

"It's Uncle David," Phoebe shrieked, racing out to greet him.

"No, it's the Creature from the Swamp!" He picked her up and swung her round then did the same for Kit.

"Shh, you'll wake Finn." Robyn lifted her face to be kissed.

"Too late," Jane said as a small figure trotted resolutely down the stairs.

"Jane did a Halloween party for us," Phoebe cried.

"It was great," Kit added.

"Great," Finn said, solemnly adding his seal of approval.

"Jane you're a star." David kissed her on the cheek but his eyes were on Anna.

"We all helped. I did—" Phoebe was explaining.

"And I—" Kit joined in.

Their voices faded. Anna was conscious only of David, his arms around her, his lips on hers.

Robyn and Jane exchanged glances.

"What did I say about families?" Robyn laughed. And Jane knew that everything was going to be all right, for all of them.

If you enjoyed this book, please review it
and spread the word.

ALSO BY MISHA M. HERWIN

BELVEDERE CRESCENT

Abandoned as babies, twins Sadie and Thea have been brought up by Great-Aunt Jane and when she dies, they inherit her house in Belvedere Crescent. They plan to sell the only home they have ever known, but the house and its past will not let Thea go.

Haunted by the woman with the red hair, Thea is drawn into half-understood secrets, and the more she probes the greater the danger. As everything fractures around her, she slips back in time where she finds herself alone and fighting for her very existence.

To save herself she must come to terms with her family history and let go of the person she loves most in world. Yet the bond between sisters is one that not even time or tragedy can break.

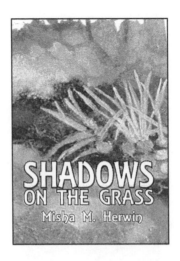

SHADOWS ON THE GRASS

Shadows on the Grass follows three generations of women. In nineteen sixties Bristol seventeen-year-old Kate is torn between the new sexual freedom and her rigid Catholic upbringing. Her parents have high expectations of her; she however is determined to lead her own life.

Meanwhile, Mimi, her grandmother, is dying and in her final hours her cousin the Princess keeps watch at her bedside. Born in the same month in the same year the two women are bound by their past and a terrible betrayal.

Caught between the generations, Hannah – Mimi's daughter – struggles to come to come to terms with her relationship with her mother and keeping the peace between her daughter and her husband. She too must find her own way in this foreign land in a new post-war world, where the old certainties have gone and everything she knows has been swept away.

PICKING UP THE PIECES

A novel about friendship, cake and the mutual support that only lifelong friends can provide.

Liz, Bernie and Elsa have been friends since their days at St Cecilia's school. Their lives had taken very different paths but they all found happiness in their own fashion. Liz is an independent career woman; Bernie a good Catholic mum with four sons; and Elsa is supported by her wealthy ex-husband.

Then, in the space of a few short weeks everything they have taken for granted is swept away. Money, jobs and partners are all gone. How will they manage when their worlds are crumbling about their ears?

Together, Liz, Bernie and Elsa have to find novel ways of avoiding disaster.

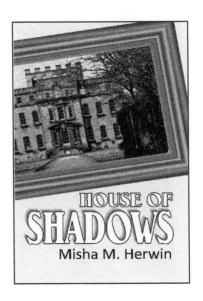

HOUSE OF SHADOWS

Brooding over the estate at Weston Ridge, the house at Kingsfield hides a violent history. Built by a slave owner for his beloved wife, it is a place of lost children, where time fractures, and two lonely girls from different centuries cut their fingers and swear to be best friends for ever.

When Jo returns as an adult, long-buried memories of her childhood begin to surface. As she slips in and out of time she realises that she has to face the consequences of her actions and a friendship forged in blood two hundred years ago will force her to make a heart-breaking choice.

Lightning Source UK Ltd.
Milton Keynes UK
UKHW040241160222
398720UK00011B/264